CATCHING OUR MOMENT

HANGING BY A MOMENT

LARALYN DORAN

A THREE DOGS DAY

For my children

1

Kelcie

My alarm hadn't gone off.

It hadn't gone off because it was missing…along with my husband.

He packed the cheap Amazon Prime special with his other essential belongings, told me he'd fallen in love, and was leaving me. "I have a chance to be happy, Kelcie."

As if my life with him was filled with rainbows and sunshine.

In the drop-off line at my son's school, I realized I'd rather relive middle school with a bad fashion sense, uncontrollable acne, and braces.

That was my new low.

I didn't even have the energy to laugh at the absurdity as I inched up to the entrance.

I didn't have any energy because I also had no coffee.

The prick snuck out with the coffeemaker too. Amber—the love of his life—had previously bragged to everyone in the neighborhood about her $800 latte machine from Williams-Sonoma—she didn't need our Keurig.

I was more upset about her having my Keurig than my prick of a husband.

Whatever. I gritted my teeth…Great, I forgot to brush them.

There was no coffee or shower, so I checked the console for a piece of gum or a mint in a vain attempt to seem somewhat civilized.

I wore my tie-dye Crocs and my University of Maryland sweatshirt that was so faded it was taffy pink instead of red. Finishing off my ensemble were the flannel Christmas pajamas I'd bought years ago as part of a matching set for our brag-and-gag Christmas card.

Look, we're so happy. Nothing is wrong. We're wearing matching pjs, for Christ's sake. How could my husband be carrying on an emotional affair if we're all wearing the same pjs?

Our picture-perfect family. Gone.

"Kelcie, are you still there?" Grace's—one of my oldest and dearest friends—voice came through the AirPods I was wearing to keep our conversation from being overheard by my twelve-year-old son, Aaron, in the backseat.

I peered in the rearview mirror and adjusted my cheap, oversized Jackie O-style sunglasses, which gave my messy bun a more purposeful and stylish look rather than the "just-rolled-out-of-bed" and unbrushed truth-of-the-matter.

"Yeah, I'm here."

Aaron sat in the backseat with his headphones on, an accessory that had become a necessity to block out the noise from an overwhelming world.

Could I get away with that for a few days? Could I walk around with massive headphones and listen to audiobooks about fictional lives?

"I just conferenced in Aliya," Grace said.

"Hey, Kelce. How are you holding up, honey?" Aliya Rae Chopra's crisp voice was laced with unusual warmth and sympathy. She and Grace Madison had been my best friends forever. Aliya Rae was Bolly-wood beguiling with the mind of a wolf on Wall Street. Grace was the natural girl-next-door beauty. She was a romantic who wanted a happily ever after for everyone, even though she lost Tyler before they could start their future together, and now mourned him like a widow over a decade later.

In my current state of mind, I didn't want to talk to either of them. I just wanted to brood, grumble about the sloths and their snowflakes in the drop-off line before me, and go back to bed.

I inched my car up another two feet in line, my heavy head propped up by the arm leaning against the door.

Aliya's assertive tone demanded my attention. "Kelcie, what is going on? Are you okay?"

"Fine. I'm fine. Except, the jackass needs to shop for small appliances somewhere besides our house. I know he knows how to shop on Amazon. He still has access to our Prime membership."

"Um…okay—"

"He is in love with our neighbor, a woman named Amber Savory." I gave the name a bit of a fake, cheerful lilt. "And he's moving out so he can date her without guilt."

Predictably, Aliya's response was thick with sarcasm. "Amber Savory—is that for real?"

"Yep."

"Sounds like a stripper name," Aliya said.

"Aliya, that's not—" Grace tried to keep things proper.

"Screw that, Gracie." Aliya wasn't proper. "So you're saying that he wants to move out so he can *date* her. He's not screwing her?"

"Oh, no. He's a stand-up kind of guy," I deadpanned. "He informed me they've only been secretly meeting the next town over for coffee and drinks *for months*." I gave my words dramatic effect to convey how selfless James was in laying this out for me—yes, my snark and sarcasm were running high. "They've been going out of their way to save my feelings, and it doesn't define an affair because he hasn't actually fu—" I glanced in the rearview mirror to check on Aaron and questioned the noise-canceling effect of the headphones. I lowered my voice. "Regardless, he thinks everything he's done so far has been fair, and I have no right to be upset."

"He's ending your marriage and thinks you should be okay with it?" Even level-headed Grace seemed put off by this conclusion.

I shrugged as if she could see me as I pulled into the roundabout that led to the front of the school. As a carefully choreographed dance, minivans and SUVs stopped, kids spilled out with their bags, and doors slammed as they walked up the sidewalk leading to the school entrance. The cars drove off, and another set of cars moved up.

That was until…Serina Shiffner and her son, her special snowflake.

This was not the day I wanted to be stuck behind them.

I slammed my hand on the steering wheel. Was there such a thing as drop-off line rage?

As Aliya and Grace outlined all the ways we could get away with maiming my soon-to-be ex-husband without being caught, the woman in front of me exited her car. She opened the passenger door, chauffeur style, for her very capable seventh grader. She grabbed his lunch and musical instrument, handed them to him, and then—wait for it—hugged him before he walked away from the car and closed the door. With a slew of other cars waiting for her to move her designer yoga pants-wearing butt, she stood there and watched him leave. Then she waved before casually getting back in her SUV with a goddamn smile on her face, as if it were their first day of kindergarten, not a Wednesday in April.

Nope. I was done. Four-letter words exploded as I lost control of my mouth and mind. As my hand reached for the horn, a far steadier one landed on my shoulder and settled me.

Once again, I knew that even the most effective noise-canceling headphones couldn't keep Aaron from hearing me. His ultra-sensitive hearing was his superpower, his curse, and sometimes my burden.

I turned my head and peered into the same eyes as mine. "It's okay, Mom. Relax."

The administrator knocked on my window and motioned me forward. I pulled the car up as Aaron undid his seatbelt, ready to do our part in the drop-off dance.

Through my earbuds, Grace said, "Tell your boy Auntie Gracie loves him."

"And his Auntie Aliya," Aliya interjected.

He opened the back door and jumped out, slamming the door behind him.

"Aunt Grace and Aliya said to have a good day," I shouted, but he'd already been herded into the pack heading into the school.

"Is he gone?" Aliya asked conspiratorially, ready to move on with more James bashing.

With a quick check in my rearview mirror, I put the car in drive—

"Oh, crap!"

Aaron's lunch bag was dead center in the backseat.

If Aaron realized he'd forgotten his lunch, that simple change in his routine would unravel his morning. Even if I brought it into the office afterward, it would throw off his routine, which could spiral through the rest of the day.

Not today. God, help me. I couldn't deal with a call from the school today.

"What? What is it?" Grace said.

Hard stop. I leaned over the passenger seat, and my eyes darted around for Aaron as he approached the entrance. The administrator was two car lengths ahead and not close enough for me to flag down. "Son of a bitch." I threw the car in park and cursed like a sailor as I took off my seatbelt, reached behind me, grabbed the lunch, and threw open my car door. Grace's voice cut out as I ran in my tie-dyed Crocs and not-meant-for-public ensemble, passing the line of cars up the sidewalk and to the school entrance, waving the lunch bag at my son like a surrender flag.

"Aaron, your lunch!"

I practically horse-collared my baby boy, tugging on his backpack to get his attention, and shoved the lunch in his hands. Without a hug, additional words, or an awkward goodbye, I walked out of the school with all the moxie I could manage.

…and only one earbud in my ear.

I grabbed my empty ear for the missing earbud, wishing for it to appear before feeling around my sweatshirt and retracing my steps back to the car.

There it was…about ten feet away from my car. Oh good. It looked undamaged. But wait. Why was there a crowd gathered around my car? Administrators, teachers, and even parents from other cars had gotten out and were coming close.

My face burned as I approached, and I was positive I would be publicly flayed for violating the car-rider line protocol.

"I'm so sorry…" I scooped up the missing earbud off the ground, taking the other out of my ear and tucking both safely in my Christmas pajama pockets. No one was paying attention, and there weren't any snarky remarks or even dirty looks.

Grace's and Aliya's voices blared from my open car door through my car speakers like a female-centric, girlfriends-giving-it-to-you-straight style podcast.

"So let me get this straight…" Aliya was ramping up. "A stripper named Amber Saaavory," she drew out the name with exaggerated, comedic enunciation, "tempts your husband into an affair, tells him she won't fuck him unless he leaves you—"

"Aliya, there's no need to be so crass," Grace countered.

"Girl, there is some sketchy shit of what defines sex going on there. He's getting something from her besides a coffee date." Aliya didn't do tame or censored when she got going. And she was just warming up.

I scrambled toward my car and tripped past the wide-eyed administrator, afraid of what would come from Aliya's mouth. Maybe I should have mentioned that Amber was the beloved PTA president and knew everyone in the school and neighborhood.

It also would've helped if I hadn't had their voices broadcasting out of my car speakers.

"Kelce. Let Savory Amber have that pencil dick," Grace said.

I rounded the car, almost face-planting when I misjudged the step off the curb.

I dove into the car and started pushing all the buttons on my dash, trying to disconnect my call. "Do we need to come down there?"

I grabbed my phone and pushed multiple buttons before it disconnected, and then I closed my car door to lock out the world.

Cue the horns and shouting from the parents behind me.

The entertainment I provided to liven up their morning was over, and now, I was Kelcie Byron, the pathetic woman whose husband left her on a promise of sex with the PTA president—and I was ruining the car-rider line.

I needed caffeine. I needed a new life.

2

—————

Kelcie

The repercussions of the drama in the drop-off line hit hard and fast.

James came home in the middle of the day, not just to abscond with more small appliances, but to ream me out for publicly humiliating Amber.

Our broadcast made it through the halls of the middle school quicker than wildfire. Being PTA president, Amber was volunteering and spent the morning in the teachers' lounge, crying.

It was my fault.

I'd humiliated *her*.

After all, it wasn't her fault my husband fell in love with her.

It wasn't her fault our marriage failed.

Because, after all, she wouldn't have sex with him if we were together. She had done the right thing. She wasn't an adulteress or anything.

I didn't say a word. I just crossed my arms and leaned against the wall while he listed how I had behaved immaturely and explained how this didn't have to be filled with so much drama.

"I'm sorry if you're hurt or if you have unresolved feelings for me, Kelce, but don't take them out on her."

"Oh, I have unresolved feelings, alright," I murmured. What I gave up for this man…for this idea of a happy family. He was acting like he had sacrificed. I tore my heart out of my chest to marry him and put my whole self into our family.

I bit down, burying those feelings like I always had. "James, I'm fine. It was a mistake. I explained the situation to Grace and Aliya, and they reacted to the news. The car speakers kicked in. I didn't intentionally set out to do it."

"Oh, I can only imagine what your friends had to say."

"Like you've ever cared what my friends thought of you."

He opened his mouth to respond, and my phone rang. I held my hand up and leaned into the kitchen to grab it off the counter.

Shaw—as if summoned at the exact time it would hit the hardest. Dawson Shawfield. My former BFF and the most popular tight end in professional football. One of the sacrifices—*the sacrifice*—I made when I married James.

I closed my eyes. If he was calling, it meant one thing: one of our big-mouth friends had told him. And I couldn't handle hearing his voice. Not now.

I sent the call to voicemail. I'd rather deal with the appliance-creeping James.

I continued holding my hand up to James and, with a steady voice, said, "Listen. You've dropped a bomb on our home, on our family. Just back off. I deserve a moment to digest this. Give me that without pillaging our home."

He closed his mouth, put his hands on his hips, and nodded once. In utter silence, we stood in the foyer of our home—the one we'd shared—and I ran my hand over my still-disheveled hair.

Damn, I needed a shower.

A text came through.

> GRACE
>
> Shaw heard. He's going to call you. Please talk to him.

ME

How did that happen exactly?

I did not need my friends circling the wagons and having Shaw come riding in on a white horse. I'm sure James and I could settle this, with Aaron's best interests in mind, if I could have a moment to get my bearings. But if my friends got involved, and Shaw stepped in, things would…escalate.

GRACE

It wasn't me. I swear. It was Wyatt.

ME

Yeah. And how did he—

Out of the corner of my eye, I saw movement in the kitchen again. James was on his knees in the pantry, pulling out the KitchenAid mixer.

"You've got to be kidding me." My voice was on the verge of maniacal laughter, and James jumped like a child with his hand in the cookie jar. The KitchenAid mixer crashed to the floor and narrowly escaped his foot.

"Son of a bitch, Kelcie," he growled at me.

I threw an accusing arm out at him. "You don't even cook, let alone bake. Put it back."

"You only use it for—"

"Put. It. Back."

My phone chimed again with another text message, and I held the phone to my forehead, praying for patience. "So help me, James. Enough with pinching the appliances."

Another message came in. And another.

I checked my phone. Multiple messages from the group chat— Wyatt, Gracie, Aliya, and Shaw—coordinated how they were each going to eviscerate James and explained why I wasn't responding.

ME

Excuse me. Back off. I'm handling it.

If they came here, I'd be attending bail hearings instead of defending my home from my soon-to-be-ex's petty theft of small electronics.

My mouth opened, and the words popped out: "I'm going to go home for the weekend and take some time—" Time to stop the planned public evisceration.

James's expression opened with optimism. "I think that's a great idea. Go home and be with your friends. Take Aaron—"

"I was going to see if you wanted to stay here with Aaron and spend some time with him. Talk to him about what will happen with you moving out."

His hands went back in his pockets, and he shifted on his feet. He stared over my head.

"You have plans." I thought out loud.

"I'm going to move into the condo I rented…so, yeah."

Bullshit. Having dropped the D word on me, he was hoping to drop his D on her, obviously. He was hoping to get laid.

Surprisingly, I didn't care. There was no punch to the gut. My frustration, anger, and maybe embarrassment grew at this further proof that he had his whole life planned out, and my head was still spinning.

"Fine." I put the KitchenAid mixer back in its place and firmly closed the pantry door.

The phone rang again. I didn't even look at it, just sent it to voicemail.

"We can discuss Aaron's schedule when you get back." There was relief and hope in his tone that I wouldn't be "difficult."

I nodded. "Whatever." My new favorite word.

I wanted to take my shower.

I halted. "Just one thing. Not in my house, James. Go to her place or your new love nest. But at least have respect for me, for our son, not to have her in *my* house. Don't even pull up in the driveway with her. I don't want the neighbors talking more than they will be."

He walked past me but wouldn't meet my eyes. "Then, let me get a few more things."

I followed him down the hallway and stood quietly.

Another text came in.

GRACE

I tried to talk Shaw down. But he wants to talk to you.

If you don't answer, he will just come out here. He and Wyatt are making plans.

Dammit. Wyatt was the brother I never had. He was the kind of guy you always wanted on your side and at your back, because loyalty to him was a commandment. Once Wyatt got involved, things happened. Nothing you could necessarily attribute to or pin on him. But they happened.

In school, a bully would mysteriously appear to wet himself during a school assembly, or your rival would finally get caught for cheating on a test and be cut from the team.

Once, we complained to Wyatt about a teacher who stared at our chests and made inappropriate comments. Within a few days, that teacher was arrested for soliciting a female police officer working undercover as part of a sting targeting online predators.

I wasn't saying he set it up—it could've been a coincidence. But when we heard, he looked at his watch and said, "Good response time."

So, I had grave concerns about unleashing Wyatt.

Besides, I was a bit insulted. They thought I would fall apart.

ME

Tell them to stand down. I'm OK—no need to sound the alarm. James is here now. Aaron and I will come there for the weekend so I can regroup. Can we stay with you?

GRACE

Of course. Pack a bag and get up here.

ME

I'm serious, though. Please tell them to stand down. I'm fine. I have enough on my plate right now and don't need them stirring the pot.

GRACE

I'll see what I can do, but Shaw is already on his way, honey. You know they care about you and Aaron.

ME

Yeah. And they knew this day was coming. I bet they even had a plan already drawn up. I wonder if they had money on how long it would take before my marriage failed.

GRACE

Honey. It's not like that. Please don't be mad at them.

Tears welled in my eyes for the first time as all the emotions surfaced at once—anger, embarrassment, shame, sadness…and, dammit, failure.

When I first found out about my pregnancy with Aaron, I postponed my physical therapy career. I burned my friendship with Shaw after he offered to slip into the role as baby daddy and, instead, ran to James the minute he wanted to give marriage and parenthood a shot. All to have it fail.

When it came down to it, marriage to James was like driving an economy car when what I'd walked away from was a fully loaded luxury vehicle.

And seeing Shaw was a reminder of the choice I'd made—the leap I failed to take. I chose what I thought was the safe path, and it blew up in my face. Seeing Shaw was my reckoning, and that pain would be salt in the wound that was the failure of my marriage.

ME

I don't want this to be a thing.

GRACE

Honey, you didn't answer his call. That's all
he needs to know. It's a thing.

My thumbs hovered over the screen. Maybe if I texted him, it would be enough. I could tell him I was fine and that I'd contact him once things settled. I heard he was on the West Coast doing promos for some new sponsor, and his model girlfriend was keeping him occupied. His schedule was too full for him to be involved in my domestic nonsense.

I tightened my eyes. I could've used one of his amazing bear hugs. I'd bury myself in his chest, and he'd lean down, whispering that everything would be okay and that he had my back. My last hug from Shaw had been the night he was drafted into the professional football league, back when I was pregnant with Aaron.

I took a cleansing breath and released it then investigated the noise from the master bedroom. James was kneeling in the closet, rummaging around.

I didn't want to encourage further conversation with him, so I sat at the kitchen counter.

Hopefully, Aaron would be amenable to traveling. He didn't like sudden changes in his routine, so I tried to think of what I could do to distract and entice him to make the transition easier. Maybe some chicken nuggets for dinner.

James came out of our room with a few clothes on hangers and the Roomba tucked under his arm.

"Uh-uh. No." I followed him and grabbed the robot vacuum. "No way."

I grabbed the beat-up toaster his mother had given us for our wedding over a decade ago, yanking it out of the wall, crumbs scattering, and placed it in his arms. "If you need an appliance, take this." I tamped down my frustration, determined to get him out of the house before we wrestled for the air fryer or the indoor grill.

Growing up with a father as a football coach, I knew how to drop a shoulder and take down a guy twice my size—hard. I channeled that energy into using his body as a tackling dummy and shoved him out the front door, slamming it on his protests.

I managed not to throat-punch him. So there was that… Yay, me.

I leaned against the door and let the realization sink in that, after a decade of being a wife in a loveless marriage, this was an opportunity for me—and a small victory. I could quit pretending I was happy and seek out change for myself.

I stared at the front door and let my gaze linger over the house. It was no longer home to me.

I straightened, took in a deep, cleansing breath, and made a mental list of what to do next.

I needed to shower, pack…and plan.

But first, I needed to make a few calls.

3

Shaw

I disconnected the call with one of my oldest friends, Wyatt Fortner, and paced the floor, staring out the palladium window overlooking Los Angeles, digesting the news he'd given me.

"How soon can you make it back home?" he had asked.

Home. He didn't mean Charlotte, my current residence where I played for the professional football team. He meant Keysville, Maryland, where we all were tethered. Kelcie, Wyatt, Grace, Aliya, and Tyler. Our friendship and experiences together were the foundations upon which we built our futures. I would never be where I was without them, especially Kelcie.

Grace had called Wyatt with the news, and Wyatt called me because Kelcie wasn't about to pick up the phone and tell me her husband was leaving her. The world could have been on fire, and she wouldn't make that call.

But I was in Los Angeles—on the other side of the United States—and something was going on with Kelcie. *My* Kelcie. The person who was once my best friend.

Hell, she wasn't answering my calls.

I slide my cell phone back into my pocket to resist crushing it with the hand that palms footballs for a living.

This was bullshit.

I needed to get home.

I needed to get my girlfriend out the door.

"Riles, the car is downstairs waiting for us. We gotta go."

"I'm almost done," Riley, my girlfriend who considered Charlotte living in the boonies, called back from the bathroom.

"Is your bag ready? I'll take it down—"

"Almost…"

I rechecked my watch and flicked my wrist, stretching my neck and shoulders as I continued to pace.

Knock-knock.

"Riles, the guy is here to take the luggage. We gotta go."

"Okay, take the suitcases… Just finishing my face."

"We're just going to be on a plane," I said, striving for patience, but the irritation was seeping through.

She poked her head out the door, her long, freshly styled blonde hair falling forward, reminiscent of a shampoo commercial. Actually, I think she *was* in a shampoo commercial.

"Yes, but baby, this is LA. LA has paps swarming the airport. You never know when you're going to be photographed. I always have to be perfect when I am in LA. I've told you." She popped back into the room. "This isn't Charlotte."

I turned my back so she missed my eyeroll. "No, it is not."

I would not miss LA.

"I'm going to miss LA," she sighed. "Are you sure we can't stay any longer? Spring training doesn't start for a few weeks yet."

"I do other things besides football training," I said—*like not living in LA.*

I came out here because of my sponsorship deals. I had to shake hands, make guest appearances, do a few commercials, and have a photo session. Of course, then there were the obligatory parties and club appearances. But I was a football player, not a celebrity. Still, according to Riley, it worked the same way for players in the league.

"You have to have something to fall back on when you retire. You should capitalize on your celebrity with your looks, charm, and social media following."

Right now, all I wanted to do was get out of LA.

Riley craved all of it. I craved the football field and missed my home.

My pocket vibrated with an incoming call. Grace.

"Hey, Gracie, what's going on?"

Knock-knock.

As I headed over to answer the door, her light, melodic tone greeted me, "Hey, Wyatt said you're in LA?"

"Yeah, heading home shortly..."

The bellhop sat at the door with a luggage cart. I motioned to him to come in and pointed out the ridiculous amount of luggage we had for the short trip. "Getting ready to head to the airport."

"How about a stop in Baltimore?"

The bellhop went to work. I pulled up short as her words registered.

"Is she okay?" I asked, my hand rubbing at my forehead.

"She's coming home this weekend, and I—"

I closed my eyes. "So, he is really leaving her?"

"Um, yes."

I looked at the sky in front of me. "Is she okay?" I asked again.

"She says she is. She's taking it all in stride. You know, Kelcie."

Yeah. I know Kelcie—or at least I did.

"Anyway, I thought maybe some friendly faces could be distracting—"

Riley came strutting out in her stilettos, the latest designer purchase, and two hours of prep work to get on a cross-continental plane ride. "Shaw, baby, I'm ready."

"Is that Bailey?" Grace said.

"Riley...yes." I grimaced.

"Oh...well, bring her," Grace said. Her sincerity was forced but appreciated. My girlfriend and friends had nothing to discuss past greeting each other.

I glanced at my beautiful girlfriend, who was every teenage boy's dream—outrageous body, flawless skin, cascading hair. She was easily one of the most beautiful women I'd met. She wasn't bitchy or cruel. She wasn't dumb or a big partier. She was unapologetically ambitious and driven.

But she wasn't exactly subtle, and since she considered Charlotte a small town, she definitely wouldn't want to spend any longer than it would take to fill a gas tank in my hometown.

I told Grace, "I'll let you know when I land."

"Ok, Shaw. Sounds good."

I hung up and turned to Riley. "Riles, how would you like to stay in LA for a bit longer?"

4

Kelcie

Aaron took some coaxing and the promise of a McDonald's Quarter Pounder, but we set off for my hometown with his headphones on and electronics in hand.

Keysville was smack in the middle of the mid-eastern part of Maryland. Equidistant between the mountains and the beach, it was a crossroads for Washington D.C. and Baltimore to anyone heading west. The town was rich in Civil War history, having spent its childhood witnessing monumental battles that made up each turning point in the war. Today, it was a bevy of contradictions—a haven for families escaping the city life, a charming historic downtown filled with antiquing weekenders, acres of farms still fighting for their way of life, and a booming biomedical research and business corridor.

But for our crew, it was the soil from where we sprung and where our roots still resided.

My father was semi-retired, and he and his wife were touring the United States in an RV until the end of the year. But Grace's Aunt Maeve lived on a decent-size homestead that butted up to a historic battlefield and always had room for us.

It was at that little farm, the surrounding woods, and the battlefield that our hellion friends spent their youth with Ms. Maeve doing her best to keep us out of trouble. Even though she was Grace's guardian—she had no children of her own—we were all her kids: me, Grace, Aliya, Shaw, Addison, Tyler, Wyatt, and a few stragglers in our motley crew. From Memorial Day to Labor Day, we probably spent more time on her property than in our own homes.

"Well, hello there," Maeve said with a huge smile that could melt any cold heart, and a soft voice that could soothe a wounded soul. But you didn't want to cross her or talk to her about her land. In the twilight, her warm brown skin still managed to glow, and her long braids were tied, cascading down her back. She held her arms slightly open, giving the invitation but not pressing as she waited to see Aaron's reaction. Sometimes, Aaron was okay with physical affection, but he had to be the one to initiate it. "I was so excited when you called."

Aaron methodically walked toward her, head down, watching a video with his earphones still in. "Hi."

"Aaron." I touched his hand. "It's time to put that away until later. We need to greet Aunt Maeve."

He glanced up and dropped his gaze just as fast, putting his phone in his pocket and slowly drawing his headphones down to rest on the back of his neck. He stepped forward, climbed the stairs, and leaned in, then wrapped one hand around her and hugged her briefly. "Hi, Aunt Maeve," Aaron said, stepping away before she could fully return the embrace.

"Hello, darling." She smiled, transferring her affection from a hug to the gaze she gave him. She held open the door and ushered him inside. "Go on in. I got some of those cookies you like."

He walked in, the storm door slamming behind him.

Simultaneously, we both yelled at Aaron.

"You may have two," I said.

"Take three," Maeve said, winking at me.

Her warm gaze turned to me as I trudged up the stairs. Over the years, I'd climbed, walked, stumbled, raced, and leaped up those stairs more times than I could possibly count. Now, my feet felt like they were made of concrete, and I wasn't sure I could lift them to the familiar heights.

She came down to meet me, not waiting for my approach. She enveloped me in a hug. "Oh, honey."

I wrapped my arms around her and let myself be comforted, because explaining to Maeve that I didn't want to be pitied wouldn't go over well. "I'm fine, Aunt Maeve. Really."

She leaned back, searching my eyes, but she wasn't convinced. "I know you are." She lied as well as I did.

"Come on, let's get inside and get you some food. Those girls are coming to steal you from me in the next half hour, and if I know them, you'll need something in your stomach before they get here."

An hour later, I had my stomach filled with Maeve's cooking, and two of my oldest friends and I were walking into the Brewer's Pub in the middle of town.

Grace's tawny skin was a beautiful canvas for her big brown eyes and the naturally curly hair she let loose and wild after years of trying to tame. Grace was the quintessential bookstore owner with her swaying sundresses and ever-ready smile. She already lived her romantic story, and even though she'd lost the love of her life at a young age, it didn't deter her belief in love. She worked part-time as a romance editor and wanted to watch her friends find their happily ever after, even though she believed her own chances were over.

Bollywood-beautiful Aliya Rai carried herself with the confidence of a 90s supermodel—tall, the kind of curves men loved, and the face of a seductress who didn't need make-up. Being an only child to first-generation parents from India, she had been raised to be the success her parents couldn't be. Not only was she to marry well, but she was also to thrive in every aspect her parents could measure—valedictorian, homecoming queen, MBA, and now soon-to-be engaged to a successful businessman from a prominent family.

And then there was me. Pregnant at twenty-one years old, I married a man I didn't love. Once Aaron was settled in school, I squeaked out a degree to be a physical therapist. Now divorced on the other side of thirty, I was redefining what my future would hold.

But I had these ride-or-die friends ready to battle for me if needed. Sometimes, though…I didn't want it.

To strangers, we were an odd trio—the sweet-as-sunshine editor, the sharp-witted businesswoman with a sharper tongue, and the slightly reformed tomboy-turned-mom—causing heads to turn whenever we walked into the pub.

Grace wove her way between tables to one in the back corner, waving to the bartender as she walked by, "Hey, Nick."

"Hey there, Grace." His smile kicked up a notch, veering into Hollywood bad-boy territory as he nodded at me. "Who's your friend?"

"Oh, don't you worry about her. She's off limits," Grace said, not even turning his way.

"Hey…" I half-waved at the handsome bartender, trying to keep up with Grace as she beelined to the back. "Technically, I can start scanning the menu again," I told her. "And he looks yummy."

She ignored my appreciation of Nick's tempting smile as she reached a large round table much too big for us.

I scanned the area. "Let's get a booth. We don't need a table this big."

"We're fine here," Grace said, pulling out a chair.

Aliya strutted over as if she were on a catwalk. Her hair—and other parts of her—joyfully bounced and caught the attention of every warm-blooded man with eyesight.

The wattage on Nick's smile went full tilt. Obviously, he was one of those warm-blooded men who appreciated the performance. His deep voice raised just loud enough for Aliya to hear him over the music playing but not loud enough for us to discern what was being said.

She didn't break stride but threw a knowing smirk over her shoulder. Then, her attention was entirely on us. Her performance was over.

Nick shook his head, still smiling. He put his hand over his heart, as if he'd just taken a hit, then turned to take the order of a gaggle of women at the end of the bar.

"Is there something going on there I need to know about?" I whispered.

"It's their way of flirting," Grace said.

Aliya flashed her a death stare. "I am not—"

Grace perused the drink list. "You flirt as easily as you breathe." A waitress took our drink orders: wine for Grace and me, and an old-fashioned for Aliya.

"So…" Grace checked her phone and then folded her hands on the table. "Onto the topic of the evening. What's next for you and Aaron?"

Aliya rested her chin in her hand and eyed me.

I folded my hands in front of me, wanting my drink before we got into this topic. "I don't know. I just found out he was divorcing me twenty-four hours ago. Do you want to give me a few minutes to digest that?"

They eyed each other. "Are you going to stay in Virginia—in the house?" Aliya asked.

"I don't know. We haven't gotten that far. We agreed to talk when I get back."

"Do you want to stay in the house?" Aliya asked. "Because I know a lawyer and can get you the house if you want it." She pulled out her phone and started typing. "I already told him I'd be calling. He has some free time tomorrow."

I held up my hand. "Let me think about things first."

"Honey, he's had all the time he's needed to get his affairs—" She cringed, her eyes darting to Grace and then to me. "Sorry, poor choice of words. But he's had time to get his thoughts and papers in order. You haven't. We need to play catch up." The "we" in her statement did not go unnoticed, and while it was appreciated, it just made me more anxious. "You need to get copies of all your financial statements. You probably should've done that before you left," she said, her eyes flashing with a plan of action. "We should run back to your place tomorrow. That asshole could be hiding everything from you as we speak."

Grace held up a hand. "I think Kelcie needs some time to let this process. Maybe we could try to just support—"

Aliya turned her phone over and put it back on the table, obviously ready to jump in the ring now. "No, she doesn't have time for sulking. We need to do this now."

"Fine." She sat back. "But we're calling my guy tomorrow. You can bitch me out now, but you will thank me later. I have Jorge on speed dial. Best in the state."

"You have him on speed dial? A divorce lawyer?"

"I'm in real estate." She shrugged a shoulder. "Of course I do." She waved us off. "How do you think I get the best listings?"

We sat sipping our drinks, catching up on gossip, and talking about changes in town when it suddenly dawned on me what was going on. I checked my phone, put it face down in front of me…and waited.

The drinks arrived, and we thanked the server.

"Have you spoken with Shaw?" Aliya asked.

Grace took a sip of her wine, staring at the table.

"No. I have not spoken to him. I did talk to Wyatt. Maybe he called him off."

"He's very worried about you," Grace said. "We all are."

"I appreciate that." I sat forward in my chair, splaying my hands on the table. "But I don't need him or any of you getting involved in this. It'll only make things more complicated." I turned my phone over, face up. "It's under control. If you guys get involved—"

A larger-than-life shadow fell over the table. "If we get involved, that needle-dick asshole will know not to fuck with you." The voice behind me was deeper than I remembered, and I didn't hear the teasing tone I was used to. Even without setting eyes on the man, I instinctively knew exactly who it was.

Dawson "Shaw" Shawfield was arguably the best professional tight end in the league, one of the most sigh-worthy players…and my former best friend.

I pushed out of my seat, stood on shaky legs, and gathered the courage to face him. Shaking my head, I said, "Wyatt really shouldn't have called you."

This was what happened when Wyatt Fortner was ignored: one hint of trouble, and he sends in the cavalry. My white knight. The man who captivated me long ago as a skinny, long-legged teenager whose only magic showed on the football field and in his ability to have women fall at his feet.

Now, he was one of the most eligible bachelors in the country with his sea-glass green eyes; tousled, dirty-blond hair; square jawline… And don't get me started on that biteable bottom lip.

I glared at Grace and Aliya. They were staring at their drinks as if they were crystal balls unveiling the future.

Grace threw a gesture over her shoulder, her voice a bit higher-pitched than usual, and she said to Aliya, "How about we go see what Nick is up to?"

Both stood and ran off, practically knocking over their chairs. Shaw caught Grace's chair, straightening it and settling his large form into it before saying, "Sit down, Kelce." And like a pouting teen being called to the carpet, I did.

"You're right. Wyatt shouldn't have called me." He leaned both forearms on the table and shifted even closer before tilting his head up, his dangerous green eyes flashing just enough emotion to communicate his displeasure. "You should have."

And just like that, I forgot what we were even talking about.

I leaned away from him so I could breathe. Then I crossed my arms over my chest and let out an annoyed breath. "Why? So you could drop whatever multi-million-dollar photo shoot you were doing just to run back here and hold my hand?"

"If that was what you needed, yes."

I glared at him. "Do you think so little of me that you believe I can't handle my own crappy life?"

He sat back, tilted his head, and crossed thick arms over his equally massive chest. The effect was much more noticeable than it was when I did it. "I didn't say you couldn't handle it, Kelcie. But you don't have to handle it alone."

We narrowed our eyes at each other—as was our way—in a silent test of wills.

I hadn't seen him in person in years, and my gaze wandered…

down his chest, shoulders, and forearms back to his chin and the tilt of his cocky smile.

"You looked away first," he whispered.

Ugh.

He ran his hands down his chest. "It was always the chest. Got you every time."

"Shut up." I smacked him in the arm.

It was like hitting a thick tree trunk.

He caught my arm and held it gently, "What's going on, Kelce?"

Kelce.

Other people sometimes shortened my name to Kelce, but it didn't sound the same as when Shaw said it. There was just something about the warmth he injected into it. As we grew older, it began to send shivers down my spine. That was how I knew things had changed between us, at least for me.

"I'm fine," I said between gritted teeth, tired of repeating myself.

"Kelce. What happened?"

"No one has died. This isn't a funeral or wake." I threw my hands out. "My husband is divorcing me. Big deal. You hated him. You all hated him." My impatience had my volume drawing attention. "You said this would happen from the day I told you I was—"

He punched a finger at the table before me to make his point. "I said he wasn't good enough for you." His voice quieted, and he gained control. But it was the tightness in his jaw and his voice that hinted we were walking into territory neither of us was prepared to discuss. Not here. Maybe not ever. "And yes, I stand by that statement. The only good thing that came from that man was Aaron."

Whether it was our body language or the volume of my voice, Aliya and Grace returned to the table. "Everything okay over here?" Ever the mediator, Grace slid in next to me.

Shaw's head was down, staring at the table, probably rethinking his return flight time.

I was staring at the top of his beautiful hair, wanting to touch it, even yank on it like I used to when I was teasing him or wanted his attention.

"This hair is too beautiful to belong to an ox like you...it makes you too pretty..."

I used to tease him, but only because I was envious. Not just of the hair but of the girls who got to run their hands through it.

"Kelcie, Shaw is here to support you like we are, honey. There isn't any reason to be upset," Aliya said.

Flashes of those unrequited feelings mingled with the humiliation of my failed marriage and became doused in guilt over the way I left things with him when I decided to marry James. It was a lot for my already weakened heart to manage. I was envious of his life's success, and my pride stung at how low I'd sunk.

I stared at my three friends. "I know I have Wyatt to thank for getting Shaw to fly out here and—" I couldn't finish my statement without being harsh, so I shut my mouth, trying to find words for the emotions coursing through me. I stood, pushing back my chair and finishing my wine in an attempt to gather my composure.

I pointed at Shaw, but my attention was on Grace and Aliya. "He's here." Out of my peripheral vision, I caught him folding his hands, settling in for my oncoming tirade. "He's here because you think I'm going to fall apart. Or is it because Wyatt has a plan to castrate my ex and needs your help to carry it out, figuratively or literally? Either way, it probably doesn't fair well for the father of my child."

He lifted his hand and opened his mouth to reply, but I stopped him.

At that moment, my phone dinged with the anticipated notification. I tapped a couple of buttons and, without looking up, said, "I'm not going to fall apart. For God's sake, I've been through worse than this." I stood as I slipped the phone into my back pocket. "Having a child before I was ready, juggling raising a child on the spectrum and trying to finish my degree. And this joke of a marriage..." I shook my head and gestured with my hands. "This was just the cherry on top of my last decade." It was a good idea to take a step away from my friends before they could delve deeper into any part of that statement. "I'm getting another drink."

If they pushed, I'd say something I would regret.

I'd contemplated walking right out of the bar but stopped myself. That was too dramatic, even for me.

Besides, Grace was my ride.

As I approached the bar, Nick quickly placed another glass of wine in front of me. I couldn't look at him—or anyone. "Thanks, Nick."

I never yelled at my friends. I was always the level-headed, laid-back, boring one of the bunch. The voice of reason. The logical thinker.

I checked to make sure my ringer was on before taking a healthy sip of my wine. I took a few more "healthy sips," which brought on a coughing fit. Yeah, there were reasons I shouldn't chug wine.

Great job, Kelcie—really badass.

A giant, warm paw began to softly pound on my back while another one, large enough to palm a football, grabbed the dainty wine glass out of my hand and set it on the bar.

My friends thought they'd called in the big guns when they told Shaw. But with everything left unsaid between us, we were more like unstable, emotional explosives.

5

———————

Shaw

Her face was red from the effort of channeling indignation over any other emotion.

God damn that man all to hell.

I stuffed my hands in my jeans pockets and didn't immediately reach for her. My instinct was to wrap her in a bear hug and comfort her. Before, I would've been the one she ran to, but not now.

Now, I was powerless to help. It was another figurative kick in the ass.

When she'd stomped off toward the bar and the exit, Grace stood to go after her.

"I've got her," I said, taking a deep breath and wondering if those would be my last words. Taking on a few three-hundred-pound linemen sounded more enticing than dealing with Kelcie right now.

Kelce was a woman of average height, but she seemed tiny next to my unusually tall frame. She had an inherent athletic build from years of sports, which had given way to some attractive curves, whether from maturity or from having Aaron. She wore her chestnut-brown hair in a high ponytail—a carryover from her youth. It had been fun to yank on when we were teenagers.

After initially attempting to inhale her wine, I rubbed her back as I held up my hand to Nick. He stepped away. "Kelce, honey."

Her hand went up. She cleared her throat, stepped away from my touch, and faced me, staring at my chest instead of looking up at me. "Shaw, I appreciate that you took time out of your busy schedule to come all the way back to town. I know Wyatt probably told you I was despondent and needed you, but as you can see, I'm fine." She held out her arms, still not making eye contact.

"Kelce, it's not like that—"

A notification buzzed on her phone and grabbed her attention. She shifted and closed her eyes. "Seriously." She pinched the bridge of her nose. "This wasn't a surprise. It wasn't as if we married for love. We married because of Aaron."

"It doesn't matter. Promises were made."

"Having a child takes a lot of wind out of a marriage."

"Kelcie, stop." I held up a hand.

"And it wasn't like we had a strong marriage to begin with…"

"He was wrong to—"

She turned around, finished what was left in her wine glass, and began to text someone. She said under her breath, "Yeah, well. I wasn't exactly easy to live with—"

"That's it." I knowingly let her make the mistake of marrying him years ago under the assumption that this was the best thing for every-one. Now, I was hearing about the way her life really was and how she accepted his cheating as inevitable. No.

Once she finished her text, I asked, "Is everything okay with Aaron?"

Bemused, she said, "Yeah. This isn't about him. Don't worry about it. I just need to take care of something that is time-sensitive."

"Are you done?"

"For now."

I grasped her hand and began pulling her toward the back. As we passed Grace, I slid Kelcie's phone from her hand and passed it to Grace.

"Hey! I need that," she protested. "I'm expecting a call!"

"Grace, watch her phone. We'll be outside," I said over my shoulder.

She grabbed the door frame before we made it through and called out, "Grace, if it rings, answer it and bring it to me, no matter what."

"Come with me." During the summer, a small patio was set up outside with string lights and picnic tables. Luckily, it was pretty empty, and I found a quiet corner where I could turn my back for some privacy. She needed to hear what I had to say, and I didn't want to compete with bar noise.

She pulled out of my arm. "Will you please stop manhandling me? I'm fine."

I put my hands up in defense. "Fine. You're fine."

"Yes, I am. This isn't a big deal." She walked past me and over to lean against the table, crossing her arms over her chest. "Aren't you supposed to be in LA or something?"

Staring up at the heavens, I prayed for patience, trying to remember how to deal with obstinate Kelcie. I was a little out of practice. I narrowed my eyes, mimicked her words, and growled, "I'm fine."

"You're impossible," she said, but the fight had left her tone. She punctuated her words with a slap on my shoulder, and we were back on solid ground.

I stepped toward her. "I didn't come here to upset you." She stiffened, and I stopped. "I didn't come here because I thought you were breaking down." She tilted her head up to prove she was made of stronger stuff.

I slipped my hands in my pockets and rocked back on my heels. "I came here because you were—are—my friend. No matter how much time has gone by or how things were left, you're important to me, and I wanted to see you with my own eyes. I needed to see—" I bent my head to stare down at her. "I wanted to see *you*, okay?"

She studied me, not giving away anything.

"And if there was a possibility of James's ass being handed to him, literally or figuratively—whether it's done by you, me, Wyatt, or a combination of all of us—I didn't want to miss it."

"Shaw—"

I quirked one side of my lips. "I'm kidding." I stepped into her space, slowly putting my hand on her shoulder, pulling ever so slightly to see if she would take the cue and move closer to me. It was a dance we used to do with each other.

One of us would be angry, vent to each other about what angered us, or rage against the universe to blow off steam. The other would listen to a point and then tell them to move on. It always ended with a hug.

I was testing the waters to see if this Kelcie would fall into the end step of our dance and let me hold her.

My fingertips rested on her shoulder, and my other hand tipped up her head to meet my eyes. She was still as beautiful as ever. The years had transformed her from pretty and adorable to beautiful and enchanting. The cool air of the night brushing against our skin, with minimal light casting shadows all around, made it almost feel surreal to be standing there in front of her.

I leaned close and whispered to her, "Regardless, I'm here. We're all here. So, stop being a schmuck, and appreciate the effort."

She swatted my hand away and gave a half-hearted shove to my midsection, and I caught her fighting a smile. Her touch was familiar and something I missed more than I'd realized. "I appreciate it, alright?"

My finger gently coaxed a wayward strand of hair that danced around her face to behind her ear. My focus darted between her smile and her captivating eyes, seeing that resilience and a glimpse of who she used to be, knowing that my Kelcie was still in there... She'd be okay.

"Just you wait. This will be a whole new beginning for you and Aaron."

She forced a positive tone. "God, I hope you're right. Because I need something new in my life."

I wrapped her in my arms, and she let me. I don't know how long we stood there, me rubbing her back, my chin on her head, her head on my chest, arms unable to wrap around me.

"You didn't need to come," she said against my shirt. "After everything, I wouldn't have expected—"

"Shhh. We aren't going to talk about that right now," I said. All that was important was having her back in my life—to fill the void of the friendship I'd lost and could never get over. She had been in an impossible situation. So what if I didn't agree with her decision? I wouldn't throw her aside for it. I was a bigger man than that.

She kept squeezing my middle and letting go, and then she said, "Jesus Christ, Shaw, what the hell have you been eating? You're as big as a house. I can hardly get my arms around you."

Yep. She hadn't changed that much.

I leaned back. "They literally pay me to be this size."

"Yeah, I know. Obviously. But my God." She broke the hold, stepping back. "Do you live off those protein shakes you advertise? Personally, I think they taste like crap." Even though I was happy that her mood had changed, and she was back to teasing me, I missed holding her. Not knowing what to do with my hands, I shoved them back in my pockets and leaned against the table she sat on.

"Are you in the habit of tasting crap?"

"No, but do you really eat the things you promote? Or just cash the checks?"

I shrugged. "They are really big checks."

"Seriously? You've become that guy?"

"You've been keeping an eye on me, Kelce?"

That got her tongue to stop wagging. She closed her mouth and shrugged. "I'm just making conversation. It's kind of an awkward moment."

"Uh-huh…" I couldn't hold back my smile. "You've been watching me."

"Aaron follows football quite religiously." She winced. "He's a Baltimore fan."

I shot to my feet. Blasphemy! Baltimore was a huge rival for Charlotte. "What? Why? Why would you let that happen?"

She stared at her shoes, glanced up, and winced.

"James," I answered for her. Of course. "Okay." I clapped my hands. "Well, that's unacceptable. We'll have to fix that—whatever it takes, Kelcie. And I don't care how much it angers your ex. If you won't let me maim James, at least let me make Aaron a Carolina fan. I can't get arrested for that.

She tilted her head back to me, her eyes brightened, and her smile grew. It was a shot of sunshine peeking through the gloom. James hadn't silenced her or dimmed her light completely. She was in there, that mischievous, determined, strong-willed girl who'd always led the charge.

I made her smile. I could still make her smile.

Mirroring my stance, she shoved her hands in her pockets and rocked back on her heels, making me wonder who originally had that habit and who'd picked it up from the other.

"Well," she said, her entire demeanor lightening, "I believe that is one revenge plot I can get behind."

Grace's head popped out of the back door. "Hey, sorry, guys, but..." She hesitated, grimacing to Shaw. She held Kelce's phone. "Um, the police are at your house, Kelcie."

The blaring noise from the speaker had us both on our feet with athletic speed. "What the hell?" I said.

Kelcie's lips were tilted to one side in a knowing smile. "This"— she walked around me, gesturing for the phone—"is why I kept telling y'all I had things under control."

"What is going on?" Grace asked, hesitantly handing her the phone.

Kelcie ignored us and hit the speaker. "This is Mrs. Byron."

"Yes, ma'am. This is Officer Wills of Alexandria Police," a no-nonsense female voice sounded. "We were called to your residence this evening after a security alarm was set off. A gentleman claiming to be your husband entered the house without the proper code, setting off the alarm."

"I am her husband. If you let me go to my goddamn car, I can get my identification."

"Sir, I'm speaking to your *wife* now," Officer Wills sternly said to James.

Returning to the phone, she said, "Sorry, ma'am. I must commend you—this home security alarm is impressive. It seems to have woken half the neighborhood. In fact, most of your neighbors are outside with their cell phones catching the drama. Also, having the sprinkler system turned on the door was a nice touch."

Kelcie's smile was positively devilish. "Officer Wills, was anyone with my husband?"

"Excuse me?" the officer said.

"Was my husband alone?"

The officer chuckled and lowered her voice slightly. "There are reports of a woman fleeing the scene and running barefoot through the yards."

James swore obscenities in the background.

"I see," Kelcie said.

"There was mention of uploading footage to YouTube. I'm sure you can Google it," the officer said conspiratorially.

"What about all the shit she took?" James shouted.

"I'm getting to that," Officer Wills said. "Mrs. Byron, do you know anyone who would've burglarized your house? There wasn't any sign of forced entry, but Mr. Byron claims the place was cleaned out."

"I can't find the CrockPot! Where is the VitaMix? Why don't you ask her about that? And the towel warmer!" James shouted.

The officer let out an audible sigh. "Mrs. Byron, do you know—"

"They are still in the house. I haven't taken a thing, as per our agreement. He, on the other hand, agreed not to come over this weekend and swipe things behind my back," she said, her teeth clenched. "Obviously, things aren't going to be amicable. I apologize, Officer. We will handle this as a private matter. The objects in question are locked in the basement. The code is the date of our first date. If he can remember it, he can access it."

"Oh, good one," the officer whispered.

"May I speak to him, please?" She stared at her feet as she pushed a few rocks around with the toe of her shoe.

"You are such a jealous bitch."

I lunged for the phone, and Kelcie dodged me better than a wide receiver, glaring at me like a mother would a naughty child.

"No, I'm just not as stupid as you were hoping I'd be," Kelcie said. "You chose the field, and you set the rules. Don't get your panties in a twist when you can't play the game."

"This isn't a game. That's my stuff."

"It's *our* stuff—thirteen years of it. As we agreed, we will sit and sort it out like grown adults. Now stop trying to screw me and work on screwing your girlfriend."

"Vindictive bitch—"

"Whatever." Her voice was tired and bored. She punched the end button, crossed her arms over her chest, then fell onto a bench, her feet outstretched, and sighed deeply.

Grace, Aliya, and even Nick stood with me in silence, wide-eyed.

"What?" she asked. "Did you think I would walk out of that house assuming that he'd play fair?" She focused on me and repeated, "I told you I was fine."

6

Kelcie

June

When I returned home, James had the divorce moving full steam ahead. Amber had been humiliated by her own actions this time—although she would never admit it—and was eager to have me out of town. This, in turn, made James eager to divorce me with all expeditiousness.

I planned on moving back to Keysville. This did not go over well with James because of the inconvenience it would cause him. But when faced with alimony payments to support me while Aaron and I lived in our current home, he dropped the issue, and we split the house sale.

Shaw's brother, Dylan, owned a duplex property he was renovating—two attached homes that shared a porch. He was done with one half and had been working on the other half for a few weeks, so he offered to let me live there at a reduced rate while he finished the other side.

James was too busy with his new life to interfere with Aaron and me as we acclimated to our new routine and environment. I started my new job with the physical therapy practice in town, and Aaron spent his days with Grace's Aunt Maeve until school started.

One day, Shaw texted me, asking if Aaron and I had a minute to jump on a video call. Curious, I called Aaron into the room and pulled up my laptop. Shaw hadn't seen Aaron since he was a small child and only in passing at a few events the whole group attended. He'd never made a point of mingling with us, trying to minimize the drama.

I'd known Shaw as a skinny, pimply teen with a squeaky voice and feet too big for him to run a straight line without falling. But I'd seen him bulk up in size and confidence. I'd held his head when he had the flu, and I'd held his hand the night he was drafted, reaching his lifetime goal of playing professional football.

Yet, the man's smile always took me by surprise. When he smiled at me, for a heartbeat, I'd lose my ability to form words. He'd appear happy to see me, and for the briefest moment, all the history between us would fade.

For a few seconds, I could pretend he wasn't a celebrity football player but just a boy I'd grown up with, a man I'd fantasized about.

Then my brain would come back online, reality would hit me upside the head, and I would remember who I was to him. I was the friend who found a date for him to take to prom, the pal who'd helped him pass high school English so he'd get his scholarship.

I thought back to the day I ran to his house to tell him I got a lacrosse scholarship from the same college he was attending—something we both had wanted. Then I heard him in his locked bedroom with Maxine Vanderson and knew I couldn't go through four years of that.

The tears that had welled in my eyes at hearing him with another girl…again. It just hit me—I wasn't just one of the guys. I felt more than friendship for him. We needed—no, I needed—to go in a different direction. It was time.

My dad had been right. We needed to live our own lives. I tore up the letter and never told him about it. From that moment on, everything changed.

And even though he still managed to take my breath away with that dangerous smile, I needed to salvage our friendship first. Then, with luck, I'd be able to face my unresolved, unrequited feelings for him later.

"Hey, ya'll, how's it going? How's the summer been so far?" I'd video-chatted with him a few times since he started training camp, mainly updating him on how we were settling in.

"Good," Aaron and I chimed together.

Shaw began walking again, but a door shut behind him. Keys rattled on a table.

"Where are you?" I asked.

"Just finished my afternoon workout. I'm home and about to get cleaned up, but I wanted to catch you two while I had a chance."

He stopped for a moment. "Aaron, my man. Good God, now that you are standing by your mom, I realize how big you've gotten. Are you taller than your mom?"

"Not yet. I'm five feet two inches, and she's five feet five inches. But I'm close."

"Well, if you take after your mom's side of the family, you will bypass her by the summer's end. Your grandfather is almost as tall as I am." Shaw drank some water and was walking around what I guessed was his home in Charlotte.

"Dad says I'm more like him than Mom's side of the family."

I gritted my teeth and said nothing. Shaw was quiet for a moment, and the tension in his smile indicated that he was biting back a snarky remark, too.

He managed to resist. "Yeah. Okay. Well, your mother told me you were a Baltimore fan."

"Yes. Dad and I love Baltimore football."

Shaw tilted his head, narrowing his eyes at my son in mock seriousness. "Well, you know I play for Carolina."

"Yes, you are number 88." My son settled in to give Shaw a rundown on himself. "Drafted in the first round ten years ago and traded to Carolina two years ago for a draft pick. In 130 targets last year, you made eighty-seven receptions and ran for 1,100 receiving yards, scored—"

I touched his arm gently. "I think Shaw knows his own statistics, honey…"

"That's alright," Shaw said, trying unsuccessfully to hold back his amusement. We hadn't been around Shaw in the last few years, and if I was reading his reaction right, Shaw was entertained. "You know how much I love hearing about myself."

"I'm sure your ego feeds off of it," I added. And because this was Shaw, I couldn't hold back the dryness in my tone.

Ignoring me, he focused on Aaron. "We're coming up to play Baltimore in a few weeks. I was wondering if you'd like tickets?"

Aaron's expression went blank. He sat back, grew quiet, staring down at his hands that were folded in his lap. Then he began to fidget with his fingers. Without looking up, he asked, "Could my mom come?"

Shaw's smile faded as, even over the video feed, he picked up on Aaron's change in mood.

"Yes, of course, buddy. I wouldn't forget about her. You know she used to be my biggest fan?"

Aaron picked at his fingers, deep in his thoughts, bit his lip more, and shifted in his seat. He was getting unsettled.

I leaned over and whispered, "We don't have to go."

"I want to go," he whispered back, leaning closer. "But…you know what Dad says"—he shifted closer and glanced up briefly at Shaw—"about the stadiums being too loud for me and how they would hurt my ears."

That was going to be an issue. Aaron's hearing was extremely sensitive, keeping us out of movie theaters, sporting events, and concerts. We watched everything at home, where he could control the volume and take a break when needed.

Unsure of how to handle this, I turned back to the screen, ready to ask Shaw for time to think about it.

"Hey, guys, I forgot to tell you the best part. I got you a box. Do you know what that means?"

Aaron shook his head while my mouth was unable to form words.

Shaw chuckled before continuing. "It means you, your mom, Grace, Aliya, Aunt Maeve, and maybe my pain-in-the-butt brother can all come to watch me play. I got a suite, and you can sit in a separate room that looks over the entire stadium and watch the game. It has doors so you can go inside. There will be food and drinks, so you won't have to stand in lines." My heart melted at what he must have done to get these tickets.

Aaron stopped biting his lip and turned to me for confirmation. I nodded. "They are some of the best seats in the stadium," I reassured him, "I think we can do this. I have a few ideas."

My hopeful boy stared back at Shaw. "Okay. I want to go to a game —especially a Baltimore game."

Shaw grabbed his heart and winced. "You're killing me, my man. Please. Please. Try to keep your favoritism to yourself that day. Give me and Charlotte a chance…"

Aaron shrugged, but there was a hint of a smile peeking through.

Shaw pointed at the phone. "I'm going to make you convert—just wait." He turned his focus to me. "I already told Grace, and she will coordinate the arrangements. I will have a car service pick you guys up and drive you to the stadium, so hopefully, I can see you before and after the game."

"Shaw, that isn't necessary. Baltimore isn't even an hour away. We can handle it—" I began to argue.

He held up his hand. "Already ordered. This way, you all can relax and not worry about driving home."

Aaron was still fidgeting with his fingers. He was obviously still worried.

I opened my arms. "Honey, we got this." He stepped into my hug but didn't wrap his arms around me. I squeezed him gently, hoping the pressure would reassure him. "It will be fine. We will talk about it and come up with a plan." He responded best when things were laid out as a plan.

He nodded, stepped back, and glanced at the screen but could not hold direct contact. "Shaw, I would love to come see you play."

"I am so excited for you to watch in person. Now, here's the deal.

The only thing I need you to do is promise me not to wear anything with Baltimore's logo. You'll kill my reputation."

Aaron's smile grew. "Okay. Deal. But I may still root for my favorite players—just quietly."

Shaw gave an exaggerated side-eye. "I see I have my work cut out for me. But that's okay. Challenge accepted. I will become your favorite player." He winked and clapped his hands together. "Okay. I have to go. I will be in touch and see you two in a few weeks."

"Thank you," Aaron said, quickly jumping off the stool and running out of the room as if he had something pressing to do.

Shaw and I both waited for his door to shut. Then Shaw's face fell, and his real thoughts showed. "Should I not have done that? I thought it would be a fun surprise."

I let out a beleaguered sigh and shook my head. "No, it was sweet, and we do appreciate it. Aaron has always wanted to go to a game. But James was afraid to take him."

"Afraid?"

I shook my head and waved my hands to dismiss that conversation. "It will be fine. I have an idea that may work. We will have a blast. I appreciate you doing this for us."

He leaned back in his chair, rubbing his hands through his hair as the word *Carolina* that was scrawled across his t-shirt stretched over his broad chest. "I just thought you both could use a distraction, and it would be something fun for him to do after school starts."

I nodded. "It will be fun."

"I can't believe how grown-up he's becoming," Shaw said, and I didn't miss the melancholy tone in his voice.

"Yeah, I know. He's like a little man now." My heart ached that he'd missed out on knowing Aaron all these years. "I wish—"

Then a feminine voice said, "Shaw, honey, we have to get you dressed and ready." Shaw turned his head. "We have to go in forty-five minutes."

Riley, with long blonde locks of hair, entered the frame. She leaned over Shaw's arm to see who he was on the call with.

We'd met only a handful of times, and she had a quizzical look on her face, indicating I wasn't that memorable. Shaw helped her out. "Riley, this is Kelcie. Remember, she's one of my friends from back home."

And that was what I was—just an old friend from home. Nothing more or less. Someone he was helping through a tough patch. Her face brightened with understanding. "Ohhh! Yes." She nodded and flashed me a sympathetic but no less dazzling smile. "Hi, Kelcie. I'm Riley."

"Yes, I—"

Shaw interrupted before I could explain how we had previously met. "Kelcie, her son, and a few others will be at the Baltimore game."

"Oh, what fun." She stared open-eyed at him, as if trying to say something. "Umm…but I'm going to be sitting with the—"

Shaw shook his head, lowering his voice. "I got them their own box suite. They'll sit with Grace, Maeve, and the group. You can hang out with the wives and girlfriends in their section."

She straightened then smiled again. "Oh, oh. Okay." Then, she began shooing him off the call. "Nice to talk with you, Kelcie, but I need to get this guy in the shower and ready for the evening."

Get this guy in the shower. I'm sure she did.

Stop. It.

I plastered on a "you-two-are-so-cute-I-could-puke" smile and said, "Have a great night. Thank you for the invitation, Shaw. We will see you in a few weeks. Night!" and I closed the laptop before I said something I shouldn't.

Believing I was alone, I gagged at the computer.

"Mom, are you going to puke on the computer?" Aaron snuck up on me. "Are you sick?"

I stood, pushing the offending laptop away. "No, darling, I'm fine. What's up? I thought you were in your room." I went into the kitchen to make him a snack, hoping against hope that he wouldn't share my reaction with Shaw when he saw him.

7

————————

Kelcie

September

"Mom…" Aaron came into the kitchen, holding his headphones. "Do I have to take these?"

I opened the dishwasher and started to put the dishes away but turned to give him my full attention. He usually took his earphones everywhere without issue, especially somewhere unfamiliar and with a very loud, very big crowd.

Even after years of various therapies, noise was still extremely difficult for him to handle. The fact that he was even willing to try to attend the game was monumental.

I leaned across the counter and put the drying towel on my shoulder. "Do you want to take them?"

He stared down at them, shifting on his feet. "I want to take them because I need them. I just don't want to need them."

I walked over to him and touched his shoulder. "First of all, I think it is a very mature thing that you recognize that you may need them."

He didn't say anything but continued staring at the headphones.

I put a hand on each shoulder, facing him but not forcing him to look at me. "I think taking them would be a good idea."

He nodded. "Okay."

But he didn't turn away. He kept stroking the top of the earphones. "Other boys don't wear them. People look at me."

This was the part I hated. Sometimes it was very frustrating to have a child on the autism spectrum. As he got older, he became aware of his differences and, too often, had those differences blatantly pointed out as unacceptable. I realized I couldn't change how the world reacted to his perceived quirks or his needs—the ignorance and cruelty of others weren't within my control. The best I could do was prepare him for how to deal with it.

I opened a drawer, took out a small container I recently bought, and handed it to him. "These are earplugs used by men who work in really loud places—like with jets and construction sites. They are made of foam, so they are more comfortable than what we tried before. Do you want to try them?"

He reached for them and studied them.

"They can fit in your pocket," I added. "Why don't you go in the bathroom and see if you like them? I think there are instructions for how to place them in properly."

He nodded but hooked his earphones around his neck, keeping them with him like a security blanket.

"You know, we don't have to go—"

He immediately shook his head. "I want to go. I want to go to a game."

"Okay, then we'll go. We can take it one step at a time. Remember I showed you what the suite would look like." I reached into the fridge to grab some juice. "We'll have snacks and drinks in the suite, and we can watch from the seats outside or go inside if it gets too loud." I grabbed a glass and poured him some juice, setting it down in front of him. "And Shaw sent us jerseys with his number so we can look like him. But if it's not comfortable, we can—"

"I want the jersey." He drank his juice.

Of course he did. I nodded. "Okay, then. We have our wardrobe arranged."

He finished the juice, and his face lit up. "So, we'll be the same." He smiled.

In the past, anything that reminded James of how close Shaw and I used to be was an automatic invitation to drama. I'd had to leave all my Shaw memorabilia with my dad—photos, college jerseys, mementos. Nothing had come with me.

One silver lining to the divorce: none of that mattered now.

I was reclaiming a part of who I used to be, the piece of the person who was so interwoven with Shaw that it had become part of my identity—Shaw and Kelcie, Kelcie and Shaw. Well, alright, we weren't anywhere near that now. But going to his game, wearing his jersey to cheer him on… That seemed like a first step to reclaiming who I used to be because, throughout my high school crushes and his college hook-ups, we always had a spot for each other.

Until James. Until Aaron.

When I chose to marry the father of my child, I disengaged from Dawson Shawfield's rising star and did not saddle him with my burdens, but I left a piece of myself behind too. Now, without James's demands and conditions, maybe reclaiming that part of myself could help smooth out a decade of change, and we could establish at least a newly defined surface friendship. It would have to be rewarding enough. Considering how different our lives had become, it would be enough of a blessing. I couldn't bring myself to wish for more.

I smiled back at him. "That sounds like a great plan."

8

Shaw

The night before the game, I called to check in and see if everything was set for the next day. I'd talked with Kelcie about what to expect at the stadium and arranged for a driver to pick them and the rest of our crew up. Aaron and I had started texting regularly as he familiarized himself with my team's roster, and I was more than happy to bring him over from the dark side.

"Did you get my package?" I'd called Kelcie to check on the matching *Shaw* jerseys and t-shirts I'd sent.

"Is that the price of the ticket?" she teased. "We're all supposed to be your box of groupies? Don't you have enough of those?"

"Yeah. Yeah. But did they fit? I wanted to know what Aaron thought—"

"Oh, Aaron has lots of thoughts. He's been following the IR list and all the latest films from the last few games. He has lots and lots of thoughts."

I guffawed. "About me?"

"You. Your QB, your defensive line... I told him he couldn't have your cell number because you were on electronic lockdown to avoid press and focus on the game."

"You lied to your son?" I produced the most pathetic pearl-clutching gasp I could manage. "Shame on you, Kelcie Byron."

"Trust me. It was in your best interest. After the game, I will buy you a beer or a six-pack, and he can break it all down for you."

"That sounds like a plan."

"You don't believe me?"

"Kelce, he's what, twelve? I've been grilled, picked apart, and fried in the press, during interviews, and by public opinion. I'm sure I can handle it."

"I'll bring a box of tissues, just in case."

"Come on…"

"Shaw, he's Holden Hammer's grandson. Do you really think he'd mince words about sports?" Holden Hammer was Kelcie's rough-around-the-edges bear of a father who'd also been my coach and mentor. After several high school state championships, Coach Hammer had been pulled up the ranks in the college system. He'd honed his no-nonsense approach to coaching with me. With my father not in the picture, I had been an unfocused, misdirected lump of man-clay Coach had set out to mold into not just a player but also a decent man—just not a man decent enough for his daughter.

That had been one of Hammer's unspoken rules—maybe his only one. His daughter was not going to get wrapped up with a football player. And that included me.

"Give him my cell."

"Shaw—"

"I want to hear what he has to say."

"Okay. Don't say I didn't warn you," she sing-songed.

"So, you all set with the driver and everything tomorrow?"

"Yeah, the gang is coming over, and we'll leave from here."

"Great. I'll meet up with you all after the game. If he's up for it, I'll send someone up to the box to get you to come down to the locker room."

"Oh, boy. That may be too tempting for him to resist. He might be jockeying for a coaching job before we leave," she joked. Then she sighed. "Most likely, he will be done by the second half, but we can see how it goes."

"Okay, well, I want him to have fun, so whatever it takes."

"Thanks, Dawson. Seriously. We've been looking forward to this."

"Wow, pulling out the first name. I can't remember the last time anyone called me Dawson."

She was quiet, and I kicked myself. She was one of the few people who'd called me Dawson. It didn't happen often, but her slight Southern drawl made it uniquely hers. Hearing it from her filled me with nostalgia.

"It's going to feel like old times, having you at my game, cheering me on."

She was still quiet, and I cursed myself for not FaceTiming instead of just calling on the phone. I wanted to see the expression that accompanied this unusual response.

"I'm glad you—and the rest of the gang—are coming," I added. "I'm thrilled it will be Aaron's first game." I paused because I wanted her to know what reconnecting meant to me. "But seriously, Kelce, I didn't think I'd ever see you again in the stands, rooting for me. So, thank you."

"I've always been rooting for you," she said softly then added, with a lift in her voice, "After all, I was your original fan."

"I guess you were."

"Anyway, we will see you tomorrow. And you know..." She lowered her voice and whispered into the phone, "Kick some ass."

"Absolutely." I stared at the phone in my hand, failing to control the excitement growing inside me. Because while I knew I'd eventually make it to the Super Bowl, I wasn't so sure that I'd ever get Kelcie at one of my games.

"Shaw, my man, what's up with you and that goofy-ass smile on your face? Was that Riley? Did she tell you how much she l-o-v-e-s you?"

Davy Johnson, the team's veteran running back and my pain-in-the-ass friend, was making kissy noises and puckering up in my face—not many men were brave enough to do that—as I walked into the trainer's area in the locker room on game day.

"Cut it out, man," I said half-heartedly, my mind on my guests in the skybox, settling in for the game.

Honestly, even with my girlfriend, Riley, or anyone else, I never got nervous or excited before a game. But today… "I just got off the phone with Kelcie, setting things up for her and her son. Good call on the skybox."

Davy nodded once, knowingly. "Glad it worked out. We used to have to do it when my nephew came to watch. Even then, getting through the crowds was rough, and some days, he just wasn't up for it."

I nodded. I was feeling entirely out of my depth. I wasn't even a father, so how would I have any experience with helping a child on the spectrum deal with challenging environments?

"You are more skittish than a long-tailed cat in a room full of rocking chairs," Davy said when we both were laid out on the trainer's table, getting our ankles taped before the game.

I cracked my knuckles and shook out my hands. Mo, my favorite trainer, stared at me with impatience in her eyes and a scolding tone. "Don't look at me like that. It's not my fault you're running late."

I grimaced. "I know. Sorry."

"Is everyone settled?" Davy asked, leaning back on the table.

I shifted so the trainer could tape my foot. "I got Aaron and Kelcie matching jerseys—well, I got the whole crew jerseys. When I called to check on them, Aaron was watching game footage in the box, waiting for the game to start, and eating French fries." I cracked my knuckles again. "Kelcie didn't think it was a good idea for me to see them before the game."

"Too much stimulation for the kid?"

"No. She was afraid he'd mess with my mojo. She said he would pick apart my game and get in my head." I shrugged.

Davy stared at me, bemused. "What? He's just a kid."

I shook my head. "I know, but that's what she said. And trust me, if he's anything like her or her dad, his filter will be nonexistent when they are talking football. Kelcie's nickname in high school was Sergeant for a reason. She made guys cry before they made it off the field."

"Dang. And you had a thing for this girl?"

I shrugged, and the routine response came easily. "We were just friends," I said, studying the trainer's work on my foot.

"You never—"

"Nope. Nothing."

"You ever think about it?"

I stood up, refusing to discuss this with him. "We were kids. It was a lifetime ago."

"Yeah, you thought about it," Davy said, and I heard the smile in his tone as I walked away to get dressed for warm-ups.

As I made my way to the field to stretch for the pre-game, I looked up. There wasn't anyone in the seats, and the sliding door to the interior of the box was closed. Kelce told me they would sit inside and allow Aaron to acclimate. I wished I had seen the matching jerseys…

It'd been so long since she'd worn a jersey of mine. It had been a long-held tradition that she was the only girl who ever got to wear my high school and college jersey until my number had been licensed and sold to the public. Then, I lost all control of who could buy it. But I never gave another woman a jersey of mine to wear. Only Kelcie.

I'd lost girlfriends over that. I could give them my sweatshirt, jacket, whatever, but the minute they started to demand the jersey… well, it was an issue.

When we first started dating, Riley wore my jersey to the first game. But once she was invited to sit with the WAGS (wives and girlfriends), that stopped. She said she wanted to look her best for me, not like just another fan. I think it had more to do with the fact that the camera occasionally cut to the WAGs' suite when one of us made an amazing play, and Riley always wanted to stand out.

As I stretched out my calves, my mind wandered back to that

skybox and the day we'd first met during the first high school football practice.

Kelcie ran the warm-ups and did stretches with the guys like a boss. Half the size of most of the boys on the team, she demanded their undivided attention and their submission.

I walked on the field with Tyler as the new kid in town. Tall and thin enough to be blown over in a summer storm, I had enough trouble walking with my disproportionately large feet, let alone running drills, without tripping.

I shifted into lunges as I smiled at the memory of her yelling at me when I wasn't doing a stretch correctly, singling me out, and the heat on my face hadn't been from the summer sun.

I snuck another peek up to the box.

Did she ever watch the games when she was with James? Did he really make it an issue? Screw him. I wish I could put her on the Jumbotron in my jersey and send a photo to him.

I stopped stretching and stared at the Jumbotron above me, thinking about the possibilities. I bet Wyatt—our enigmatic techie friend— could manage it.

A groan escaped me as I lowered myself to the ground to stretch my legs, back, and hamstrings.

Jeez, since when did I start groaning like an old man? I attempted to turn it into a growl. It was weak.

Please, God, don't let the rookies hear me.

"Need some Bengay over there, Shaw?" Our first-round draft had the balls to poke at me.

"Did they make sure your diaper was secure for when the Baltimore defense makes you shit yourself, Thomas?" I shot back, not even looking up at him.

This led to other jabs and taunts among the players, and I phased out of it. When I stood, I stared up at the skybox again then swung my arms out to stretch my shoulders.

"Hey, did Riley make the trip up here with you?" Lance, a young safety, had a not-so-discreet crush on my girlfriend. Most of the male population was envious of my life and the drop-dead gorgeous girl-friend who'd moved in with me.

"Where is Riley?"

"Hey, Shaw, is Riley with you?"

The questions came at me all the time. I was a serial monogamous, one-woman man. If there was a commitment, I upheld it. I never bought a ring or came close, but I'd met some good women who'd tried to persuade me.

"Yeah, she came up for the game." I pointed my finger at him, half-joking. "So don't make an ass of yourself."

After completing stretches and running to warm up, we disappeared into the locker room for final instructions and to mentally prepare. Some guys needed to get in the zone—meditate, use positive imagery, listen to loud pounding music, joke around, or do whatever it took to focus us.

As for me, I switched on my music, adjusted my headphones, leaned back in the chair by my locker, and closed my eyes. I pictured the plays, reaching for the ball, running the ball, blocking the opponents, engaging my body, and pushing them back. I imagined the power in my legs and the weight in their blocks and called on my body —getting old with use and abuse—to do right by me today.

A tap on my shoulder pulled me out of it, and I slid the earphones down to my shoulders. "It's time. Let's go."

Time to earn my paycheck.

9

Shaw

At this point in my career, I wouldn't say I was desensitized to being in front of 70,000 people in the stadium and another 10-20 million televised, but I'd learned to block most of it out and focus on the opponent.

After all the pomp and circumstance of the opening, I stepped into the huddle, shaking out my hands as our quarterback went over the first play—a short jet sweep to Davy. My job was to block for him.

Done.

We gained a few yards in the next two plays but nothing to cheer over.

Back to the huddle a few more times. A few more plays—some good, some not so good.

I got to seven minutes left in the first quarter when I was on the sidelines, and curiosity got the better of me. I turned to look up over my shoulder to see if my gang was out in the seats.

Grace and a few of their friends were sitting by the railing, talking but watching the field. Aaron and Kelcie were in the doorway, Aaron leaning against the frame, my jersey proudly displayed. Kelcie leaned over to him, pointing my way, saying something to him, and waving. I held up my hand and was relieved when he straightened and waved back.

Okay. Things were okay.

Davy smacked me in the chest. "Come on. We're up."

After making progress down the field, we finally reached the seventeen-yard line. The coaches called for a play that was my specialty.

I lined up for the snap and took off running alongside our fastest wide receiver, who cut to the outside—a decoy for the defense to chase.

I cut off the midfield and saw my quarterback scrambling before he launched the ball to me. I had enough time to eye a defender on a collision course with me from the right. I lifted my hand in the air, grasped the ball with my fingertips, and pulled it into my chest just as I juked him to the right. Within two strides, I reached the end zone for the touchdown.

I stopped on a dime, and with the ball in my hand, I pointed at the skybox where Kelcie and the crew were. This was for them.

Without them, I wouldn't have been on this field. Without them, I don't know where life would've taken me. When I'd first moved to town with a single mom and a younger brother, I'd been a lost, shy kid with a bad haircut and big ears. Kelcie and the gang had practically enveloped me and became the family I'd made. Summers down by the river, we all begrudgingly became friends.

Tyler, Wyatt, and I would escape to the woods behind Grace's aunt's farm when the girls were being weird, and we needed to do boy stuff. Grace tutored me in math, Tyler introduced me to football, and Kelcie ran laps with me on the track. And then there was Wyatt, who was different than most kids—hell, than most adults. When Grace's aunt offered him the kindness the world had never shown him, and we all followed suit, we became his family, and he was the glue that kept us together all these years.

I tossed the ball over to a ref while my teammates Davy and Braydon smacked my helmet in appreciation for the TD. They fell in line while I did my signature Shawfield Shuffle—a bit of a two-step with swag. I didn't do it as often as I used to, but the roar of the fans— even at the rivals' stadium—was louder when I did. It was a special occasion, after all. I had to ham it up for Aaron and Kelcie.

The rest of the game was competitive but relatively uneventful. With Baltimore up and one quarter to go, the score was twenty-one to twenty-seven.

I wasn't worried. Our offense was closing in, and if our defense could hold them, we'd be okay.

I glanced up at the box again, wondering how Aaron was handling it.

A hand smacked the back of my helmet. "Come on, man. We aren't quite done yet," one of the receivers said.

More blocking. More running.

Baltimore was forced to sub in their rookie linebacker when their starter went out injured. And now I was forced to deal with a smack-talking kid with a lot of ego and not a lot of sense. "Hey, old man, let's see you run that play again with me on the field this time."

The problem with hot-shot, first-round rookies was that they were used to being the best. From their middle school years through college, they'd been rock stars. But now they were in the big leagues and had to prove themselves. Talking shit to veterans didn't earn respect, yet each year, some young fool tried it with me, and today, it looked like it was going to be this linebacker with something to prove.

I shook my head and lined up across from the tough-talking rookie. "How about I give you a heads-up when that happens?" I replied, *asshole* left unsaid at the end of my statement.

He lined up and sneered at me from across the line. I rolled my eyes.

Davy finished the latest drive with a beautiful run, and we got the extra point. We were up twenty-eight to twenty-seven.

I was running on the field and glanced at the skybox, wondering if Aaron could make it through the whole game. I wanted to spend time with them afterward and see what he thought of being at the stadium.

Head in the game, Shawfield.

The quarterback gave us the play, and we broke the huddle. I put on my game face, ignoring the rookie's incessant bantering. Sure, I might be older. I may even be slower at this point in my career…but I was more experienced. The quarterback took the snap, I juked to the inside, and once he gained momentum, I cut back across his back, opening myself up for a long pass to what seemed like an open field.

This would be great. Another TD for them to see. This would clinch the win.

BAM.

What the fuck—

BAM.

Well, this sucks—

WHACK.

Fuck—

10

Kelcie

"I don't think this is a good idea," I said as Shaw's younger brother, Dylan, gently propelled me through the double doors leading from the garage to the hospital elevators. He pressed the button and stared at the descending numbers, ignoring my protests.

Grace was getting Aaron something to eat. They would meet us here later because nothing was keeping Aaron from checking on Shaw.

Dylan herded me into the elevator's cabin when the doors opened like a border collie would a wayward sheep. A smaller version of Shaw, Dylan Shawfield's body was cut from days of physical work, not days in the gym. Bearded, tanned, and a little more rugged, the younger brother had always gone his own way—more subdued and maybe a little more laidback. Even his walk conveyed ease as he smiled and greeted everyone.

"It's probably best if we just wait until he's home. We can call there to check on him," I said, trying again.

He repeated the movement inside, not acknowledging my weak protestations.

"I know your brother. He's going to hate visitors," I said, adjusting my tote bag.

Dylan stared at the ascending numbers over the doors, a slight tilt of his lips. "You either forgot who you're talking about, or you're lying to yourself."

"He's probably in pain, or maybe he's resting…" I mumbled.

He ignored my protest.

Then, another, more likely, scenario occurred to me. I huffed and turned to him. "He's probably with Riley. Maybe they want some time alone. His people are probably very concerned—"

That got his full attention, and he zeroed in on me. "*We* are his people." The elevator dinged. Dylan took a step out and then stopped abruptly to cock his head at me. "Aren't we?"

"Yes, of course." I thought so.

No. He was right. Before the fans, bright lights, agents, and all the extras—before his fame and success—we were his people.

I followed Dylan, fighting my default response of minimizing my importance in Shaw's life. It had been ingrained in me for the past decade because he was a multi-million-dollar household name and a celebrity football star, while I'd been a regular mom, married to a man who didn't appreciate the friendship we once shared.

We were once each other's people. Now, we were heart-warming nostalgia with a dash of regret and awkwardness.

Nostalgia wasn't what Shaw needed now, and time had changed both of us. We'd outgrown each other. I wasn't the person he'd relied on, and our support had limits—didn't it?

We stopped in front of a hospital room, and I adjusted my tote, straightened my back, and smoothed my ponytail. Dylan viewed me over his shoulder with his hand on the handle and an

almost devious half-grin on his face. "Besides, my brother wanted to see you and Aaron after the game. He'd be disappointed if you didn't come." Then Dylan stepped into the room.

"Well, good morning, man." Shaw's booming voice was a bit hoarse as Dylan preceded me. "Did you bring me anything? I'm starving."

I forced a smile and stepped forward, pushing the privacy curtain out of my way to see Shaw sitting there in a hospital bed. His smile was a bit loopy but completely brilliant.

I wanted to hug him and tell him he would be fine. I wished to God this chasm I felt with him would just disappear. Did he feel it?

Eventually, we'd fill it. We had to. *I* had to.

"I brought you a surprise," Dylan said and followed up, in a completely deadpan voice, "just not something you can…necessarily…eat."

"Dylan!" My indignation flew out of my mouth before I realized I had given in to his innuendo. It would've been wiser to ignore his smart-ass remark. Heat traveled up my neck and over my cheeks.

Dylan's smile was broad and unrepentant. Then all other repercussions were cut off with the arrival of Shaw's girlfriend, Riley Lynn—model/media personality/aspiring actress. The woman made entering a hospital room an event. She was gorgeous—and not in a fake way, but a genetics-jackpot kind of way.

We parted for her like the Red Sea as she eyed us, politely smiled, and casually dismissed us as unimportant.

Her act was wasted on us. "Shaw, baby." She strutted to his bed in faux-leather pants, high-heeled boots, and an amazing blouse that probably cost more than my entire wardrobe—including my purse and what was in my wallet. She leaned over and gave him a light kiss on his forehead, brushed away her lip gloss, and patted his hand. "How are you, honey?"

Shaw held the same dopey gaze. "Hey, Riles."

His eyes traveled back to focus on Dylan and me. "I'm good. Look, Dylan and Kelcie came to visit me."

"I see that," she said with a sweet voice that didn't do anything to authenticate her acting credentials. She scooted herself up to sit on his bed. "Has Ayva called? What about your doctor? What did they say about your prognosis?"

His dopey smile was still in place, and his eyebrows reached higher as his eyelids drooped lower. He seemed to be trying to focus on her. "Hm?"

She spoke slower and louder, jutting her chin out closer to his face, as if he were hard of hearing. "What did the doctor say about when you will get out of here?" Then she lowered her voice, pointedly keeping her back to us to keep the conversation private. "What did they say about how long you will be out for?"

Dylan cleared his throat and sat in the chair behind him, beside Shaw's bed, crossing his leg over his knee and making himself comfortable—he was staying a while.

Riley glanced over to us, her fake smile slipping.

"Who is Ayva?" I whispered to Dylan. I, on the other hand, didn't feel comfortable sitting here while they were trying to have a private conversation.

"His manager." Dylan typed something on his phone, quirked an eyebrow at me, and motioned for me to sit in the chair next to him. Since he was my ride and we were waiting on Grace and Aaron, I guess we would be staying for a while.

While he diligently typed on his phone, I tried to find a reason to leave the room, fidgeting with my purse to pull out my phone. I should check on Grace…only my call wouldn't go through. "I think I'll try to find where Grace and Aaron have run off to."

I shoved the phone back in my purse and went to stand up, but Dylan's hand closed over my arm to still me. His phone was still in front of him, but his eyes studied the couple. "Wyatt is caught up in Seattle, but he hopes you are on some good drugs," Dylan said, leaning around Riley to catch Shaw's attention.

"Wyatt?" Shaw said.

"Yes. He saw the game and was wondering how you were. He said to let him know if you needed anything and to keep him updated."

"What could Wyatt do from the other side of the country?" Riley said, dismissing the offer out of hand just as her phone rang.

Dylan put his phone back in his pocket, trying to hide his growing smile. He said under his breath, "You'd be surprised."

Luckily, the doctor walked in with a trail of underlings behind him. They unsuccessfully hid their gawking as their eyes grew bigger, dancing between the beauty of Shaw and Riley.

"Good morning, Mr. Shawfield…" The interns ran through his diagnosis, treatment, and finally, prognosis.

The petite doctor with the corkscrew curls turned to the team of interns, giving the rest of us her back, and asked for the others to present his case. I listened while Riley, Shaw, and Dylan whispered about what Shaw's manager was saying about the team and speculated on his return to play.

From what I was hearing, it wouldn't be anytime soon. In layman's terms, Shaw had done quite a bit of damage—a broken clavicle, herniated disc, and a decent concussion. They had done surgery to pin the bone in his clavicle, but now only rest, physical therapy, and time would take care of the rest.

"It may be time to consider a change in profession and leave this job to the younger men," the doctor said to Shaw, who guffawed exaggeratedly, looking like an adorably intoxicated Yeti.

"I heal fast." He tilted his chin up as she examined him, checking his pupils and then his reflexes.

"Yeah, well, don't be in too much of a hurry. If these injuries don't heal properly, you could be back on my table with a laundry list of things to be taken care of," she said as she looked over the shoulder of the person inputting the information into his chart.

"Doctor, when can he leave?" Riley stepped into the room far enough to ask the question.

The doctor looked at her and said, "I'd like him to stay another twenty-four hours just to ensure we've got everything under control." There were whines and groans from Riley and Shaw before Riley pivoted and put the phone back up to her ear.

Shaw attempted to sit up straighter in bed, and Dylan jumped up to help support him in his efforts. But when his pain was too intense to push his body up physically, I stood on his other side and grabbed the bed controller to raise the bed slightly.

"How's that?" I asked him as I held his hand. I was surprised at the clarity in his eyes.

"Is that okay?" I asked quietly.

Our eyes met briefly as he sighed, "Yes, that's perfect. Thanks, Kelce."

My name in his husky voice sent a warm feeling through my body. Caring for him, even in that small way, felt right.

Riley stepped back into the room and closed in on his other side, reaching for his hand as they discussed next steps. I stepped back and retook my seat even as my clinical ears perked up.

The doctor discussed concussion protocol, immobilizing the arm and shoulder, intense physical therapy…need to watch over the next eight to twelve weeks, minimum."

"So he's out for most of the season?" Riley's face fell.

"We will have to see, maybe more, depending on an MRI. I don't like the numbness he had in his arms after the hit. But I'm afraid so—"

Shaw's head fell back against the pillow, his eyes closed. "But the numbness is gone."

"That's probably from the anti-inflammatories we've been pumping in your body." She motioned at the IV. "It doesn't change the fact that it was after an impact strong enough to break your clavicle. And your body, including your spine, has taken a lot of abuse."

Shaw took his hand from Riley's and ran it over his face.

The doctor continued talking to Shaw and Riley about what was planned for the next day or two and when he could be expected to leave. Shaw stared at his blanket, a grim expression on his face. He did this when he didn't want to hear what was being said to him—it always reminded me of a petulant child.

Dylan's chin was cradled in his hand, but his leg was shaking with impatience as he studied his brother.

I glanced at Dylan and whispered, "You're being awfully quiet."

He shrugged. "Just waiting."

"For what—"

Riley was full of nervous energy. Shifting and fidgeting, she jumped when her cell phone rang. "Oh, baby, it's my agent," she exclaimed as if it were Christmas morning and Santa was calling. "I'll be right back."

Dylan stepped forward and began asking questions about his restrictions—driving and the limitations of using his arm and shoulder. I asked about the kind of PT he would need and the follow-up schedule. The doctor smiled at both of us. "You seem to have a hell of a team working for you already, Mr. Shawfield."

Dylan laughed. "We don't work for him. I'm his brother," he said.

"Is she his sister?" A pretty intern gestured to me.

"Definitely not." Dylan let out a surprise laugh. "There is no brotherly love there."

I stepped away, going back to sit and stay out of everyone's way. What was I doing here anyway? I knew I shouldn't have come. I stared at my useless phone, trying to find a graceful way out of there.

An intern finished typing some notes on the keyboard by Shaw's bed as the doctor headed toward the door. At his obviously glum look, she added, "It's best you stay for another day or two. We have people whose entire career revolves around pain management. If we send you home, it will be with Tylenol." She clapped the guy at the computer on the shoulder and looked over at Shaw. "I'll come by and check on you later today. Let the nurses know if you need anything. It's nice to have you here—even if Carolina beat Baltimore." With a quick smile, she was gone, her entourage shuffling quietly after her.

As soon as the door closed, Dylan turned on me. "Kelcie—jeez, you look like someone kicked your dog. I was just joking. I meant you're not family because he never thought of you as a sis—"

"Dylan, just shut up," Shaw groaned.

Dylan sat beside me and quietly added, "I'm sorry. I didn't mean it—"

I patted his arm. Being the younger brother, Dylan often teased Shaw and me about the time we spent together. *"Shaw and Kelcie sitting in a tree...k-i-s-s-i-n-g..."* and all the things little brothers do. "It's okay. I know what you meant. But enough years have passed, and I think teasing him about me has had its time. You can give it a rest."

Dylan winked and whispered to me, "Never."

The door burst open, and Grace and Aaron barged in. "Shaw. Shaw.

Are you okay?" My son ran past me and straight up to Shaw's bedside, scanning everything around him but not quite looking at him.

"Yeah, my man, I'm fine," he said. "Come on over here and tell me about the game."

"We left when you got hurt," my son said matter-of-factly.

"Yes, but did you like the game?"

"Until you got hurt. Yes. I liked it a lot," Aaron said and nodded emphatically.

Riley stormed through like a whirlwind, her hands flapping. "Oh. My. God. Baby!"

She pushed past Aaron and threw herself at Shaw, forgetting all about his sling. He grimaced in pain.

Dylan pulled Riley back off Shaw. She stumbled in her heels and adjusted herself. "I'm sorry, I forgot myself. I'm just about to burst!"

Shaw shifted in his bed, and I reached for the controller to lower it for him. He gave me a grateful nod before turning back to his girlfriend.

"What is it, babe?"

She began jumping in her stilettos, clasping her hands to her chest, and screamed piercingly, "I got the part!"

Shaw's head tilted slightly, his brows drew together, all his concentration on the bouncing woman. "Part? What part?"

"When we were in LA, all that networking and stuff we did… someone mentioned me to the producer of *A New Adventure*—you know, that reality travel challenge—and they called my agent!" She began pacing around his bed.

"Oh. Did you try out for it or something?" Grace asked.

Riley didn't turn to acknowledge who asked but just waved her hand, dismissing the ignorant question. "No, no. I guess it's all about who you know. They want celebrities on these shows to get people to watch them."

Was she a celebrity?

Ok, that was unkind. She was an influencer and, you could say, a model. I guess they were automatically celebrities.

"Well…um…that's wonderful," Grace responded since no one else seemed in a rush to say anything.

Shaw ran his good hand over his face again. Poor guy. His world seemed to be changing every five minutes. Being doped up on pain medication probably wasn't helping him process everything.

I stepped up next. "Congratulations, Riley. How exciting." I threw in as much excitement and joy for her as I could because…good for her. This obviously meant a lot to her. There was a fair amount of envy on my part, not just because she was beautiful, and not just because Shaw loved her, but because she was passionate about achieving her dream.

She tossed her hair over her shoulder and said, "Thank you, Kelly."

Okay. I tried.

A slight noise came out of Grace, and I glimpsed over to see her covering her mouth, hiding her amusement.

Shaw shook his head, blinking his eyes slowly, but caught up enough to take my cue. "Yes, honey. Um…congratulations." He reached over to beckon her down and kiss her gently on the cheek. "I'm very happy for you." Was it just fatigue or medication that held back his legendary enthusiasm? Maybe his own dilemma was over-shadowing his joy for her. This lack of excitement wasn't like him.

We all went around offering our congratulations.

"So, when does it start?" Dylan asked, leaning against the sink.

She stilled, her head dropping as she hesitantly walked over to Shaw and took his hand. "Well, that's the thing." She cupped his hand in both of hers. "They want me in LA tomorrow."

"Tomorrow?" His brow furrowed, confusion returning.

"Yeah. I'll be gone for three to four months of shooting."

"Three or four months?"

"Yes. We are going to be traveling all over the world. A new adventure each week. New challenges and things to do, tasks for them to film…" It was clear she already had one foot out the door. "And since it's a contest…"—she winced—"we can't communicate with people at home."

"Riley…" Shaw's voice faded. "This is awfully sudden, isn't it? I mean, you aren't even packed."

She became more animated. "I know!" She paced around the bed. "I need to run back to Charlotte and get a few things." She plowed around everyone in her path as she paced. "My agent booked me on a flight this afternoon. I have a few hours in Charlotte before I get on a late-night flight to LA." She walked away from his bed, her fingertip to her lips. "This is crazy, isn't it?"

Silence fell in the room.

Shaw studied Riley.

Riley studied the floor.

Dylan, Grace, and I studied Shaw.

Aaron voiced the question we were all wondering. "But who will take care of Shaw?"

Riley's head popped up, and she rushed to sit at his bedside. "Oh, baby…what about you?"

And there it was. She finally thought about him and the fact that he was currently lying in a hospital bed.

"If I leave, who will take care of you in Charlotte—take you to your PT appointments and make sure you are eating and feeling okay?"

She turned to Dylan. "Can you take care of him?"

"Me? No, Riley, I own a business. I work—"

"You're a contractor. You work for yourself. Surely—"

Shaw held up his hand to stop them from going down that bumpy road, and his smile was sad but resolved. "I'll be fine." He lifted his hand and caressed her cheek. "I'll be okay, honey."

"But in Charlotte—"

Aaron stepped forward. "He can come home with us."

Five sets of eyes swung to Aaron and, in unison, said, "What?"

Aaron walked over and took my hand in his, his gaze resolute. "Mom and I can take care of him." He stood shoulder to shoulder with me. "Mom is a real good physical therapist, and I can babysit him after school.

Oh my God, my son with the heart of gold… I was going to kill him. "Aaron, I don't think Shaw would want to live with us. We don't have a lot of space, and he's used to his privacy—"

"Mr. Dylan, what about the other side of the house we live in?"

"The other side of the duplex is finished, actually." Dylan brightened, his back to Shaw, knowingly putting me on the spot.

Aaron squeezed my hand. "See. It will be perfect."

My phone chose that moment to work, ringing with a shrill sound that I thought was saving me from an uncomfortable situation. Then I looked at the caller ID.

James. My stomach clenched. What did he want?

I sent the call to voicemail. I could only deal with one situation at a time.

My moment of distraction solidified Dylan and Aaron into a united team. "He'll come home with us," Aaron said, and Dylan put his hand on Riley's shoulder.

"Don't worry about our guy here. We've got him. He'll be back on the field in no time."

Riley perked up at that idea and began gathering herself to leave. She cupped Shaw's face and kissed him deeply. I closed my eyes, wishing I didn't have to witness this.

"Alright, then, I see you are in good hands. I'll call you, baby, when I get to LA and let you know more of the details."

I turned away from them in disbelief. How could she just leave him in the hospital?

Grace gently added, "Hey, guys, I heard traffic getting to BWI may be an issue. Riley, you'd better get going."

She bounced on her toes. "Uh. Okay." Pulling on her hair, she turned back to Shaw, kissed him again, and began walking toward the door. "Are you sure?"

"Go," he whispered, as if he would ask her to stay at this point.

She slung her purse over her shoulder and stepped backward to the door. "You get better, and by the time I get back, you'll be back on the field. I will email you my emergency contact information and try to call when my contract allows."

"Sounds good." He gave her a small wave, as if he were sending off a colleague, not a woman he'd been in a relationship with. "Be safe."

And with a flourish—but without a backward glance to the rest of us—she exited, stage left.

Dylan offered a respectful twenty seconds of silence before clapping his hands then turning to the rest of us. "Okay. So, here's what we are going to do…"

"No." Shaw spoke to all of us but was looking at me. "You all don't have to do this. I don't need a babysitter." He shifted, grabbing the bed controller and raising it some more. "I'll just go back to Charlotte. I'll be fine."

"You can't drive," Dylan pointed out.

"I'll hire a car service," he countered, smoothing out his bed sheets.

"Don't be ridiculous," Grace said. "You can't take care of yourself with your shoulder that way—"

"I'll be fine." Shaw was digging in his heels.

Grace, Dylan, and I glanced at each other. "I'm going to take Aaron for a walk," Grace said.

"Sounds like a good idea," I said.

Aaron walked over to Shaw's bed. "When I don't feel good, I watch television and eat my favorite foods. Mom makes me oatmeal chocolate chip cookies that are so good."

"Is that so?"

"Come to our house, and Mom can make you cookies. We can eat ice cream and order pizza, and we can play video games and watch football, and it will be fun."

"Ah. Well, I can't eat all that stuff right now."

"Why? You can eat whatever you want when you aren't feeling well."

"Because when you play football, you're on a strict diet."

"But you're not playing football anymore."

Silence. The doctor's words about his days of playing football coming to an end haunted the room.

"Hey, how about we go find Shaw a healthy snack for now?" Grace said.

"I'm going to make a few calls," Dylan said, eyeing me as he walked by. "You're up. Work some of that mojo on him."

That left me and Shaw in a hospital room. Alone.

If I knew where my mojo was hiding, I would've pulled it out months ago for myself.

"So, um, before I forget, I wanted to thank you for the tickets to the game. You were right…it was a memorable experience, to be sure."

He let out a chuckle as I pulled up a chair next to his bed, taking the controller in my hand and lowering the head of the bed. "You have a concussion. You need to rest," I said matter-of-factly.

"Can you show me how to turn on the television? I want to check the scores."

"No. No television."

"What? Why not?"

"Come on. You're a football player. You know concussion protocol. No electronics. Just rest."

He harrumphed, and I swore his arms moved to cross over his chest, but he stopped, given the pain in his shoulder.

"Come home with us," I said.

"Don't be ridiculous. I'm a grown man. I will be fine."

"I know you would be fine. But you don't need to be alone," I said.

His bottom lip jutted out, and it was almost adorable. I tried not to laugh.

"Shaw. You are a hypocritical pain in the ass," I shot back.

That got his attention.

"That's not nice. You're supposed to be nice to an injured man."

"I thought you were fine?"

He glared at me.

"When you heard about James, all you kept saying was that I needed to let people help me. 'Move home,' 'Let Dylan help you find a place to live,' 'Let Grace help with job search,' 'Let Maeve help with Aaron,' and 'Let us help.'" I scooted closer to the bed. "You wanted to be there to support me. Now, tell me what makes you so great that you can't accept the same support and help." I stood and put my hands on my hips. "I could've done it without any help. But I tell you what…it was a lot easier and less lonely with all of you hovering around."

"So, I was right?" He smirked. "You needed us to help you?"

"If you weren't already in a hospital bed, I'd put you in one, you pain in my ass." I threw up a hand. "Of course, you 'being right' was what you got out of the conversation." I shook my head. "No. It was that I could've done it alone, but you convinced me to accept help from the people who cared about me."

With eyes hidden under thick lashes, he peered up at me. "I hate when you turn my words around on me to make a point."

I held his hand of the non-injured arm. "So, how about we do each other a favor? How about you become my lean-to person again, and I'll become yours—at least until Riley comes back home."

He squeezed my hand gently.

"Maybe by spending time with each other again, we can find a way to make up for those years we've lost."

"Man. You are really giving me the hard sell," he said, his speech getting slurred and his movements slow. He was exhausted.

"Is it working?" I squeezed his hand.

"Will you bake those cookies for me?"

"Um, sure…but I thought you just said you had to watch what you ate during the season. I'm not going to be your dietitian—"

He shook his head. "I guess I'm not playing for a while, so to hell with it. Throw in the cookies, and you've got yourself a deal." He leaned back on his pillow with a satisfied, cat-who-at-the-canary expression and closed his eyes. "You can take care of me."

"Well, we know there isn't anything wrong with your ego. I guess that's a good sign." I let go of his hand, sarcasm lacing my words. "Alright, I'm going to go"—I stood and slung my tote over my shoulder—"and let you rest. I'll call tomorrow to see if they are going to let you leave."

He rolled his head my way, wincing slightly. "Hey, Kelce—"
"Yeah."

"Thank you. I'm…I'm glad you were here."

"Me too, big guy." I closed my eyes before he could see how close those words were to dragging tears of relief from me. Unsure how to hug him without hurting his shoulder, I leaned forward, giving him a quick kiss on his forehead, like the affectionate ones he used to give me when I was upset. "We'll have you juking linebackers before you know it."

As I walked to the door, I added, "I'll see you tomorrow." The hope of salvaging our friendship had me turning, and without even thinking about it, I added the familiar words, "And don't worry, we got this."

11

Shaw

Dylan and I had time to catch up on our drive to town without anyone else around. He gave me an unfiltered update on Kelcie and Aaron and how they were handling things.

"This is perfect. You'll be a good distraction for her."

"Dylan—"

"I mean, she could be helpful to you with rehabbing your injury and policing you from pushing yourself too fast. But you could also distract her from the crap her ex is pulling," he said, throwing on his turn signal as he merged off the highway and onto a main street leading into the downtown area.

I sat up straighter. "Like what?"

Dylan glanced over at me. "Just divorce crap. Jerking her around about living up here and his visitations with Aaron."

"So, James is being more of a dick than usual," I mumbled, surveying our town for any changes since I'd been back.

Dylan grunted in affirmation. "Honestly, I think her stress comes from trying to hold in her aggravation so Aaron doesn't pick up on it."

"How is Aaron?"

"Hard to tell with him." He shrugged. "Kelcie won't talk about it, but we can all feel her tension when the weekend rolls around. That is why I think it would be good for someone to live close to her. Maybe help her distract Aaron from some of the divorce drama."

I stared back out the front window, mulling that over.

"I doubt me being next door is going to *lessen* the drama," I said.

James wasn't my number-one fan. It wasn't like Kelcie and I saw each other much, but I knew that me moving next door would stir up some animosity. I never asked Kelcie how much she'd told James of what happened between us before he stepped up and took responsibility for her and Aaron. And I often wondered if that had been what had made him propose to her.

Dylan shrugged again. "Frankly, who lives next door to them is none of his business."

James never deserved her or Aaron—we both knew it.

We pulled up to a stoplight. Autumn was around the corner—the perfect time in mid-Maryland. It was still warm out, but it had the promise of being a cool, beautiful evening. We drove down Market Street, the center of town, flanked by intersecting streets, filled with historic buildings that housed small restaurants, boutiques, antique shops, and even theaters and art galleries. Surrounding the town were a small college and a variety of neighborhoods. Even farther out were historic Civil War battlefields and landmarks.

It really did have a lot of charm that, as a child, a teen, and even a young adult, I'd never appreciated.

Maybe Aaron, Kelcie, and I could spend time exploring this place as if we were new to it. We kind of were. It would be a good distraction for all three of us.

Dylan took a left off Market and pulled up in front of a duplex. The left side had flowers in pots on the shared front porch. The right still had a ladder and other construction paraphernalia lying around on it.

As Dylan pulled up in front of the house, I stepped out of the truck, rolling my head over my shoulders and stretching.

My left arm was in a sling to stabilize my shoulder, and my head ached.

Dylan popped the trunk and pulled out my luggage. "This is it—the new duplex I told you about. I bought it earlier this year and was going to flip it." He motioned to the house.

We both started to walk toward it. "Kelcie's side is completely finished. Your side has a few cosmetic things left to do—a small punch list I can do at your convenience. No rush."

I scratched at the beard I'd unintentionally begun growing over the past week and tried to piece things together. "So, are you renting it to her?"

"For now. Until she figures out what she wants to do."

"I could buy it from you if you want." We walked toward the steps when the light came on from the left unit. The storm door flew open so fast I thought it would break.

"And be her landlord? Yeah, I can't see that going over well," Dylan said. Aaron crashed through the door and ran down to us.

"Shaw!" he said. "You're late." Aaron grabbed the railing with one hand as he flew down the steps, coming to a halt one foot in front of us. "But Mom said you're always late, so nothing is new."

I glanced up, and Kelcie stepped out of the door, slower than her son. She stopped at the top of the stairs, leaning on the railing, a small smile on her face.

I cleared my throat. Not for the first time, I couldn't help wondering how this was all going to work out. I tried to lean forward and come down to Aaron's level, but I was reminded of the throbbing pain in my head, not to mention the dizziness, which was how I got here in the first place. I straightened.

"Well, my man, first, I wasn't driving. So, if we're late, it's because of him." I threw my thumb over my shoulder toward Dylan. "Second, your mother is mistaken." I shot her a side-eye. "I was always waiting for her."

Dylan walked behind me, carrying my bag up to the front door. "You were both always late."

"Hey, did you know DeeJay Mullins is playing your position this week?" Aaron blurted out, walking alongside me. "Analysts are saying it's going to be a test to see if he could handle filling your shoes permanently."

Ah, yes. Aaron's bluntness.

"But Mom said he's not taking your shoes. It means he may replace you." He tilted his head as if trying to understand me better. "Are you leaving football, Shaw?"

I pretended to yawn as if I were tired and not trying to avoid answering.

Kelcie knew my tactic and intervened. "Aaron, honey, I think we need to give Shaw some space. I'm sure he's tired." She hesitated to approach, waiting for us to reach her.

Did she regret our arrangement? Did she have second thoughts? I'd been pretty drugged up when it was all being discussed.

I took a good look at her, comparing her to my memory. The setting sun still pulled the chestnut color out of the hair that escaped her ponytail, and she was in worn jeans and a t-shirt. But her bow-shaped mouth, instead of being ready with a witty comeback, lacked something and seemed less familiar.

After a few heartbeats, with Dylan and Aaron discussing my epic comeback when this was behind us, Dylan suggested we get my stuff inside.

Ignoring his mom's suggestion, Aaron said, "Mom ordered pizza. Do you all want some?"

Kelcie snapped out of it, holding the storm door to my new place open for us. "I figured you all may be hungry after driving. I put some cold beer in the fridge too."

I stopped in the foyer and took in my new home as they stepped around me.

"What are you going to do about a car? Is Dylan giving you one to use?" She surveyed the fridge. "What do you want to drink? Soda, water, juice? You should probably avoid the beer while on concussion protocol."

"Is there any flavored water?"

"No, sorry. I haven't done much shopping yet."

"Just water, then. As for the car"—I pointed at my shoulder—"I'm afraid I can't drive right now. Between the concussion and waiting for my collarbone to heal, it's a non-issue."

"Oh, yeah. Right. I forgot. I think that falls under my Florence Nightingale routine."

Yeah, and that wasn't happening. I waved her off. "That's what car services and my brother are for."

My brother cleared his throat in protest.

She filled a glass from the water dispenser in the fridge and gestured to the stool by the island. "Pull up a chair. I got sausage and pepperoni from Lucia's before remembering that you are on a strict diet. Is that okay? We could order a salad or something, and I can go pick it up."

"Don't you dare." My mouth started salivating as soon as I caught a whiff of my favorite hometown pizza. I managed to scoot onto a stool and made grabby hands. "Gimme." She handed me two slices on a paper plate as Aaron saddled up next to me with a slice of cheese.

He took a bite and maybe chewed twice before hitting me with football questions.

"Do you prefer running a corner route or on the inside? Did you think you should've gone to New England in the draft instead of Washington?" He grilled me about all things football, checking my knowledge while also gauging my opinion. Eventually, Dylan bowed out and took off, stating he'd be around the next day to clean up the front porch.

Aaron, the analyst, wasn't giving up. "Why have your stats fallen in the last year? Are you afraid of being replaced?"

Kelcie, standing on the other side of the island, coughed on her beer. "Aaron. That's rude."

Luckily, I didn't have a mouthful of food, or I might have choked.

"It's true. His statistics—"

I held up my hand as Kelcie opened her mouth to reprimand her son. "It's fine. It's a legit question. I get asked it every press conference," I said to her.

I turned to Aaron and leaned forward on the counter, "I'm going to tell you what I tell the press. I always do my best on the field. Some seasons are better than others, but I will learn from last season and apply it to my training for this coming season."

He cocked his head. "How?"

"Maybe you and I can discuss what you think I need to do later. We don't want to bore your mom."

"Oh, my mom has lots of opinions on what you should do. She—"

Kelcie's voice boomed as she grabbed his plate. "Okay. How about some dessert? Then it's time for bed."

Aaron jumped off his chair and followed his mom into the kitchen. "Mom, you should tell Shaw what you said to me about the game against New Orleans."

Kelcie stood and cleaned up the counter, keeping her back to me. "I'm sure he has enough coaches telling him what to do. He doesn't need our armchair advice."

I leaned back in my chair, tempted to cross my arms over my chest until I remembered my bad shoulder. "I'd love to hear your thoughts— and Aaron's too."

She paused and then turned. "Well, as you suggested, let's save that discussion for another day. I'm sure you're tired and sore, and Aaron needs to get to bed as well."

She handed Aaron a cookie, almost handfeeding it to him, then placed a few in front of the two of us—possibly to quiet us both.

"If you want to give me a list of groceries or things you need, I can swing by the store tomorrow on my way home after work."

I nodded.

"What are your plans tomorrow?" I turned to Aaron.

He shrugged. "Going to Maeve's, I guess. Mom thinks I'll get bored sitting at home alone. I think she's afraid to leave me alone, even though I'm a teenager." His expert eye roll proved his age.

I nodded again. "Maybe we can—"

Kelcie cut me off. "You'll be resting tomorrow. I have the instruc- tions from the doctor. Until your concussion clears up, you are supposed to rest—at least another five days."

I waved her off. "I've had concussions before. It's not a big deal. I know when I've pushed it too far."

She was about to put a cookie in her mouth and stopped to stare at me in disbelief. "How many have you had? Besides the one in college?"

I shrugged again. Honestly, concussions came with the territory, but I knew this wasn't a discussion I wanted to get into with her.

"Fine, I'll rest tomorrow, alright?" I mumbled like a petulant teen as I bit into my cookie.

I caught Aaron's chocolatey smile and quiet giggle at me being chastised.

I winked at him then leaned over and whispered, "There will be plenty of time for you and me to hang out."

He didn't answer but just kept chewing his cookie and smiling. "My dad is coming to get me next weekend, but we can hang out before that."

Kelcie's head dropped to the counter, and her body stiffened.

"Whenever you want, you know where I'll be."

We sat quietly, and it was like déjà vu—Kelcie and I sitting at a kitchen counter eating cookies and talking shop—with the addition of an inquisitive boy who kept me on my toes.

It niggled at me, taking me down the "what if" road. What if James had just stayed away? Would this have been us?

12

———

Shaw

After a few tortuous days of people checking on me, boredom had become my enemy. I wasn't someone who ran with an entourage, but even during the off-season, I usually had things to do when I got up in the morning—workouts, film, meetings, promotional appearances, etc. So just sitting here all day was killing me.

Unfortunately, until I was cleared by the doctor, Kelcie wouldn't let me work out. She gave me a few light stretches to keep my muscles from stiffening, but because of the concussion, no cardio. I couldn't even take a long walk yet. I wasn't supposed to be on the computer or watch television or use any type of electronic. I had all the blinds in the house drawn shut because the brightness of the sun had been an issue, and I was held up in the house like a damn vampire. Kelcie and Aaron were at work and school, and I didn't know what to do with myself.

Even if I didn't have anything on my agenda, Riley usually had somewhere we "had" to go, or my agent would come up with a place I had to make an appearance. There hadn't been any word from Riley on how things were going with her and the reality show. It was strange how things had changed so much in the last two weeks. Yet, somehow, it seemed…not so weird. Riley and I were great partners. We loved to travel, enjoyed good food, and explored new places. She respected the work I put into the season and understood the off-season wasn't all fun and games.

Not everyone saw past her superficial veneer, but Riley was smart and driven. She had ambition besides just being my girlfriend and wasn't looking for me to put a ring on her finger.

I missed her, but mainly, I hoped everything was going well for her.

All I managed to do today was shower and get myself dressed, which, with a broken clavicle and concussion, wasn't easy. In fact, it took up most of the morning. But by lunch, I'd resorted to seeing how many mac and cheese elbow noodles I could fit on my fork.

So, while I valued my quiet time, not having a set agenda for anytime in the foreseeable future was unnerving.

I had too much time on my hands. Time to think.

I stood in my quaint kitchen in my hometown, living next door to Kelcie, one of my most beloved but disconnected friends.

Twelve birthdays had passed, twelve holiday seasons without her. Twelve football seasons without her smart comments or "suggestions." And now she and her son were living next door to me. It was as if life had put her in front of me and said, "Fix this."

Thursday? It was Thursday.

Thursday night football was on in an hour or so. I opened the refrigerator and pulled out a bottle of beer. If I'd been in Charlotte, there'd be wrapped custom-made meals by the chef who came to my house every few days.

I ate whatever he made, but rarely did I ever drink a beer in season.

Now, it was all I wanted, and yes, I knew I wasn't supposed to have one now, but who was around to tell me not to?

I stared at it, trying to figure out how to open it with my arm in a sling.

Damn. I put down the bottle, cursing at it as I fell into the chair at the counter.

I could make some dinner, and the evening was warm enough to have a beer on the back porch—if I could open the damn thing.

Well, now…that sounded like a plan.

Warming up a piece of lasagna from the dish Maeve sent over, I brought my feast out on the back porch, closing the slider behind me with a bit more power than I meant to. Kelcie's kitchen light was on, and there were sounds of movement, probably from her making dinner.

As I situated myself at my table and dug into my homemade lasagna—still staring at my beer, willing it to open on its own—I imagined Kelcie pacing back and forth in her kitchen. Thinking of her there, talking and pacing, brought a kind of comfort and familiarity I'd missed. Being so close to her felt more like home than my penthouse with chef-created meals overlooking downtown Charlotte ever could.

I shoveled in another bite of lasagna and glared at the bottle of still-closed beer with the condensation dripping down the sides like tears from not being opened.

If I asked Kelcie, she'd yell at me and confiscate the beer.

It was relaxing to be back in town, with my friends—the people who knew me best. Being around Kelcie, though…it was still not… right. It was nice. It was surface.

While we weren't strangers, we still weren't *us*.

We were nice neighbors; the type you'd shovel the sidewalk for or maybe even give Christmas cookies to. But we weren't us yet.

For the most part, we'd waved good morning or thrown out an occasional, "How are things going?" She'd asked me if I needed anything as she walked out to her car with Aaron, and I'd replied, "I'm good. Have a good day," while drinking my morning coffee. So friendly and so…surface. She'd check in on me when she got home and offer me whatever they were having for dinner. We'd talk about what level of activity I could engage in and what lingering symptoms I would still admit to experiencing.

There hadn't been any inside jokes, no snarky comments about my hairstyle, or texts to check in with each other. We didn't have that smooth, effortless friendship that felt like an extension of our personality—the foundation of our identity. The kind of friendship that was so deeply ingrained I never remembered not having it.

It wasn't anything I could complain about. Change happened. People had their own paths to take. This was just weird and, well, unsettling because this surface shit wasn't us.

I finished the lasagna, and Kelcie's form disappeared before I found the balls to knock on her door and ask her to open my beer, so I walked my sorry ass, my empty plate, and my pathetic, weepy beer inside.

I wanted us back. I wanted that friendship back, the ease of the ebb and flow that we had. I wanted her to give me shit about my hair, the way I ordered my food (everything on the side), and I wanted to share our inside jokes that no one else could ever understand.

I wanted to be able to go ask her to open my goddamn beer and not feel like I was intruding. I even wanted to argue with her about the fact that one beer wasn't going to damage my brain more than it already was.

I put the bottle in the fridge, pulled out a can of soda, and promised myself to only buy canned beer until I recovered. I'd become a pro at opening cans one-handed.

I walked back onto the screened porch and settled with a groan on a chair, crossing my ankles comfortably over the ottoman before flipping on the TV Dylan had helped set up. I was ready to be on the other side of football for the evening and trying not to think about it being a permanent arrangement.

About halfway through the first quarter, her back door opened and closed. Aaron was on his porch, watching the game over my shoulder.

"Hey, buddy. What'cha doing?" I sat up and turned around to face him.

"Mom is talking to Dad. She didn't want me to listen, but it's hard not to."

Damn. She'd mentioned his sensitive hearing.

"You want to come over here?" I stood and walked over to my porch door, unlatching it as he scrambled down his steps and into my yard.

Without further words, he settled into the chair next to mine, and we resumed watching the game. He sat on the edge of his seat, studying the plays.

"Do you want a drink or something?"

He shook his head.

"Did you tell your mom you were coming over here?"

He shook his head again, his focus completely on the game.

I pulled out my phone and shot Kelcie a text.

ME

Aaron is over here on the back porch, watching the game with me.

I enjoyed watching football with my new companion, who only spoke to the television, giving play-by-play commentary and analysis for himself. When I tried to interject and ask questions or give opinions, I was given quick monosyllabic answers to satisfy the social necessity, and then, he returned to his own world of commentating.

So, I just listened and learned.

At half-time, I gave in and went to check on her. And yes, I was curious as to why "talking with his dad" had made him leave the house.

I knocked on the back door, but there was no answer. I knocked again, this time opening it and announcing myself. "Kelcie...it's Shaw."

"I'm downstairs. Is Aaron okay?"

"Yeah, he's fine. Watching the game."

"Okay, great. Thank you for letting him hang out." Her voice was strained, and there was a pause. "Let me just change this load of laundry, and I'll come nudge him home."

"No rush. I just wanted to let you know where he was. He's welcome to stay and watch the whole game." I walked farther into the house—the layout a mirror opposite of my own—and I looked down the stairs to the basement to see if I could find her.

I spotted her pacing from one room to another, folding and refolding a towel. "No, no...he needs to get to bed."

"Kelce, is everything okay?" I said from the top of the stairs.

She froze, realizing how far into the house I'd come and not being happy about it. She tried not to scowl at me then ducked her head and walked into the laundry room, wiping her eyes with one hand and waving me off with the other. "Fine."

I slowly descended the stairs as if walking into a lion's den—or, in this case, a lioness's den, which was likely more feral. "Aaron said you were on the phone with James." I turned the corner into the doorway of the laundry room, wishing for a shield to protect myself. "Is everything okay?"

A sigh that was a mixture of exhaustion and exasperation was meant to cover up her true emotion, and it came out of her as she closed her eyes. "Damn."

"Kelce—"

"It's fine. It's just hard to have a conversation about your son when he is smart, has supersonic hearing, and knows when he's being discussed."

I shoved my hands in my pockets to stop myself from cracking my knuckles. "Can I do anything?"

"It's fine." She resumed pulling clothes out of the dryer and haphazardly folding them. "I was trying to make arrangements for this weekend's visit." She began shoving clothes into the basket without folding them. "Or was trying to."

I leaned against the doorway on my good shoulder and attempted to cross my arms.

"What happened?"

Kelcie's lips thinned as they did when she was willing her mouth to stay shut.

"Kelcie—"

She shoved the remaining clothes in the basket, slammed the dryer door, and stood.

"He missed the last two weekends because of 'work,'" she said, using air quotes. "He doesn't work weekends. But he said he couldn't get off work early enough on Friday to beat traffic up here, and heaven forbid he wastes time in traffic." She picked up the basket so fast I thought it would go flying. "He didn't think it was worth bringing Aaron down for one night on Saturday just to drive him back Sunday morning." She rubbed her hand over her face. "Not worth it... He lives forty-five minutes away, and you'd think I was asking him to travel halfway across the mid-Atlantic."

"But—"

She held up her hand. "That's not the problem. The problem is he is punishing me for moving up here, and he's making a point. That's the first issue."

I remained quiet. I understood my Kelcie well enough to know when she needed to get it out.

"The second issue is..." Her voice began to break, and her lip began to quiver. She ran her hand over her face again and walked by me into the den that was furnished with a desk and a small sofa. But instead of sitting, she began to pace. I didn't move and stayed in the doorway of the laundry room.

This was familiar ground to me. She was sangry—a mixture of sad and angry. She was hurting and furious that she was letting it get to her. She didn't feel in control and didn't want to let go. Sometimes, I'd stood back and let her blow. Other times, I'd stepped in, held her, and let her get it out with me there to help her. Tonight, my instincts told me to stay back.

I stood still and let her pace, running her hand over her ponytail.

"What's the other issue?" I asked softly, so quietly I wasn't sure she could hear me. This was a third way I helped her—I poked the bear and ignited the fuse. Right now, I could tell that this was what she needed.

She stopped, and with the fury of Hades in her eyes, she said, "Because he doesn't want to deal with him this weekend."

I dropped my head so she didn't see the fury building in my eyes.

"His girlfriend's son has a double-header with his travel team. He wants to go to it on Saturday, and he doesn't think it's a good idea for Aaron to attend." Kelcie's eyes were glassy as her words hitched.

"Why not?" I said, my eyes still fixed on the floor.

"He said Aaron would be bored, and it would be a long day for him. But really, it's the crowds. He's worried Aaron will get agitated and make a scene…" She let out a shaky breath. "And he doesn't want to deal with it."

"Aaron sometimes would disagree with the umpire's calls and was vocal about it," she continued. "He'd get stressed and have meltdowns. It's the reason he can't play team sports, even though he desperately wants to. Most of the time, he just gets overstimulated."

So why would the man choose something that makes his kid uncomfortable? What an ass. "Okay, well, what about—"

"Last weekend, Amber's kids were with their grandparents so that they could have some time to themselves—'for once.'" She used air quotes. "The weekend before that, it was another excuse."

I drew in a deep breath and looked away, reining in my true thoughts.

"Yes, that's the man I was married to—one that is embarrassed by his son."

"That wasn't what I was going to say." I shook my head. I was going to say I wanted to stomp on his face.

She shook her head and froze. She lost all color, and a look of horror crossed her face.

I turned to find the cause.

Aaron was on the stairs, staring at both of us.

13

Shaw

"Why do I embarrass my dad?" Aaron asked in a monotone voice, tilting his head. "Have I done something wrong?" He turned to his mom. "I don't understand." He pulled on his fingers.

Panic was written on Kelcie's face. Her mouth opened, but words were not coming out as she tried to walk toward her son.

I stepped forward. "Hey, buddy. What's the score of the game?"

"21-17, Washington," he said succinctly, though his gaze was still focused on his mother.

"Is it still half-time?" I asked, trying to buy Kelcie some time to gather herself.

"Yes. So, am I not going with Dad this weekend?" He walked down the stairs and stood in front of her. He was almost up to her nose. His shithead of a father wasn't that tall, but his grandfather, Kelcie's father, Holden Hammer, was a former football player himself and was almost as tall as I was.

She hesitantly put her hand on his head, threading her fingers through his hair. "No, not this weekend. Your father is busy, and we can't seem to arrange it. But we will find something fun to do around here—"

It infuriated me that she shared the blame.

"Where is he going that I would embarrass him?"

"Honey, I didn't mean that—"

I couldn't leave her dangling. "Oh, you know, probably some dry business function that would bore any teenage kid to tears. There'd be nothing else to do but stir up trouble." I waved it off.

"I don't get in trouble."

I took a step back in surprise. "You don't? Seriously?" I studied him. "Why not?"

"Because you aren't supposed to break the rules. That's why there are rules."

"Are you sure you're your mother's son?" I deadpanned. He furrowed his brow to understand me better. "Oh, dude…how do you have any fun without breaking a few rules?"

He narrowed his eyes at me, still fidgeting with his fingers. "I don't understand."

Kelcie put her arm around Aaron. "Shaw's joking with you," she whispered.

"Is he making fun of me?" he whispered back, but loud enough for me to hear.

I shook my head. That wasn't where I was going with this. I remembered Grace telling me to be direct with Aaron. No sarcasm or inferences.

I squatted down, giving him a higher position. "No. No. Not at all. I was joking because I was trying to make you laugh. Because I was a bit of a rule-breaker when I was younger. Your mom—" I glanced up at Kelcie, whose eyes began to warm because of the effort she knew I was making. "She liked to have everyone believe she was a *major* rule follower. But really, she led the charge in finding ways around the rules rather than breaking them. It's how we were such good friends."

"My father used to pay me an allowance to keep Shaw out of trouble." She tapped her hand on his shoulder, pointing at me. "It was my first babysitting job."

"Wasn't Shaw my age?" he asked sideways over his shoulder at her.

She nodded, smiling, and winked at him.

"Oh…I get it, because he was immature like a child." He put his hand over his mouth to try to hide his laugh. "Shaw, she said you behaved like a child." He guffawed.

I jokingly glared at Kelcie but then shrugged and smirked because Aaron was amused. My mission of removing James's taint from the evening was accomplished.

"Yeah, well, if it wasn't for her keeping me out of trouble, we probably wouldn't have made it to the state championships our junior year…"—I narrowed my eyes as if concentrating—"and maybe our senior year either."

"Definitely senior year. Remember? You always wanted to skip fifth period with Mandy O'Hare," she said, hand on her hip.

I smiled up at her with devilish amusement. "Oh, yeah. Good ol' Mandy."

She rolled her eyes at me, but I saw the tilt in the corner of her mouth.

"Tell you what," I said, wanting to maintain the momentum, "how would you like the job of babysitting me?"

Aaron chuckled, and Kelcie's brows drew together. She was obviously wondering where I was going with this.

"I'm so bored." I stood and threw up my arms in exasperation. "How about tomorrow you come home from school and keep me company?"

"He goes to Maeve's after school, until I get off work."

"Even though I told her I could stay by myself. I'm not a child." Aaron glared.

"Of course you're not," I said.

"And you aren't supposed to be driving yet," Kelcie countered.

"True…"

"I can walk a few blocks by myself, Mom," Aaron grounded out.

Kelcie shifted, closing her eyes to this well-worn argument.

"Or I'll meet him."

Kelcie produced a side-eye glare for me.

"Or we can meet each other halfway. I think we can manage between the two of us, boss." I resisted the need to tug her ponytail like I used to when I'd won an argument. "We will call you when we make it home, okay?"

Aaron's face lit up, and he began to nod vehemently.

"Maybe we can go to the park and find something to do that is fun," I said and then held up a placating hand, adding, "without breaking rules."

She opened her mouth, a slew of excuses undoubtedly ready to come out. "But—"

"Kelcie…" I rolled my eyes with great drama. "I'm bored to death. I can't exercise except to do a few stretches. There's only so much binge-watching of reality TV I can do. I hate reality television."

"Your girlfriend is starring on a reality TV show."

I opened my mouth, pointed at them, and said, "Not the point."

Then, my eyes darting between the two of them, I pled the rest of my case because this was the best idea I'd had in a long time. "Everyone is working... It really will keep me out of trouble."

"Mom, please. I'm bored at Maeve's."

I pulled Aaron gently toward me, put my hand on his shoulder, and surprisingly, he let me. We were a united front.

"We can talk sports and maybe take a walk downtown. Give us a list of rules, and we will follow them. It would be a good change—a distraction—for both of us."

"You can't go for long walks yet."

"Then we will find a park bench and sit on it." I gave her a pointed look and nodded once. I would make sure to distract him from his father not coming tomorrow.

She studied us both, her eyes darting from me down to her son and back. She took in a deep breath, relaxed her shoulders, then closed her eyes, and I knew I had her. "Okay. We can try it."

Aaron tilted his head up to smile at me and then over to her.

Yes. This felt right.

"Aaron, honey, why don't you go upstairs and get ready for tomorrow? I'm going to walk Shaw out." We all turned and walked upstairs. Aaron continued up to his room, and Kelcie and I walked toward the back door.

"Okay. Bye, Shaw," Aaron said.

"Later, my man."

Once we walked out onto her back porch, she crossed her arms over her chest and stared out into the backyard. "I appreciate you stepping in, but it really isn't necessary."

"I wanted to. I think this will be perfect for both of us."

"It was my fault he overheard me. I let my emotions get away from me." She moved toward the railing and ran her hand through her hair, pulling on her ponytail, "God, I should have known better."

I walked up behind her and jammed my hands in my pockets. "It doesn't mean he heard everything you said."

She nodded. "He did. You may as well be warned. He could hear our conversation out here with the TV on in the kitchen. He has unbelievable hearing. His brain can't filter background noise, which makes his life difficult and overwhelming, but it also means he hears *everything*. We've had to invest in several decent noise-canceling headphones for him.

I leaned against the railing, facing her.

"Really?"

"Yeah." Her voice dropped to almost a whisper, and she kept her back to the closed sliding door. "When he was younger and couldn't communicate how uncomfortable it was, life was hard for all of us. He'd get overwhelmed, the noise would get to be too much, and it would send him into meltdowns that we couldn't always predict or understand. Daycare was out. Going out to eat didn't happen. Playdates with other screaming kids were a definite no."

"That couldn't have been easy," I said quietly, glancing at her, wanting her to talk but not wanting to hear how hard her life had been.

"It wasn't. It's why I stayed home for so many years." She leaned her arms on the rail and continued to talk into the darkness. "Once he was older and able to express himself, he was able to predict when something wouldn't work for him, or I would be able to anticipate signs of stress in him."

I shifted myself closer to her, my hand inches from hers. "Like going to the game with 75,000 screaming people? That must have been overwhelming. How did he manage that, anyway? Did the box help?"

She met my eyes from over her shoulder, and in that moment, I saw how hard things had been for my girl.

"Oh my God, he was trying so hard, Shaw." Her voice hitched with pride. "He wanted to go so badly. I bought new industrial earplugs for him to use."

"Did it help?"

She nodded and glanced up. "It did for the first half. He would step out onto the seating area for a bit and then back into the quieter room to take a break. He did an amazing job of managing himself. He wanted to watch you in person, so he kept in his earplugs and did his own commentating, which was fun to listen to."

"I caught some of that this evening. He's quite good." I grinned at how he'd imitated the voices of the other commentators in their intonations and cadence.

She straightened and turned toward me. "He got agitated once you were hurt. His sense of right and wrong kicked in, and he wanted justice for you being hit. He insisted it was a penalty. We left quickly, and Grace stuck around to see how you were doing. It was a tipping point, and he needed to decompress after that. That's why we needed to go straight home." She crossed her arms over her chest, leaned a hip on the rail, and stared at her feet. "We were really worried about you, though. I knew you had a lot of people around you…"

I reached for her hand, holding it gently, wanting her to look at me.

"I am sorry he had to witness me getting hurt. I'm sorry you both did. But thank you for coming to see me. It meant a lot." I motioned with my other hand.

She squeezed my hand, and the corner of her mouth tilted up.

"Not that I want to get the crap knocked out of me, but at least something good is coming out of it."

She shrugged. "That's true. At least we both are at a point that we can be here for each other like we used to be. And I get to boss you around again. That's almost worth it."

Yes. Exactly. This is what I wanted—to have her back in my life. "Come here." I couldn't not hug her. I wrapped her in my arms, ran my hand over her hair, and breathed in her scent. It was like fitting another piece of myself back in place. I closed my eyes, tucked her head under my chin, and stared up at the night sky—the same night sky that had seen me do this so many times in the past. And I…well…I felt more like myself.

No lights, no glam, no stress to impress. Just Shaw with his Kelcie.

"God, I missed this."

And she squeezed me a bit tighter in response and mumbled, "Me too."

14

———————

Kelcie

When I was young, my whole world revolved around sports. My father was the local hero and state champion football coach, two of my best friends were star Division One football players, and I was even a state-ranked lacrosse player.

Growing up surrounded by athletes, I knew I wanted to be a physical therapist. And after two successful lacrosse seasons, good grades, and being accepted into the physical therapy program—which would require years of education and semesters on rotation practicum—my future seemed laid out before me.

And then everything went off the rails. One of our closest friends, Shaw's best friend and Grace's boyfriend, Tyler, died tragically while away at college. Suddenly, our rosy-colored sunglasses of the perfect future were gone—none of us were guaranteed an easy road.

James had been on the men's lacrosse team. He'd been so handsome, and we became fast friends with a lot in common. His schedule had been as rigorous as mine, and he was as dedicated to his degree and to his future as I was to mine. We fit.

There had been mutual respect, and we loved each other the way untried couples believed they did.

But our trial came right before Thanksgiving break when I discovered I was pregnant—

I cut off the bitterness the memory sometimes evoked. While having Aaron was the best thing that ever happened to me, even if the timing wasn't ideal, the following events were difficult to remember.

Telling James. Telling my father. Telling Shaw… How differently they'd all reacted. James had refused to deal with it. My father had stormed off and wouldn't talk or look at me. Shaw had wrapped me up in his arms and told me we'd get through this—*we* would get through this—as if the baby had been his and mine.

James didn't say that. He didn't reassure me. But Shaw did. He'd always been my rock. Except, as my father pointed out, that rock was not meant to gather moss. Shaw wasn't meant for a quiet life, which was where I was headed.

I pulled into my garage, pushing away the memories. It was done, and there was no going back. I went into the house to find the guys— my guys.

Tossing my bag and keys on the table, I found the remnants of a snack and a note in Shaw's angular print. "Went to the park."

A few minutes later, a chorus of laughter and shouting greeted me as I rounded the trees and bushes that outlined the park. I immediately zeroed in on him. With his back to me, Shaw pointed with his uninjured arm as he shouted at a group of boys running up and down the field. I quickened my step until I stood beside him, scanning the area for Aaron. Where was he? I looked over at the benches.

Shaw stepped away and onto their makeshift field. "Hey, okay. Come here, and let me explain this better." He motioned the four boys over.

I was prepared for him to lie to me about Aaron when I saw his good hand land on my son's shoulder. He was one of the four boys, and he was holding the football.

"Jacob, after you hand off the ball to Aaron…" Shaw's voice faded out as he squatted down and, at that level, was practically eye to eye with them as he pointed out plays, the boys following his instruction with rapt attention. "Okay, let's try that again."

"Yes, sir, Mr. Shaw," the boys said in unison and smiled at him with stars in their eyes.

Aaron caught my eye and became hesitant. He hugged the football close to his chest and stood by Shaw, as if he would block for him if he had to run from me.

What the heck?

I walked toward them, finally gaining their attention. "Hey, guys. What's going on?"

My son didn't play football. He didn't play sports at all.

Shaw's smile was uncertain. "Hey, Kelce. You're here. I guess I lost track of time. Sorry about that."

"We're playing football," Aaron said with force, squeezing the football closer to his chest.

I clasped my hands together and tried to ease my tone. "I can see that."

"We were out for a walk, and the boys came over to say hi," Shaw tried to explain.

"They're boys from my class. They know Shaw is a big football star."

"They were throwing the football around—" Shaw continued.

"And they wanted him to throw with them, but he can't because of his injury. So, I did. They let me play instead."

And there went my heart, broken in two.

I swear pieces of my heart broke so often for my boy and his pure, painful words each day. It was amazing I had anything left of it at all.

I took a deep breath through my nose, willing the tears not to appear.

Aaron rarely got asked to play or join other kids. The cadence of his voice, the volume he spoke at, the quirkiness of his interaction, and the topics he chose to discuss were all different from those of most kids. Some were still young enough not to mind it, but older ones, who'd rather die than be associated with someone "weird" …they were usually cruel and ostracizing, as if being seen with someone "different" would condemn them to social Siberia.

I nodded.

One of the boys called Aaron's name.

"Why don't you work on that play I showed you guys?" Shaw said and waved Aaron off in the other boys' direction.

I tracked Aaron as he ran to the boys, still clutching the football to his chest.

Shaw stared down at his feet, poking at the ground with his shoe. "Kelce?"

I watched my boy interact with the other kids, relinquishing the ball to one of them and lining up for the snap. Tears finally came as I saw him act like a neurotypical preteen.

"Kelcie, did I screw up? You have that look, like I did something stupid."

I shook my head. "I—" There was a slight hitch, and I cleared my throat. "No. You didn't—"

He gestured at Aaron, who took the ball and completed a jet sweep, dodging the other boys and avoiding their touch before running into the imaginary touchdown zone.

Shaw began to cheer, and I clapped for him.

"I thought you said he couldn't play sports. He seems like a natural."

I shook my head. "He *is* a natural. He's very coordinated. And he's fast." I subtly wiped away the tear that was escaping, pinching the bridge of my nose as if I were tired. "But he has trouble being on a team. He has trouble with the crowds, with all the noise, and most of all, with the social expectations."

Shaw shrugged. "He seems fine now."

The flippant comment seemed to minimize the past twelve years when my son wasn't "fine," and my tone turned sharp. I gestured to the four boys. "Yes, this is fine for now, until one of the boys disagrees with him, or a referee makes a call he doesn't like, or they start to lose because a teammate screws up, or—" I broke off, realizing I was ramping up too much and toned my voice down to explain it better. "He will dig in and not back down. It's not fine then."

Shaw looked at me and then at Aaron and shrugged. "Well, this is just having fun."

He didn't get it. "It's fun until it isn't. It's like setting him up to fail. Dangling something in front of him that we know will set him off. Yes, he wants to play football. Yes, he wants to play team sports. But sometimes, what you want and what you can deal with are two completely different things."

I stepped around him as the boys lined up. It was Aaron's turn on defense. "Aaron, honey, it's almost time to go. Please make this your last play."

He ignored me.

Shaw clapped his hands. "Boys, let's wrap this up, and maybe we can do it again this weekend."

This was met with a mixture of groans and nods, except for Aaron, whose expression remained blank as he stared down at his feet, refusing to look our way.

Shaw turned back to me and lowered his voice. "I didn't mean to overstep my bounds or do anything that would hurt Aaron. He told me on the way home that he didn't have anyone to play with after school. These boys approached us, and I thought it was a good opportunity—"

I shook my head at him and waved him off. "No. I know. I didn't mean to snap at you. It's just frustrating that I'm always the one to tell him no."

We watched as the boys ran each other down, and Aaron touched the receiver with both hands. Aaron's legs were long, like mine. With two parents who were lacrosse midfielders and a grandfather who was a college football player and coach, Aaron had sports in his DNA.

"Then why always tell him no?" Shaw said softly as we watched the boys cheer each other on and compliment Aaron. All seemed more than a little surprised at his athleticism. I let that question hang in the air. "You know he's a natural…"

I nodded. "James and I agreed years ago that we wouldn't encourage team sports. He's tried swimming, karate, and other individual athletics, but nothing has captured his attention. We just thought he'd grow out of it."

"Seems he hasn't…"

I let out a huff. Clearly, with a professional tight end living next door to you, losing interest wouldn't be happening anytime soon.

Shaw stood with his good hand on his hip, the wind blowing his hair out of his face, and a contented smile. My heart warmed. He was enjoying this. Aaron was enjoying it. I should be too.

Lost in thought, I missed it when Shaw put his arm around my shoulder and tried to shake off my mood. "I'm hungry. Want to get some dinner?"

"You're always hungry." I pushed my hand against his rock-hard abs in the most pathetic attempt to separate us.

Aaron came running over, and the boys walked in opposite directions. "Derrick, Jacob, and Henry asked if we could come here again on Sunday. They have a game tomorrow but want to play again on Sunday if we can come." He looked up at Shaw's towering frame and not at me. The fact that he was asking Shaw and not me said more than I wanted to analyze.

Shaw glanced up at me, hesitating. "Let's see what your mom has planned."

His arm was still around me, his hand lazily hanging off my shoulder. I faltered slightly as my stomach flipped, and I couldn't help but smile. How had I gone this long without him? As we turned to walk back to the house, just as I was deciding whether to wrap my arm around his waist, he stepped away, giving us space.

Aaron jumped in front of us. "Can we? Can we come back Sunday?"

"We can talk about it later. How about thinking about dinner? Your coach here is starved." I resisted the urge to smooth a hand over Aaron's tousled, sweaty hair.

Shaw nudged my son's head instead. "You were amazing today, buddy."

"Thank you," Aaron said. "Can Shaw eat with us?"

"Sure. I think he mentioned pizza."

"Why don't you two come to my place, and we will order some?" he suggested.

Aaron loved pizza. "Yes!"

We ordered pizza, and while Aaron showered, Shaw brought out a few beers, and we settled in to enjoy the evening on our front porch.

"Tyler would've gotten a kick out of watching him today," Shaw said as he lowered himself into a chair beside me. "He wouldn't have been sitting on the sidelines like me. He would've been in there, throwing the football for them—sending them sprinting down the field for those long passes that all boys love to catch."

I took a sip of my beer then leaned my head against the chair and studied Shaw's silhouette. We didn't talk about Tyler often. He had been one of us. Shaw's best friend, the love of Gracie's life... But after he died, it was too painful for any of us to speak openly about him.

Tyler had been the one who'd introduced Shaw to me. He was the kid who'd told Shaw to come to football tryouts. He had been the quarterback to Shaw's receiver. And like so many good men, he'd died far too young. It had been just days away from his visit home from college to see Gracie when the accident had happened. It had wrecked all of us —tore open our cocoon of safety and ignorance of how cruel the world was.

Enough time had passed that Shaw's mention of Tyler's memory now only drew a sad smile from me. "I really wish he'd met Aaron."

Shaw was looking out at the street. "Me too."

The strangest thought almost made it past my lips. *"I wonder how our story would've played out if Tyler had been around to intervene."* Instead, I asked, "What do you think he would've thought about you and your career?"

"Oh, he'd have a lot to say," he chuckled. "Sometimes I have dreams about him giving me shit. *"What the hell were you doing in that game last night, taking a merry stroll? You run like an old man..."* He imitated Tyler's tone and cadence, which differed from Shaw's slight drawl, and made me smile wider. "He'd have kept me grounded, I think."

We sat with that in silence.

"He wouldn't have let you marry James, that's for sure." One side of his mouth tilted up in a mock smirk.

"Shaw…"

He took a pull on his beer then swallowed and added, "Just saying. He would've had the guts to stand up when the preacher asked, "Is there anyone here with a reason for these two not to be married?"

I stood quickly, not wanting to have this conversation. I wasn't ready. "There wasn't any reason for James and me not to marry."

Aaron walked out. "Is the pizza here?"

That wasn't enough to stop Shaw from having the last word. In a low, rumbly voice, he said, "You had me."

———

After dinner, we cleaned up, Aaron went to watch TV, and we both grew quiet. "I'm sorry about before," he said with his back to me, tossing the paper plates in the trash. I took a perfectly nice evening and ruined it by bringing it up."

I shook my head and waved him off. "If we want to be real with each other, I think I need to apologize for leaving the way I did and when I did."

He shook his head, wiping down the counter with a towel. "You should've talked to me."

"I'm sorry—"

He threw down the towel. "No. Wait." His voice began to rise before he caught himself. He looked over his shoulder to see if little ears were going to catch him.

"Aaron, we will be back out soon," he said. With a hand on my back, he guided me into the backyard for our best chance at privacy. In the moonlight, he turned me around, raked his hand through his hair, and said, "I would've done it, you know." He gestured to the house. "I would've been his father. I would've done the diapers and the midnight feedings. I would've helped with the carpools and anything else—"

"It wasn't your responsibility—"

"I never said it was." His hand flew up, his voice impatient. "It wasn't about responsibility. I never thought of him as a responsibility. I never thought of you as a burden." He cupped my arms with a gentleness that didn't match his tone and leaned into me. "I wanted to do it. I wanted to do all of it."

I guess we were doing this. Fine.

I stepped back from him. "Shaw, I love my son with my whole heart, but I'm more convinced than ever that I did the right thing. It wasn't a cakewalk. In contrast, you had an amazing career filled with unbelievable experiences."

"It didn't matter." The words burst out of him, to both of our surprise. He took a deep breath through his nose and closed his eyes, gathering more composure before saying, "You made a decision and took off without talking to me about it."

"I did what I thought—"

"Was I incapable of making rational decisions? We were both young, but we

were adults. I was completely aware of what was at stake. I was also aware of all the zeros on my check and that my salary was enough to support us."

"You're a good guy, Shaw—"

"Oh, jeez…" He turned his back on me and covered his face.

"You would've considered it the right thing to do—to take care of me. Both because of our friendship and—"

"From the moment you told me you were pregnant, I wanted to be part of his life." He held up his hand. "Please stop telling me what was best for me."

I stepped closer. "My father and I didn't want you to feel responsible for the road I would be traveling."

"Your father…" His face darkened.

"Yes, he…" I swallowed and cleared my throat. "He realized our intentions and told me that if I truly cared about you, I'd cut you free. He was right. It was wrong of me to take advantage of you."

"That's bullshit. And I will be calling Coach to tell him that. He—" Shaw clenched his jaw and stepped away, pulling out his phone as if to call my father at that moment. I grabbed it from him.

"Shaw, don't. It's in the past."

He tore the phone out of my hands. He stepped so close I drew back. "Tell me one thing. One thing, and I will drop it."

I gripped my fingers, not wanting to hear what came next.

"Did you *want* to marry him?" He stepped even closer—closer than he'd been in a long time.

Crap. I knew he'd ask that. "What? Of course, at the time…"

His eyes were all I could see. "Don't…lie…to me." His voice dipped. "If James had never come back…if he hadn't said he wanted to marry you…"

The truth I held back for years broke out from inside me. "You didn't love me," I said quietly, pathetically. "You pitied me." The tears pooled in my eyes and cascaded down my cheeks. "I could never do that to you. I didn't want to be married to someone who didn't love me."

His expression was hard as stone, frozen in one expression. He stared at me like I was a stranger. I was the first to look away, incapable of making eye contact after he struck the blow. "But you did. You married James."

We stood for an indeterminate amount of time until I said, "This is pointless. It's history. It didn't work out. I have a wonderful son I adore, and you can say, 'I told you so.'"

I took off inside the house and beelined to my room, acting like the teenager I'd been when we'd loved each other so well.

15

Shaw

I walked back to my side of the house reluctantly. Everything in me wanted to follow her and finish this conversation. Because it mattered. It was what needed to be said to move forward.

But Aaron shouldn't be within listening distance.

In my bedroom, I went to the desk drawer where I kept important items and pushed aside a small, smooth, gray river rock she'd given me when we were young. She'd called it a worry stone. "Hold it tight and put all your worries, all your negative thoughts, negative energy, into the stone." In high school, it gave me something to do with my hands when I fidgeted—to help me focus in my classes. When I was older, it helped me settle down when I got nervous. It was my lodestone, my lucky rabbit's foot. It was a damn rock, but it was my last connection to her. All these years, it had traveled with me and stayed in my pocket with my keys and wallet, always a topic of interest to those around me, but never explained.

From under it, I pulled out a dog-eared envelope. It had been folded and refolded, was smooth from years of wear, and was also kept close to me but never saw the light of day around anyone. Inside was a piece of hotel stationery. The same hotel I stayed in the night of the draft. The best and worst night of my life.

I held the envelope and sat on the edge of my bed.

Draft night had started out with her next to me, holding my hand as we walked backstage with her father, my mother, and my agent. She had been beautiful in the dress we'd bought together to hide her newly developed baby bump. We'd been talking about the future, about me being there for her and the baby.

We were waiting to see what team I'd be drafted to before making any definite plans. But I'd thought she'd shared my happiness. I'd thought the promise of a future with me had quelled her concerns. I'd thought the building chemistry was seeping through. I'd allowed myself to let in the feelings—the thoughts and desires—I'd refused to recognize before. I'd thought it was the beginning of the rest of our lives.

I'd thought wrong.

I'd planned to kiss her later that night, not like a friend, not as a joke. I was going to take her beautiful face in both my hands and kiss her the way I'd dreamed of kissing her. I was going to make this real.

The most defining moment of my life was when they announced my name in the draft. I'd never felt so high. Never felt like the world was at my feet. She was in the wings, and my future was in front of me. The people around me cheered. I hugged my mom and shook my agent's hand, and Kelcie's father offered his proud congratulations. The television cameras were waiting for me to walk out on the stage and hold up my new jersey with my new team. But before I walked into the spotlight, I enveloped her in our hug—her against my chest and my hand on her head, my head bowed to hers. I kissed her cheek— not wanting our first kiss to be on national television—and whispered, "Thank you. Our future starts now. This. Us. We got this." I'd squeezed her hand, smiled at her with all my love, and kissed the top of her hand, hoping she felt everything I wanted to say. Then I walked away, stepped onto the stage, and entered a new way of life.

But the past was where she'd stayed.

When I came back, she was gone.

Her father claimed she was nauseated and went back to the hotel. He encouraged me to take in the entire experience, telling me that Kelcie would want me to enjoy every minute. I called her, texted her, and was about to head back to the hotel to find her a few times, but was caught up with interviews and meeting people. Eventually, I got a short text saying how proud she was of me but that she was going to bed, and I should enjoy myself.

The next day, I found the now dog-eared envelope slipped under my door—the one I'd carried around for the last twelve years. This fucking "Dear Shaw" note said nothing except that James had shown up and wanted to marry her. She was proud of me and wanted me to be happy, not tied down with her. It said that she was doing what was best for both of us. Finally, she told me she loved me and couldn't wait to see me reach all of my dreams.

If she loved me, she wouldn't have left.

If she loved me the way I loved her, she wouldn't have left.

But the envelope...I couldn't throw it away. It was like a scar that hadn't faded or smoothed out. It reminded me of the hit I took and never quite recovered from.

If I...if we were going to try to regain the friendship we once had, I had to let this go because, like she said, it was history.

We were back in our hometown. Hell, we lived next door to each other. But it wasn't the same. It would never be the same. We were completely different people. It had only been fourteen years, but it had seemed like almost a lifetime of growing. Yet, she was still Kelcie, and I was still Shaw, and deep down, that connection was still there. It still felt necessary. Her tenderness with Aaron, laughing with me, scolding both of us...

I stared at the trash can on the other side of the room and stuck it back in the drawer, placing it gently under the gray rock. I still couldn't throw it away. And I couldn't give headspace as to the reasons why.

16

Kelcie

Shaw and I traveled to Baltimore a few days later to visit the doctors at Hopkins and to move him onto the next stage of his recovery. Things had been tense since our showdown the other night, and we both knew we needed to clear the air. But neither of us wanted to revisit it with Aaron around, so we tried to let it go and act normally.

But with Aaron not in the car, there was no need for the pretense, and we drove in almost complete silence on the ride there. Shaw pretended to sleep while I played chauffeur.

The good news was he was cleared of the concussion, which wasn't a surprise. The bad news was what had him quiet, bitchy, and brooding even more on the way home. His shoulder was going to take another six to eight weeks to heal, and the verdict was still out on the herniated disc in his neck.

Since he was cleared of the concussion, he wanted to drive home. I had to point out that he was still only operating with one arm, and we were in my car. That didn't go over well. Thankfully, though, he dropped it. We didn't argue often, so we didn't exactly know how to make up.

With me in the driver's seat, he sat with the chair pushed back to accommodate his long legs and stared out the side window as the city changed into suburbs, and the tractor-trailers and cars kept us company all the way home. As if tuned in to his mood, the heavens opened, and it began to pour.

"How are you doing over there?" I was out of practice getting him to open up to me, and it felt awkward.

"Fine." The universal answer for, *"Of course I'm not fine, but I don't want to talk about it."*

"I wouldn't worry about anything they said today. Let's just concentrate on your recovery and—"

"It's not something I can ignore," he said, his tone deep but flat.

Okay.

"I'm not suggesting ignoring it. I'm just—"

He lifted his hand to me. He obviously didn't want to talk about it.

I let out a quiet sigh. "Okay, well, we have your new treatment plan. I will get my work schedule, and we can figure out a routine together," I said. "I can hardly wait to get my hands on you," I joked.

"Yeah, okay. Whatever you think. It's not like I have a busy schedule, so whatever works."

My shoulders dropped slightly. We were dealing with wallowing Shaw.

His phone rang. He picked it up and hit a button, cutting off the ringer.

It rang again. He stared at the screen. "Shit."

"Is everything okay?" I said, pulling the car off the interstate at our exit.

He scowled at the phone as if it was about to pick a fight with him. "It's my agent."

"Oh. Do you not like him?"

"Her. No, I like her fine enough, but she's calling about the appointment, and she's going to want to talk. Only, I don't want to talk." He dropped his head back against the headrest. "But if I don't answer, she will fly her ass out here, and then I'll have to deal with her in person. And she won't be happy about it."

He took in a breath and answered, "Hello, Yaz."

I pulled up to a stoplight. He was quiet while listening to the muffled, fast talk of his agent. He rubbed his forehead, resting his head back against the headrest. He relayed what the doctors said about his recovery time. "Yes, I realize that's most of the season."

A few minutes went by, and besides a grunt of affirmation, he didn't say anything. "Of course, I realize it's not ideal, given the status of my contract."

More mumbling from the phone.

"Yeah, she's here. We're driving home," he said. "She discussed a treatment plan we will be starting with the team at Hopkins." He listened some more, cutting a quick, sheepish glance at me, making me curious about what was being said. "Yes, the team doctor approved of her credentials. It's fine. She's a hard-ass. You'd approve."

That was a correct assessment. I was going to be extra hard on him after this sulk-fest.

There was a pause from the noise coming from his phone. "Does that mean we are done—" Then more talking. "Guess not."

"Aw, come on, Yaz—"

"Yeah, I know I'm not on vacation, but I'm also supposed to be lying low while I recover," he said.

More from Yaz. Then he tossed up his free hand. "Fine, one interview." Mumbling. "When?" Mumbling. "I can't. I am busy after 3:00 on weekdays."

I put on my blinker to make a turn, shot a look over at him, and shook my head. "You don't have to cancel plans because of Aaron."

He put up his hand at me. We were going to have to talk about this new habit of his. He was still listening to Yaz. "Tell you what. Tell them to send me the equipment, and I will do it from here."

Inaudible mumbling from the phone. "Call TJ. Ask him, or I will."

"What are you talking about?" I asked.

The muffled sounds also increased.

"No non-disclosures. These people are family. They don't need non-disclosures." Shaw's irritation was hitting heights I didn't remember seeing before. "Just send me the specifics. Talk to you later." He hung up the phone and rubbed his hand through his hair. "God dammit, I can't get a quiet moment."

Silence once again descended on the car. I turned on the blinker and made another turn. "Everything okay?" Yes, I realized I was part of the reason he couldn't get a quiet moment.

"Fine."

Okay. "Listen, if you have things you need to do, you don't have to worry about Aaron."

"It's not a big deal," he said. "She—my agent—has an interview lined up with a former teammate of mine who has his own podcast now." He grumbled to himself. "Why she thinks this is a good idea is beyond me."

"Okay, well, like I said—"

"I thought maybe Aaron would like to watch. TJ is a good guy, and Aaron would probably get a kick out of meeting him," he said. "I need to check on the time and day, but the great thing about technology is that I can do it from home."

"Um, okay." I wasn't sure how to feel about this. We pulled onto our street, and I turned into the alley that led to the garages out back. "Let me think about it."

"Yaz is going to text me the specifics later."

I pulled in the garage and turned off the car. "If you don't want to do it, why did you agree?"

"Because she's my agent, and I basically have to do whatever she says. If I have any hope of staying in this league, I need to listen to her." He opened his door while he continued to talk. Except, I thought he was talking more to himself than me. "It's about image right now as much as physical potential." As he got out, he added, "Hell, at this point, if I have any hope of a career outside this league, I need to listen to her as well."

I got out and closed my door. "Well, we have a game plan and can start tomorrow with everything. You finally get your wish—you can start working out," I said, leading up the back stairs. "Aaron should be home from school soon. Do you want to come over?"

He stood outside the garage and stared at the ground. "Nah. I'm pretty beat. Tell him I'll catch him tomorrow."

He started to walk to his side of the house, but I took two quick steps to grab his hand, digging in my heels to stop him. "Shaw. Listen, I'm sorry about the other night. I—"

"I know, so am I. Let's just let it go. As you said, it's in the past, and I think both of us have enough going on in the present that we don't need to drag that up anymore."

"Good point." Unsure of myself, I rocked on my heels. "But seriously, I am here for you, and I will get you through this—both as your PT and your friend…and your drill sergeant."

He tried a half smile, but with his shoulders slumped and his face drained, that spark in him that I knew so well was nowhere to be seen. He wouldn't even look at me. "I appreciate it." But he wasn't accepting a pep talk as he tried to pull away toward his back door.

"Hey…" Still holding his hand, I gave it a squeeze. Shaw wasn't the broody type. But even when he did get down, I used to be able to pull him out of it. I felt inept now. Who helped him when he needed it now? Did Riley do anything?

A sad thought hit my heart. After my limited interactions with Riley and all the publicity I'd seen of Shaw over the years in the media, I didn't doubt he was surrounded by people who liked him. But did anyone really know Shaw? He hadn't spoken about anyone as a close friend, a confidant, since he'd been home. No one came to visit. No one even called to check on him except for business associates—that I knew of, at least.

Did anyone really know him anymore?

I reached up with my other hand and guided his chin in my direction. His scruff was tantalizing to touch. "We got this." I wanted to assure him that I had his back, not rub my hand over his chin. I was going to hone him into a powerful machine again, make him as good as new so I could get him back on that field…so he could get destroyed again. I winced.

He was damaging his neck and his spine with the constant trauma that came with being hit by two-hundred-fifty-pound linebackers. I didn't want to fix him up and send him back out there. The thought of him doing permanent damage hit me like a kick in the gut. But Shaw not playing football wasn't even imaginable, and saying anything to hurt him now wasn't an option, so instead, I wrapped my arms around his neck and hugged him. "We'll figure it out."

He stood rigidly, breathing in deeply before he finally relaxed. His arm wrapped around my back, and I ran my hand down the back of his head. As he rested his head on my shoulder, I repeated, "We got this."

17

Kelcie

The next morning—Saturday—Shaw and I went early to my physical therapy office before it opened. He warmed up on the treadmill, we modified the stretching he normally did at home, and we worked on his prescribed physical therapy routine. When we were done, I offered to massage his neck and back.

I knew his body had changed a lot since he'd been twenty-one. It was thicker and stronger but also worn. Without asking, he reached behind him with his good arm and pulled his shirt off, tossing it aside —because nature meant for him to be bare-chested. He caught me staring, and his cheeks turned an adorable pink. "Sorry. I'm so used to stripping down when I get to a trainer's table."

I smiled. "It's fine. It's just me here." As if I was a nobody. Because I was. I wasn't a

crazy fan who would attack him. I also wasn't a model or gorgeous celebrity—stop. *You're a professional,* I yelled in my head. *Focus on caring for your friend.*

I got some lotion out from under the table and told him to lie on his chest. Once positioned on his stomach and no longer looking at me, it was easier for me to focus on my work.

Until he began to moan.

Heaven help me. Would it be obvious if I turned on the music to try to drown him out?

I shifted my legs and—

"That feels amazing."

I dug into the trigger points surrounding his neck and shoulders, each garnering a different type of moan. I wasn't sure how to handle this. So I tried to think about what I was doing, focusing on the muscle groups and calling on my training to release the compression around his spine. As he continued to moan—and I continued to get worked up —I wondered if I should call someone else to take over this part of his therapy. But then I decided against it. Because hell, if anyone was going to lay their hands on him or even hear those sounds out of him... it was going to be me.

He has a girlfriend. He's not for you.

I ran my hand down his spine because I couldn't convince my hands to stop touching him. My body, in general, wasn't communicating properly. Any grace and detachment I could possibly hope to have in this awkward moment was gone. I tried to take a step back, removing my hands from his body, but my coordination suddenly flew out the window. My ankle turned just enough to make me unsteady, causing my hand to seek something hard to hold onto. That something hard was Shaw's ass. His very solid, very hard, very...it was a very round, firm ass.

"Oh, my God!" I cried out, and my legs almost gave out again. Clearly, blood flow to my brain had been compromised. I grabbed onto the table and straightened as quickly as possible.

Shaw pushed himself up on his good elbow, wincing at the jarring motion it caused his shoulder, and stared at me. "You okay?" His hair was rumpled, and he had amazing, half-lidded, dreamy eyes. Eyes I imagined he had when he was having an amazing, sexy time.

"Yep! I'm all good," I said, way too chipper. "Just tripped over something." Like my own two feet. And then, to make things more awkward, I smacked him on the butt and said, "Okay, all done here. Get on up." As if me touching his ass was routine.

He froze.

Uh-oh. Maybe I pushed it too far with the last swat.

I reached down and grabbed a towel from under the table, busying myself with wiping my hands and taking a drink of water. "Hey, Shaw. You might want to hurry. The office will be opening soon for Saturday appointments."

He pushed up on his elbows again, and a hand went to his eyes, pinching between them. "Yeah. Um. I need a minute."

I stepped to him, coming around the front of the table so I could face him. "Are you okay? Are you having a muscle spasm? Did I hurt you?" I reached for his shoulder.

He held up a hand but didn't look at me. "No. No. Um. Why don't you get your stuff together, and I'll get dressed."

But he didn't move.

"Shaw—"

"Kelce. You were fine. In fact, you did a great job. I was very relaxed. It felt great."

"Then what's—"

He caught my eyes, and his face turned bright red. "Um. What you did to me felt really, really good." His eyes danced, and the small, shy smile on his face made him look like a teenager again. "Maybe too good. I, um...I don't want to embarrass us—well, I don't want to embarrass you. That ship has sailed with me obviously." And he dropped his head.

I let out a loud laugh. "I'm sorry." I patted his shoulder. "It happens."

"What?" He straightened more and then winced again. "You give men hard-ons regularly? Jesus, Kelcie—"

"No. Not that—stop!" My face was burning. "You're making this...ugh! I'm going to the restroom." I motioned to him, trying hard to pull back on my laughter. "Take a moment and gather yourself." I gestured to his crotch. "I'll meet you out front."

He pointed at me, trying to be stern, but his lips were twitching. "This stays between us. No one needs to know I had this reaction."

I waved him off then walked to the restroom to pull myself together, whispering to myself, "No one would believe it anyway."

The staff was at the front desk by the time we were getting ready to leave. As I waited for Shaw, I chatted with one of my co-workers.

"Hey, just the woman I was hoping to run into." Mitch Williams' slight drawl was unmistakable, and I couldn't help but smiling when I heard it.

Flirtatious and kind, Mitch was exactly the kind of guy my bruised and confused confidence needed these days. While he wasn't my client, we always exchanged flirtatious banter when he was in for his PT. His dazzling, mischievous smile only made his tall, lean, athletic body look hotter.

"Hey there," I said. "I heard you were graduating from PT. Congratulations, although I will miss seeing you around here."

Mitch scanned the open-concept PT treatment area. "Yeah. It's good to get back on both feet, but I will miss hanging out with some of the people." He turned his gaze on me, slid his hands in his track pants, and said, "Some more than others."

"I'm sorry we never got a chance to work together," I said. Though I'd always wondered why. He jumped around to different therapists, but our paths never crossed. I'd simply assumed it was because our schedules didn't sync.

He gently put his hand on my elbow, guiding me to the waiting area and away from everyone else.

"Trust me, I would've loved for you to be my PT, but my ego couldn't take it."

"What?"

He stepped closer. "I didn't want you to see me sobbing like a toddler." I started to laugh, and he leaned over, his breath tickling my ear. "Not the impression I wanted to leave on a woman I wanted to date," he whispered.

He moved back to study my reaction. I was too shocked to camouflage my expression.

"Well, that doesn't do much for my ego," he said, trying to maintain a playful tone.

I shook my head, resting my hand on his arm. "No, I'm sorry. I think you just took me by surprise."

Just touching him felt…strange. It was fun having Mitch to flirt with—he seemed like the easygoing type who flirted with everyone. But it was exhilarating to have such a good-looking man interested in me. I hadn't been on a date since… God, in over a decade. James and I hadn't had many date nights.

"So, is it a good surprise?"

Answer him, Kelcie. Don't be a dud.

"Yes, of course," I said. "That would be great."

Great. You couldn't find a better word?

Over his shoulder, Shaw's hulking form exited the changing room and was walking toward us. His shy smile caught me for a moment, and my stomach sank with a strange emotion causing me to hesitate. What was I doing? I wasn't with Shaw. If anything, I needed to start to lay down some boundaries for myself. He wasn't sticking around. He was getting better, and then he'd be gone.

I needed to date. I needed to have other things—and other men—to occupy my thoughts.

"How about I call you?" Mitch said.

"Yes. Great." I grabbed a pen and a business card off the front desk and jotted my name and number down. Our fingers touched while I handed him the card, and he held onto it for just a second as he stared at me.

"I'll call you."

I nodded. Shaw's approach was coming fast, and I didn't want them to meet. Not like this. Why did it feel like cheating, like I was stepping out on Shaw? It made no sense, but I wanted to keep those two worlds separate. I didn't need Shaw to know about my dating life —or that I was starting to get one.

"Hey, ready to go?" he said, shifting his bag on his shoulder.

"Yes." I started digging through my purse just to kill time until Mitch was in his car.

"How about stopping at the café for some coffee?" Shaw said.

"Great." I hadn't shaken off the tendency to speak in monosyllabic responses yet. As we walked out, Shaw's hand went to my lower back, escorting me through the door.

My enthusiasm about Mitch and our date slipped. Shaw's touch through my shirt affected me more than Mitch's brief touch of my hand.

Dwelling on the differences between the men wasn't very productive, and I forced myself to step away from Shaw the minute we were outside, making a beeline for the car.

Dating other people and opening myself to the possibility of being attracted to other, more available, men was a challenge I could no longer ignore—even though I wanted to.

———

Later that morning, I went to meet Aliya and Grace for a coffee while, against my better judgment, Shaw had decided to hang with Aaron and the boys at the park and play a game of two-hand touch.

It was a cool fall day, and I stepped into the cafe to find my friends in the corner, already hovering over their large drinks. Even on the weekend, Aliya was perfectly put together in a pair of yoga pants that probably cost more than my entire ensemble, with boots and a fashionable sweater. Grace wore jeans, a colorful sweater, and no-nonsense work boots with an adorable bright knit hat pulled over her curly hair. I went to the counter, got my chai latte, and made my way to the saved seat between them.

"How is it that you live in town now, and I still barely see you?" Aliya tore right into me.

"You have my address," I shot back. "You can come by anytime." I took a sip of my delicious drink.

"I wouldn't want to interrupt any 'bonding' that was happening." She waggled her eyebrows.

Grace's choking sound distracted me, stopping me from leaning over and smacking my friend upside her perfectly styled ponytail. "Stop. You know it's not like that."

Her devilish smile wasn't hidden behind that ginormous coffee cup she held against her lips. "It could be," she purred.

I glared at her. "He has a girlfriend."

Both Grace and Aliya gave each other *that* look. The look two friends gave each other when they were silently communicating about something they had already discussed.

"What?" Was this how this coffee date was going to go, starting in on me about Shaw? I wanted to talk about him but not like this. I wanted their advice on how to help him.

I focused on Grace. I knew she was the weak link. "Why are you looking at each other that way?"

She stared down at her coffee cup, turning it in circles, and said softly, "Well, honey, I just find your response interesting."

I leaned back and crossed my arms over my chest. "Really? Why?"

"Because when you defended the reason why you aren't…bonding with Shaw, you said it was because he had a girlfriend. Not because you two weren't like that. Not because you two are only friends. Not because you could never be like that with—"

I held up my hand. Okay, I saw her point. "Yes, those are all reasons too."

"But they weren't the reasons you said. Back when we all were younger, those had been the reasons you used to give when people teased the two of you about the time you spent together—when people assumed you were a couple. But not anymore, it seems. You said, 'He has a girlfriend.' It makes it seem as if you thought about it, but Rachel—"

"Riley," Grace interrupted.

"*Riley* was the only reason you couldn't think about him as more than a friend," Aliya said.

I shifted in my seat and took a sip of my very hot chai. Blowing on it for what felt like a full minute while I contemplated how to get out of this corner, I relented.

"It's not like that," I whispered, and even I heard how weak it was.

Aliya smiled softly at me. "Honey. We all know what it's like. We always have.

"Don't push," Grace whispered to her.

Aliya waved her off. "Listen, you and he have never been able to get this together." She reached out and took my hand. "You two have a connection that is so rare, so incredible. People spend a lifetime looking for it. Your timing has always just sucked."

"What Aliya is trying to say is you are both older now. You are both here. Why not…explore…"

I picked up my drink again then said very slowly so they could understand me, "He has a girlfriend."

Aliya leaned forward and added, "She's not here." Aliya leaned back, cocking an eyebrow. "She chose to leave him. And in this condition. Shame on her."

Grace scowled and said, "Bitch."

Aliya's phone pinged.

"Moving on…I think I'm going to get a chocolate croissant." I stood up, but Aliya grabbed my hand and jerked me back down to my chair.

Staring at her phone, she said, "Your excuse about Shaw having a girlfriend may have just flown out the door."

"Aliya, I told you—"

"His girlfriend has finally gotten her wish and has gone viral." She showed us her phone and the gossip column that she had pulled up. Right there, for everyone to see, was a snapshot of Shaw's girlfriend in a passionate embrace with another man. "She's hooking up with one of the guys on that reality show she's on," Aliya blurted.

Grace gasped, and her hand was over her mouth. "Oh, poor Shaw. Do you think he knows?"

"I'm going to kill her," I growled out without even thinking about it. "That self-centered skank." My hands balled into fists on the table. "They couldn't talk for the three months she's been gone. It's part of her contract. They are supposedly cut off from their friends and family and social media. Clearly, that's not the case. Someone leaked this. She's not important enough for paparazzi to be paying for it."

"But Shaw might be. Him being cheated on would be news," said Aliya.

"And this type of juicy gossip is good for the show's PR." I palmed my face. "He doesn't need this right now."

Grace's hand went over mine. "Do you think he will see this?"

"His people will, which means he will." I grabbed my phone to see if I'd received any messages. Would he reach out to me about this?

Grace leaned forward. "This is fantastic news. Then he can break up with her, and you can swoop in to console him."

I reared back. "No. What planet did you come from?"

"For fuck's sake, Kelcie, would you just hook up with that man and get it out of both of your systems? At least kiss him and see if this sexual chemistry that has been choking all of us is for real."

I crossed my arms over my chest and tilted up my chin. I was not going down that path with them. "Actually, I was coming to talk to you two about something else, but now I don't think I want to tell you. You are going to take the wind out of my sails."

"Oh, tell us. I promise we will be good," Grace said, sitting forward.

Aliya eyed me but was quiet.

I held my cup and carefully rotated it as I took my time deciding how to say this. "I have a date."

They both perked up. "What? Who?"

"A guy I met at work. He's been coming in after knee surgery. He wasn't my client, but we talked whenever he came in."

"And?"

"And his last appointment was the other day. He came over and said he never made appointments with me because he'd wanted to ask me out for weeks and didn't want it to be an issue."

"Aw, that's sweet," Grace said.

"Sounds presumptuous to me," Aliya said, taking a sip of her drink. "I mean, he's been going there for weeks. Why wait to ask you out? You're a catch. You could have been snatched up while he took his time."

"Aliya…"

She threw out a hand at Grace. "What if Shaw had gotten off his ass and kissed you before this bozo decided it was the perfect time? Would you still be going out with him?"

"I'm getting my croissant. I need chocolate."

"You need to get laid," Aliya said…loudly. "And not by a guy with a bum knee."

"He's a marathon runner," I threw back over my shoulder.

"So, he's skinny without an ass. Do you want a skinny guy who doesn't eat junk food?" Aliya said.

I returned with a warm croissant to enjoy. "Shaw doesn't eat junk food."

"Yes, but Shaw has a hell of an ass."

I pulled the croissant apart, ready to enjoy its chocolatey goodness. "What are you doing looking at his ass?" I said, beating back the memory of what Shaw's ass felt like and trying not to be possessive of said ass. I took another bite.

"Girl, every woman—and some men—watch Carolina football just to see Shaw's ass in those tight white football pants. It's a thing of legend," Aliya said. She turned to Grace, who was giggling. "Am I right, Grace?"

Grace tilted her head. "Shaw does those deodorant commercials with the towel around his waist, and there's a reason they get his backside."

I stuffed half the croissant in my mouth.

My cheeks flamed because she was right. But the fact that my friends were talking about Shaw's ass… Well, it made me see red. There was so much more to him. "I'm not discussing Shaw's ass," I said with a full mouth. But then the memory of seeing him without a shirt made me wish I'd picked up a brownie too. "I have a date next week," I said, as if I needed to remind myself.

Maybe a new ass to look at would help. I shoved the remainder of the croissant in my mouth.

Maybe the prospect of being physical…kissing…someone who wasn't Shaw, would be what I needed to stop me from going down this obsessive, dead-end road again.

18

Shaw

The news about Riley was all over the place now. I can't say I was surprised. Hell, I couldn't even say I was disappointed. I think if I hadn't been so out of it when she'd left, I would've broken things off before she dashed out the door. It would've saved all this drama.

Then again, maybe she planned it this way. She was probably feeding off the publicity it was generating.

Wyatt heard about it and called to check on me, to see if he could do anything to help. But until I spoke to Riley, I was stuck.

Riley was a live-in-the-moment kind of woman. She was beautiful and smarter than most people gave her credit for, but we both knew there hadn't been a long-term future for us.

Now, it was going to be news: *Riley stepped out on Dawson Shawfield with some Hollywood reality TV pretty boy.* So our relationship had run its course.

Riley wasn't a bad person. She just wasn't my person.

But this also meant people were going to track me down. Maybe I needed to head back to Charlotte for a bit so they didn't disrupt Kelcie and Aaron. They didn't need that aggravation. I'd discuss it with Kelcie.

My people suggested I stay out of the public eye, even in our small town. I was getting a bit bored and claustrophobic in my house, so I looked forward to any outing, even the ones in the torture chamber that was Kelcie's physical therapy office.

After last Saturday's trip, Kelcie signed me up for daily massages with Derek at her office. We went early in the morning before the office opened to utilize the cardio equipment, stretch, and work on resistance exercises. For the rest of the day, I studied film, took calls from my management team, and puttered around the house until it was time for Aaron to get home from school. Then, he and I would meet the kids for some time at the park. In the evenings, we usually ate together, then Aaron would do his homework, and Kelcie would help me with my evening stretches before I went back to my empty side of the duplex.

Tonight, however, I'd have to do my stretches alone. Kelcie had texted earlier to let me know that she had plans. When I'd asked if she wanted me to hang with Aaron, she'd said Gracie was coming by to pick up Aaron for a sleepover.

Aaron and I had just gotten back from the park—the sun was setting earlier this time of year—and were sitting in the porch chairs with our sports drinks before heading in to clean up.

"So, you're going for a sleepover tonight. What's the special occasion?" I said, leaning back in my chair. I took a gulp of my red sports drink.

"Mom has a date."

Red liquid sprayed out of my mouth, creating an abstract expressionism effect on the white railing across from me. It looked like something my interior designer in Charlotte would've insisted was just perfect for my penthouse.

I choked out the rest. "Your mom has a date?"

Aaron stared at his bottle. "Yep. You made a mess."

"With whom?"

"Some guy with a bad knee."

Then he couldn't run. I could take him.

"How…" I cleared my throat. "When did that happen? Has she dated anyone since…since you moved here?" Jeez. How did I not know about this?

"No," he said then tilted his head, looking up at the clouds coming in. "You need to clean that up."

Okay. Maybe I wasn't as out of touch with her—

"Except for when Auntie Aliya wanted to introduce her to a guy named Bob."

"Bob?"

"Yeah. But mom said she already knew a Bob and was perfectly fine."

What the hell?

"Auntie Aliya said this Bob was popular, and she really thought they should meet. He came with lots of bells and whistles."

Then it clicked. Bob. No. It couldn't be. My mouth hung open in disbelief.

I wanted—no, I needed—information…more information. But not out of the mouth of her son.

"I got the feeling he was an electrician or into computers or something. But I don't think my mom wants to date anyone like that. She told Auntie Aliya, 'I just need the basics—you know, something too technical won't work for me.' Then she said something about not wanting a Bob with a rabbit or a dolphin or anything crazy like that. Hey, are you okay?"

I couldn't breathe.

I stood up, took off my shirt, and wiped my sports drink off the railing to camouflage my expression and focused on breathing.

"No. I'm good," my voice broke, and my breathing became more labored. I was storing this tidbit of information away for just the right moment. It deserved maximum effect.

"Oh, she also said she had to make sure Bob was quiet so I wouldn't hear him," he said. "But she knows I hear everything. And why would she want someone to be quiet in the house?" He put his hands on his hips, mimicking a man three times his age. "Do you think she's sneaking guys into the house?"

I fell over on my hands and knees and buried my head.

"Shaw? Are you upset? Maybe we need to have a talk with her."

I let it out. I couldn't hold it in any longer. Tears ran down my face, and I wiped them away. "No, I don't think she's doing anything wrong."

He tilted his head, staring out. "Yeah. You're right. I'd catch her. She knows that."

I found my chair and slid into it. My hands covered my face, but I couldn't stop my shoulders from shaking.

"It's okay if Mom starts dating. She will still have time for us, you know." Aaron hunched down on his knees and bent to look at me, placing his hand on my back as if to soothe me.

God bless this kid.

I sat back and high-fived him. "I know. I was just thinking about a funny story." *Think quickly, asshole, and cover.* "When we were young, we knew a guy named Bob." I would think about Kelcie having a Battery-Operated Boyfriend later…when I was alone.

Aaron straightened. "Ohhh." He dragged out the word in understanding. "You were laughing. I thought you were upset."

I shook my head. "I'm fine."

"There you are." Kelcie found the two of us in a huddle on the porch, me with my t-shirt in hand, ruined with a red sports drink. But instead of talking to Aaron, she was staring at my chest.

My phone rang in my pocket as I stood. I pushed a button, sent it to voicemail, and used the chair as support. "I'm fine," I repeated. "Just being clumsy."

"What the heck is going on out here?" Kelcie asked. She was wearing an old t-shirt and sweatpants, her hair was in a towel, and her eyes were dancing between us warily.

"We were talking about your love life," Aaron said.

"Were you now?" Kelcie kicked out a hip in a challenge. "Since it's non-existent, it would be a quick recap."

"Not after tonight," Aaron said.

"Yeah, yeah. Go get your things together," she said, ushering him back into the house, looking everywhere but at me and my naked chest.

"So, a date?" I said.

She rocked back on her feet. "Yep. Going to The Winecellars on the creek."

"Nice. Classy choice," I said. The guy was pulling out all the stops for a first date. I was going to be sitting on the front porch with a shotgun, just to make sure she came home alone this evening, I swear to God.

I think Dylan owned a shotgun.

"Wyatt's trying to reach you," she said as she shifted the chair around and positioned herself behind it.

"I know. I'll call him. It's probably about Riley and—"

"I saw," her voice softened. "I'm sorry."

I waved it off. "I knew it was over when she left for the show. It just wasn't spoken. This is a—" My phone came to life, blaring Rihanna's song like a bullhorn calling me to my senses.

Riley. "Speak of the devil herself."

Would I exit this extremely awkward situation just to jump feet first into another one with my soon-to-be ex? Yes, please.

We both stared at the phone in my hand. "I should take this."

"Of course. I should get ready." She was gone before I could say anything to stop her.

And really, why would I stop her? It wasn't as if I had any say in her life. She should go out with someone that made her feel important. He was probably better than that jackass she was married to. I needed to stop thinking of James like that. He was Aaron's father. The only thing he did right was father that child, even if he was a crappy dad.

The phone kept ringing as her storm door closed with an audible slam.

This evening was going to suck, so I might as well meet it head-on.

"Hey, Riles," I said, walking back into my own half of the house for privacy. Thank God this wouldn't take long…

———

I was in my porch chair, beer in hand, legs propped on the railing, when Grace walked up. "Hey, hon." She came over and leaned against the railing to face me. "How are you doing?"

I shrugged and sipped my beer. I'd replaced my wet t-shirt with a flannel shirt and a pair of sweats and socks—the picture of a man without a life. "I'm fine." Poker face in place. "How are you this fine autumn evening?"

She tilted her head to the side, her eyes reading me. "I'm fine. I spoke to Wyatt on the way over here. Sorry to hear about you and Riley."

I shrugged. "It was just a matter of making it official," I said. "She wasn't meant for the quiet way of life."

"Still, it wasn't exactly fair how you had to hear—"

"Hear what?" Kelcie let the door close behind her.

I braced myself for the blow as she stepped outside. Kelcie's hair was down and in waves, shaping her face. She wore her hair up so much I forgot how luxurious it was.

My heart dropped out of my chest. I stood on shaky legs to get the full effect.

Kelcie had always been beautiful. She'd been a cute girl, a pretty teenager, a hot coed, but now…now she was a breathtaking woman.

She was a breathtaking woman who was dressed in a form-fitting, deep-blue dress and heels that accentuated her amazing, toned legs— all for another man to appreciate. She hadn't lost her athletic body, but the curves she was displaying…man, had I ever truly seen her before? I bit my lip to stop my jaw from dropping.

And since when did she have such an ample—

I closed my eyes tight, dropping my head, not wanting her to catch my focus.

I'd hugged Kelcie over the years. I knew her shape. But this felt like a slap upside the head and a grip on my cock, because suddenly, I couldn't function.

Where did I look? I had to find something else to look at…not her legs, definitely not her chest, not the hips I wanted to grab onto, and absolutely not her lips. Hell. I want to bury my hands in her hair. If I gripped the chair tighter, it was going to splinter in my hands.

Grace looked at her. "I was just talking to Shaw about—"

I cut it to the basics.

"Riley called." I pried my fingers one by one off the chair as I steadied myself to make conversation. "She's staying in LA. We broke up." I shoved my hands in my pockets to stop them from reaching for her.

Compassion softened her face. "Oh. Are you—"

Aaron stepped between us. "What's wrong with your face? You look mad at my mom."

"I'm not mad at your mom," I said.

"You look like you want to yell at her."

Kelcie intervened. "Shaw just got some news, and he's having a bad night."

I guffawed and took my seat. "I'm fine."

She stood in front of me. "Are you really okay?" She reached out to me, leaning over, aiming to touch me, but I flinched. I didn't want—didn't need—her touching me right now. She was becoming my newly branded, personal kryptonite. I thought back to the hard-on I got from the massage. It almost drilled itself through the table and never completely deflated until I took care of myself in the shower when I got home.

I was so screwed.

"I'm fine," I repeated and leaned forward enough to cover up any bulges that might have decided to appear on their own. "It was just a technicality. It probably would've happened if we'd had time to discuss it more before she left."

Kelcie and Grace stood beside each other with a quiet, communicative glance—the one women had when they thought they were being fed bullshit.

Did I look so pathetic that these women wanted to go buy five containers of Ben & Jerry's, grab their pajamas, and settle on the sofa with me for a straight-up bitchfest?

Would it keep her from going out on her date?

"The Imperial March" broadcasted from my phone. I yanked it out and sent it to voicemail.

"Wyatt?" Kelcie asks.

I nodded. "Grace, call him off from blacklisting Riley in Hollywood, please."

"You all need to stop sending him to voicemail all the time." She leaned against the railing I had just cleaned. "Besides, he doesn't know anyone in Hollywood capable of doing that."

I guffawed again. If she only knew. Not even I understood the extent of Wyatt's ways, and truthfully, I'd rather stay oblivious. "Keep thinking that," I muttered.

Grace walked over to Kelcie. "Girl, you look amazing. Absolutely beautiful." She put her hand to her chest, and affection lit up her face. Then she side-eyed me, mischief laced in her words. "Doesn't she, Shaw?"

And I felt like an even bigger schmuck because I should've been the one to tell her that first. But I was pouting like a child who hadn't gotten picked first for the game, even though I'd never even showed up to the field.

I glanced at her but couldn't hold her eyes. I tried to find middle ground between sincerity and biting back my true feelings. So, clearing my throat, I settled on, "She always looks beautiful."

I slowly walked over to kiss her on the cheek. She smelled different. Whether she used special lotion or actual perfume for this man, I didn't like it. I didn't like that she was making an effort to be someone else for him. She looked fantastic with her ponytail and yoga pants. She was gorgeous with lip balm and the fresh scent of her shampoo. That was my Kelce.

Goddammit. She was so close…but more unreachable than ever.

She was trying to start over. I was her friend, and it was my job to be supportive. But I didn't have to watch it.

"He's a lucky man. Have a good night." And I walked inside, unable to watch her walk away with another man—again.

19

Kelcie

I think I must be broken. There was a screw loose in my head. Here I was, pulling up to my house in an expensive luxury car with a good-looking, single man, and…nothing. I felt nothing.

Mitch Williams was a developer, a marathon runner, divorced, no children. He was kind, complimentary, handsome, engaging, and intelligent, and he asked about Aaron and my job. He was gorgeous with sea-glass green eyes and dark-brown hair, and I was single for the first time in thirteen years. I hadn't had sex in…I didn't even want to count how long…and I didn't want to. He was very easy on the eyes, yet there was no chemistry. Not even a spark.

All I kept thinking about was Shaw sitting at home, his sour mood, and what he was dealing with after Riley's actions. I texted Grace a few times to check on him when Mitch stepped away.

She said he was fine, and he'd told her it was her and Wyatt's constant "checking in" that was upsetting him. I got the nerve to text him before we reached the restaurant, but it went unanswered.

My poor Shaw. He had such a big heart. I knew, when she left him alone in that hospital room, it was going to end this way.

"Hey, you okay?" Mitch asked as we pulled off the highway.

I shook my head and turned to him. "Oh, yes. Sorry, I was just..."

Mitch knew I was friends with the infamous Dawson Shawfield. Shaw had been nowhere to be seen when Mitch had come to pick me up, and Mitch hadn't brought him up.

"I'm not sure if you follow social media or anything, but Shaw is going through some stuff right now."

He nodded once. "Yeah, it was even on the local news this evening."

I winced. "The thing is, I saw it coming. It was like a train wreck, but there wasn't anything I could do to stop it. Did you know she left his hospital room and flew straight to Hollywood? Who does that?" My indignation for him ran wild, along with my mouth, after months of being shoved down. "I mean, you don't abandon the man you love for a reality TV show, especially when he's literally in a hospital bed. I guess she figured someone else would step in and take care of him."

"That person being you."

"Me and his other friends."

"But he's living with you."

"He's living next door to me."

He nodded again thoughtfully. He was quiet for a minute, keeping his eyes on the road. He patted my knee gently and said, "Well, he's better off, considering the way things worked out. I mean, if she'd stayed, he wouldn't have moved next door to you."

I nodded, playing with the hem of my dress that was inching up my leg.

Having Mitch's hand on my knee felt good. Having a man touch me because he found me desirable certainly helped my ego make a reappearance. He'd chosen me. He'd asked me out because he saw something in me he liked. It had been a while since I felt special.

I crossed and uncrossed my legs as he pulled up in front of my house. Damn, what was I supposed to say? I should've planned for this. Grace had told me to give it a try, that there were lots of things I could do besides "go all the way." I internally rolled my eyes. It wasn't as if I were a naïve virgin on a first date.

"It's like getting back on the horse. You just need to learn how to walk before you gallop," Grace had informed me.

I'd never ridden a horse, so I couldn't really relate to the analogy.

Aliya had added, "No. It's like riding a bike. It's just muscle memory, and it will come back to you.

My cheeks flamed scarlet every time Mitch used the word "ride" in a sentence this evening while talking about the triathlon he'd participated in this past summer. Riding a bike, riding a horse, riding him—nope, I couldn't picture it.

Now Shaw… He'd be a bucking bronco, and that would be the ride of my life.

Was it hot in here? I fanned myself.

"Kelcie?" Mitch said, laying a hand on my knee to get my attention.

I jumped, my leg jumping up to hit the underside of his dashboard. "Oh! Yes. Um." I laughed to cover for being so damn awkward. "Thanks for the ride!"

I did *not* just say that. Kill me now. Another flash of heat ran up my neck and to the top of my head.

He held up his hands as if to calm me. "Kelcie, honey. It's fine. I realize it must be hard getting back in the saddle after your divorce." He smiled warmly at me. "I'm not going to jump you."

I covered my eyes with both my hands. No more riding metaphors —please.

"It's okay." He gently took my hands in his. "There are no expectations. Truthfully, I had none coming here. I just wanted to spend some time with you."

"I'm so embarrassed. It's just…I haven't been out…" I let my head fall against the headrest, "on a date in…God, I don't know how long. But I didn't think I'd be this awkward."

He chuckled and stroked the tops of my hands with his thumbs. "It's okay." He bent his head slightly, the corner of his mouth ticking up in what I could imagine did indescribable things to other women. "Honestly, I thought the odds were stacked against me in getting you to say yes." He raised his brows and nodded at the house where the porch light suddenly came on.

What was Shaw doing?

Mitch squeezed my hands and brought them to his lips for a gallant kiss. Then, he was out of the car and walking around to open my door, holding out a hand to help me out.

"Someone is keeping a close eye on me."

"Aaron is still at Grace's."

"I didn't mean Aaron."

When I didn't respond, he said, "Oh, Kelcie." He leaned down, his cologne heady and his whiskers teasing my skin as he gave me a chaste kiss on the cheek that was close enough to my lips and lingered too much to be considered friendly. As he pulled back, he whispered, "I don't know Shaw very well, but given that he's sitting up waiting for you to get home, I don't think he's as upset about Riley as you think."

His wink and sinful smile made my hormones question my instincts—and my sanity. He pushed his hand through his hair as he strode in front of the headlights, an excellent spotlight to his well-tailored pants showcasing a backside that wasn't anything to turn away.

I was too dazed by Mitch and the fact that I was sending him home to comprehend his words. But once he was in his car, the fog lifted, and I walked at a brisk pace up the sidewalk to the house. I caught just enough movement to notice Shaw's door close.

The curtain in the bay window moved. He needed to work on his stealth skills. But more importantly, we needed to have words about him spying on me.

I stomped up the steps to our shared porch and opened my screen door, but then thought better of it.

We were going to have words about the spying right now. I knocked on his door. No answer. I knocked again, but nothing. "Hey, 007. I saw you." I turned the knob on his door. Locked. "You aren't as sly as you think you are, so you might as well open up and explain yourself." I began banging.

He opened the door so fast I fell inside and into him. He stepped back, bracing me with his body and one arm, then juggled me into a secure standing position, maintaining his own balance. He even managed not to spill the cocktail glass he had in his other hand with the talented coordination that had made him a very rich man.

I was reminded of the reason he was having the cocktail. He was probably lonely and nursing a broken heart. The thought deflated some of my indignation, and I covered the rest by taking the cocktail from him and sipping it.

An old-fashioned. I grimaced. Yuck.

He walked to his fridge, pulled out a berry vodka seltzer—my favorite—opened it, and handed it to me as he walked back into his front room. "How was the date?"

I took a sip, not really wanting it but needing something to do with my hands. "It was good." I followed him to the sectional and made myself comfortable a few feet away from him. "How was your evening?"

He picked up the remote lying next to him, motioned to the large screen he had on the wall, and tossed the remote on the table. "Not nearly as exciting, I'm sure," he said in a monotone voice. He took another sip of his drink, and I couldn't help wondering how many he'd had.

I toed off my shoes and curled up further. "You okay?"

He let out a forced, almost cutting laugh. "Okay?" He tilted his head then finished his drink and walked into the dining room. "No. I'm not okay."

"I'm so sorry."

He froze for a minute. "About what?"

"About Riley. It was a crappy way for her to end things."

I heard ice clinking in the glass. "It's just how she is. I knew who she was when I got involved with her. It wasn't as if I was in love with her or anything."

"You weren't?"

He came sauntering back into the room, his face contorted in indignation. "No." Without looking at me, he went to stand by the mantel.

But he wasn't acting like the Shaw I knew, all stiff lines and impersonal.

"Shaw—"

"You know what I was thinking about this evening?" he asked, slowly pacing around the room.

He didn't give me a chance to guess. "I was thinking about prom." He had been prom king, of course, and his date had happened to be prom queen.

"Prom?"

"Yeah. And about that guy you went with. Brent or something?"

"Brett Miller. He was on the soccer team and in my English class."

He waved off the details. "Yes. Before he got the nerve, I thought about asking you."

"You did? Why?"

He ignored my question. "I wanted to ask you."

"But you were going with Chloe." I stepped near him.

"I wanted to ask you." He pointed at me, glass in hand. "But then that Brett guy jumped in before I got my head out of my ass." He took a sip of his drink. "So, when Chloe asked me, I said yes." He shot me a side-eye glare and shrugged.

"Why didn't you ever say anything?"

"I tried to grab you for a dance, but—"

"Chloe was climbing you the entire night," I said.

"Yeah, well, Brett almost lost his hands when I saw them on your ass."

I gawked. "That's not true." None of this was making any sense. Shaw had been the most eligible guy in our senior year. He'd grown out of his awkward teen years and had filled in that lanky frame I'd always teased him about. And boy, did he fill in. The popular, gorgeous girls had been nice to me just because I was his friend. They hadn't even been jealous, because they knew he was so out of my league. In fact, it had been one of Chloe's friends who'd set me up with Brett.

He shook his head and took another sip, staring out the window. Then he pulled out his phone and put down his glass. After a moment, music started to play through the speakers.

"What are you doing?"

"I'm prying my head out of my ass," he said as he took my hand, walked us to the back porch, and turned on the soft lights I had helped him string up a few weeks before. Ed Sheeran's "Thinking Out Loud" started to play through his portable speaker. "Dance with me," he said, extending his hand out to me as if it were a scene in my most romantic dream.

I stepped back. "What is this about, Shaw?" Was this because I went on a date?

"Kelce, honey…" He tilted his head down, his eyes glittering with the lights and the shadows softening his features. And while my heart skipped many, many beats, my mind couldn't read him.

"I don't understand…" I began, but he wrapped an arm around my waist and gently tugged me into his arms. Shaw and I had hugged often, and my body had been close to his more times than I could remember. But this was different.

He nudged my head to look up at him, and I couldn't say another word. His gaze danced under lowered brows. I touched his face, unexpectantly, to see if he was real.

"Ask me why I didn't love her," he said, his voice deep and soft. I was very aware of his hand splayed over my lower back.

"Who? Chloe?"

He shook his head, and the side of his mouth pulled up, making him even more irresistible. He caught my eye. "Why didn't I love Riley? Ask me why I didn't love any of the women I dated over the last…hell…ever."

How much had he had to drink? "You've never been in love?" My voice was a whisper.

"Have you? Have you ever really been in love?" he asked me through tight lips, his eyes narrowed.

I looked away. I didn't want to answer him. "What is with you this evening?" I asked, making a half-hearted attempt to pull away.

He swung me around and bent to my ear. "Tell me. Have you ever been in love?"

I swallowed hard.

"Because I have." His breath on my skin, in my ear, was melting me. He nuzzled my neck and mumbled, "Shit, I think I still am."

I had no words. I was speechless, afraid where this was going but wanting—no needing—for him to explain.

He pulled back, and I couldn't hide my heart as he ensnared my bewildered gaze.

A flush flew over his face as he whispered, "I can face a line of three-hundred-pound men who want to destroy me each week, but you…here you are, bringing me to my knees." The scent of bourbon was on his breath as I fought the desire to wrap my arms around his neck and thread my hands through his amazing hair.

He cupped my face and drew his thumb across my lips, sending shivers throughout my body. His gaze darted from my eyes to my mouth, his tongue traced his bottom lip, and our breathing grew heavy and in sync. "Just…" Was his voice shaky? "Let me just do this…just once. I need to know…"

Then Dawson Shaw kissed me.

He was as gentle as a naïve teen experiencing it for the first time. He was soft, moving his lips over mine in a slow dance. His hand threaded through my hair, tilting me to a better angle before his tongue parted my welcoming mouth, and we tasted each other. Each movement took us deeper, creating a greater hunger and feeding a mounting frenzy.

To stop my eyes from filling with tears at the utter beauty of him and the way he was treating me, as if I was so unbelievably special— and to stop myself from realizing I could still fall further for him—I grabbed both sides of his face, never wanting to let him go.

I felt like I was on some ethereal planet I never wanted to leave. It was the final piece of the puzzle.

With one kiss, the wall separating what we'd believed we were to each other fell. God, the fates, the stars, the journey we'd been on…it had brought us here. We kissed, and a part of me that had always been hiding emerged, feeling beautiful for him.

I felt beautiful for him, to him…because of him.

He pulled back, his eyes closed, his brows lifted, his lips parted and deliciously swollen. While his eyes were closed, mine were wide open, and I couldn't—I wouldn't—take my eyes off him. I wanted to memorize every moment with him in case it never happened again. In case the world rushed in, and this was just a fantasy. In case my life intruded and reminded me that this would never work. I just wanted to stare at this beautiful boy—my gorgeous man.

Because he would always be both to me. The beautiful boy who'd always picked me up when I fell, and the gorgeous man I never deserved.

He leaned forward, touching our foreheads together, his eyes still closed, and he lifted one of my hands to his mouth, kissing my fingers. "I don't know if I've ever known a bigger challenge than what I did just now."

"Excuse me?" I pulled back. "Kissing me is a challenge?"

"No, it's not kissing you—although making that first move did take me almost two decades. It was finding the courage to stop." He lifted the other hand and kissed it. "Because I knew as soon as I did, that brain of yours was going to hit me with all the reasons it should never have happened."

My brain still wasn't connecting the right synapses to produce cohesive sentences, so I squeezed his hands. I thought it would be reassuring.

"Say something," he said. "You're never at a loss for words."

"I have no words," I said.

He pulled back slightly, one side of his mouth tilting up. "You mean, all I would've had to do to win an argument with you was find the courage to kiss you. Man, what a coward I've been."

"Dawson, we should go inside," I said, glancing over to the back door leading into my side of the house. I feared the moment disappearing as we stepped into the house and back to reality, but I didn't want to risk Aaron seeing us.

"Dawson?" He reared back and led me back through the door.

I shrugged. "Seems like the moment called for something more than just Shaw. The world calls you Shaw." What I didn't say was that I didn't want to be like everyone else. I stared at those beautiful, reddened lips, wanting to feel them again. "How much have you had to drink tonight, anyway?"

His smile was infectious, and my libido was telling my doubts to shut the hell up. "I'm not drunk, Kelce. I may have needed a little liquid courage to finally kiss you, but trust me, I'm completely sober now."

My smile was unrestrained as I said, "Then let's do that some more…" I shrugged awkwardly. "You're pretty good at it."

He swept me up in his one good arm, pivoted, and sat on the sofa with me in his lap, mischief and seduction warring in his expression. "Honey, you never have to ask. Just grab me anytime, anywhere, and I promise I will do my best."

We touched and explored each other as much as we could in that position. He ran his hands over my calf, traveling up my leg to push my dress up just enough to touch the backside of my thigh. All the while, he was kissing behind my ear and down my throat, sending waves of heat through me.

"SHAW!" a deeper male voice shouted as he stomped through the front door. Being a small duplex, it wasn't like there was much of a foyer. So, no matter how fast Shaw was or how quickly I scrambled to get out from under him, there was no way we could stop Dylan from getting an eyeful of the two of us scrambling to break apart from each other. Instead, we wrestled to stand and knocked each other down in the process.

Shaw pushed up with his hand tangled in my hair. I pulled my leg up into his stomach and my forehead into his jaw. We both got our feet on the ground and tried to stand, only to trip over our legs, and grabbing each other for balance, we both fell to the floor. Shaw wrapped his arm around me, shifting so he was on the bottom. He let out a groan of pain as I fell on top of him, undoubtedly tweaking his shoulder.

"Oh, my God. Shaw? Are you okay?" I said, pushing up on my hands, which happened to be braced on both of his shoulders.

He let out another groan. "Shoulder, Kelce…"

I straddled his body to remove both offending hands, horrified that I was causing him pain.

He threw his head back and stared up at Dylan, who was hovering over us. "Well, well, what is going on here?"

I shifted to face Dylan. "What the hell are you doing here?" I said, in an echo of years past, to Shaw's annoying little brother.

Shaw let out another groan and grabbed my thighs. I liked having his hands on me. Dylan needed to leave.

"I could say the same for you, Kelcie. I thought you were on a date."

I shifted again, and Shaw's hands tightened.

I stared down at him under me. His eyes were closed, and he was pinching the bridge of his nose. "What? What did I do now?" I asked.

"Get out," he gritted to Dylan. His voice dropped, then he said to me, "Kelcie, darling, please sit still."

"Am I hurting you?"

He cleared his throat. "Not exactly…" He glanced down at the area of the body I straddled, and well, I saw what my shifting had accomplished.

Heat flooded through me, and my cheeks burned with embarrassment, desire, impatience…

Dylan let out a low chuckle. "Oh, I don't think so. I think I want to find out what this"—he darted his finger between the two of us—"is all about."

Nervously, I shifted again. Shaw's hands were vise grips on my thighs as he gritted his teeth. "What the hell do you think is happening? You are being a pain in the ass with absolute shit timing. That's what is happening. Now get the hell out of here."

Dylan's smile widened astronomically. "Well, hell. It's about time." He took a step back. "Here I was, coming over to console you over your break-up, but I see Kelcie has that well in hand." Dylan pulled out his phone and was typing. "Unfortunately, I owe Wyatt. I really thought you'd dick around at least until after Thanksgiving. But then Grace told me about Kelcie's date, and I was afraid you'd grow some balls and finally do something."

"Get. The. Hell. Out."

"I'm going, I'm going."

Dylan turned to the door and put the phone to his ear, "Hey, yeah, Wyatt, tell Grace to pay up. I caught them red-handed." Dylan looked back over his shoulder with a knowing smirk. "Wyatt told me to apologize for rudely crashing in on you, but…" He threw his hands in the air like a referee signaling a field goal, closed the door behind him, and shouted, "FINALLY!"

20

____

Shaw

"Today we're joined by the touchdown shuffle master himself, Dawson Shawfield." TJ "Smitty" Smith, a retired teammate and friend, drawled on my computer screen as we taped his podcast—me at home in my makeshift office with my newly set-up sound equipment, and him in his home office. Brilliant thing about podcasts and technology: there was no need to travel to a studio.

"Hey, man, how's it going?" I asked, sitting back in my chair with the haphazard background Kelcie and Grace had helped me arrange so it didn't look as sparse as it was. A borrowed bookcase from Dylan, a few books and photos from Grace and Kelcie, and, of course, a football and knick-knacks from Aaron.

"Good, man. How's the shoulder?"

I nodded with a smile and folded my hands in my lap. "Getting there. How's retirement?"

"Ah, pretty damn nice, to be honest. I went a whole two years without breaking something. Want to join me?" He was fishing. It was the question everyone was asking me, constantly.

I laughed it off. "Ha. Ha. No comment."

"I'm sure it would make a lot of linebackers and defensive coaches really happy."

"I'm sure it would. Probably my doctors and physical therapists too. I think they're getting tired of putting this Humpty Dumpty back together. But they do a good job, and I feel like a new man each time they do."

"No doubt," he said. "But seriously. Let's talk facts. You are getting up there in age for a tight end. Have you thought about giving it up and sitting back to enjoy the fruits of your labor?"

I dropped my head and then looked up at him with a smirk. "I have a few weeks to make it back to the season, and then we will see. Right now, our team is doing phenomenally, and my main focus is getting back to help them as fast as I can."

TJ had set up a nice life for himself after his football career ended, and I needed to take note of it. I'd been to TJ's mansion in Florida and knew this podcast wasn't just a hobby. His was quickly becoming the top-rated podcast on the apps, and that meant advertising money. While Riley had nagged me about moving to LA, one thing she'd been right about was that I needed an exit strategy. More and more, it was becoming apparent that my football career was coming to an end, and I had no idea what was next for me. And man, I just couldn't swallow that reality yet.

TJ glanced over at the sound booth, where Aaron was studying the soundboard, asking questions. "Clearly, you have a lot to keep you busy." I'd introduced Aaron to TJ earlier, and the two of them had hit it off, quizzing each other on team rosters and statistics. What truly impressed TJ was that Aaron could describe what plays had been called in random games from five years earlier in the order they'd been played.

"Okay, fine. But let's just theorize...hypothetically speaking...if you were to retire..."

The corner of his mouth twitched, and I dramatically rolled my eyes.

"*IF* you were going to retire...how would Carolina fill the hole left by you?"

"Come on, man, no one can replace me," I said to him, leaning back and running my hands down my chest. You couldn't be at my level and not throw down cockiness now and then.

"Yeah, but if you were Coach Lubiski, what would you do to shift the offense? Is there a tight end out there that could carry your mantle, or would it mean rethinking some of their game?"

"I couldn't begin to tell you—"

"Because there's talk…"

"There's always gossip, man," I was quick to point out. "It's what makes podcasts like yours so riveting."

He chuckled, but he was like a dog with a bone. "That big guy out of Alabama. Everyone is saying he's the next Dawson Shawfield—and he's waiving his junior year to enter the draft." TJ was backing me into a figurative corner, pointing the pen in his hand at me. "Just like you."

Aaron caught my attention from my doorway, waving his hands madly, jumping up and down. We told him the rule was he could stay in the hallway if he wanted to watch, but he had to be quiet. I'd given him a pair of headphones so he could listen to both TJ and me. In hindsight, it was probably a mistake, because Kelcie told me he'd have opinions.

Trying to ignore his gestures, I looked back to TJ on the screen. "He's good. No doubt he's the tight end to watch in the draft class."

"Nonetheless, you've had some amazing, memorable plays. Like that one you had against San Francisco four years ago when you had that slant route. Perry was forced out of the pocket, and you were open and ran and dragged defenders for forty-seven yards for the game-winning touchdown."

Aaron slowly inched in farther until he was eventually behind me, and his waving caught TJ's attention. "I think your friend there has some thoughts about our conversation. "What? Did I say something wrong?" TJ said.

I rubbed my hand over my jawline. "This is my resident expert and advisor," I said.

TJ let out a small chuckle, the type you do when you find a kid cute. Okay, then, we were doing this. It might be amusing to see Aaron take on TJ—and it would definitely take the heat off of me. "Do you mind if he joins us?

TJ's eyebrows shot up, but he was curious enough to let it roll. "Sure. Sure."

"Aaron, pull up that other chair," I said, making room for him to join me by the mic.

Aaron's assuredness halted just short of the camera shot.

"Hey, my man. What's up?" I said over my shoulder as if we were just sitting at a booth in a restaurant.

Aaron hesitated, staring at TJ and the equipment, and rethinking his action, confidence leeched from his face. "You're wrong."

"What's that?" I asked Aaron. "Come closer to the mic so he can hear you better." I motioned him forward with my hand, making sure not to touch him.

"He's wrong," Aaron repeated. "Tell him." He stared at his hands as he fidgeted with his fingers. "Tell him he's wrong. That's not what happened. It was the Denver game, and you ran forty-seven yards." As Aaron spoke, I slowly maneuvered the microphone between us.

"Perry snaps the ball—" Aaron gave the play-by-play as if it was being read back by the announcer, just like he had the night we watched the game together.

TJ leaned back in his chair, crossed his leg over his knee, twirling a pen between his two hands, sliding it back and forth while listening to a teenager school him.

Once Aaron stopped giving his dissertation as to all the reasons TJ was incorrect, he turned off his commentary and sat still with his hands clasped in front of him, chin down. I nudged him and whispered, "Good job." He glanced at me, and I winked.

TJ blinked multiple times. "What do you think was the best play of Shaw's career?"

"Dallas, last year, third quarter, second and five. Perry dropped back in the pocket, couldn't find Miller, Shaw ran a slant and broke the coverage, with a catch and run got a 43-yard touchdown," Aaron answered.

"What was the best play of my career?"

Aaron proceeded to stroke TJ's ego with a verbal highlight reel of his career, even giving statistics and comparisons that had TJ leaning back in his seat and crossing a leg over his knee.

"You seem to know a lot about football."

"Yep."

"Can you tell me the scores from last weekend's games?"

"That's too easy. You can look those up online. Ask me something harder."

"Las Vegas versus New England 2018?"

Aaron shot off. "That's easy—"

TJ lifted a hand and said, "At halftime."

Aaron lifted an eyebrow and one side of his mouth. "10-3 at the half and 20-6 final Las Vegas." His eyes lit up, and he inched up in his seat. "Ask me more."

TJ rubbed his hand over his chin, "Carolina versus Dallas, 2020 Wild Card game, 2:20 left in the half, 3rd and two—"

Aaron took a moment, looked up at the ceiling, fidgeted with his fingers, and said, "Chris Tresor ran a bootleg for a touchdown."

TJ tried again. "Carolina versus San Diego 2019 season opener 3rd quarter, following a punt return—"

"Jamar Frankis runs a jet sweep 54 yards for a touchdown." Aaron shifted on his feet, quicker and more confident this time. He turned to me, and his eyes were smiling. "This is fun."

"Is he right?" I asked TJ because I had no idea—but I thought he was.

TJ shrugged. "No idea. It's your damn team, man." And we both started chuckling.

"You're gold," he said to Aaron, leaning back and running his hand over his head. "You are blowing my mind." His eyes grew big and then narrowed as he studied Aaron. "You're how old?"

"Twelve." Aaron glanced at me for reassurance, and I reached out a hand to place gently on his back, coaxing him closer.

TJ's shoulders shook with amusement. "We're about to have some fun…"

Aaron, TJ, and I sat for an hour, talking shop. Actually, Aaron and

TJ shot back and forth. I just sat and watched, occasionally inserting my two cents.

"Okay…" TJ clapped his hands. "Well, this hour went by quicker and in a different direction than I had planned. Actually, I couldn't have even begun to come up with this. Aaron, it was a pleasure to meet you and to have you join us. Shaw, I do believe you've been over-shadowed."

I laughed. "It doesn't happen often, but yes, with my man, Aaron, it happens frequently."

"You think we can talk him into coming back?" He spoke to me but motioned to Aaron. Aaron tilted his head and furrowed his brow until we both looked at him.

"TJ would like to know if you want to come back and talk to him and his listeners some more?" I asked him.

He stared directly at TJ. "You will have to talk to my mom about it," he said. "Shaw isn't in charge."

TJ laughed, "Oh, is that right? I thought maybe he was your agent," he joked.

The joke fell flat with Aaron. "Oh, no. Not Shaw. Uncle Wyatt is in charge of any negotiations or any legal correspondence for my mom and me."

"What about Shaw…or your father?"

"No, my mom said Shaw is not my dad."

TJ's eyebrows shot up to his hairline. "Was that a possibility?"

Oh, please. I glared at TJ with my hands outstretched, asking him without words, *What the hell? You don't ask a kid that kind of question…and forget about the video camera.*

"No, he's not my father." Still speaking to his feet, in his normal monotone voice, he added, "Although, sometimes, I wish he was."

Silence.

Dead silence.

TJ whispered, "We can edit that out."

I pulled Aaron closer to my side as if to shelter him from feeling so lost and to communicate that I would always be there for him.

TJ, to his credit, jumped in. "Yeah, Shaw's a pretty cool guy. But how about I check with your mom about having you back on the show?"

Aaron nodded and stepped forward, offering TJ his hand. "Thank you for letting me talk on your show, Mr. TJ."

"Thank you, Dawson Shawfield and Aaron," he said, purposely leaving his last name off since he was a minor.

"And thank you, listeners. Join us next time on *Smitty's Smack Talk.*

21

Kelcie

"I wish I could have Thanksgiving here with you. Then I could play football with Shaw and Dylan and the guys. We could watch it and play it," Aaron said as he slipped on his jacket.

"I know, but you get to spend time with your dad and get to see your grandparents and cousins. That should be fun," I said.

Aaron ran back into the other room where Shaw was sitting at the counter, reading something on his phone. He immediately looked up.

"Will you text me?" Aaron asked, running over to him.

Shaw's eyes grew wide, and he put his phone down, giving my son all his attention. He sat forward, extending his hand. "Of course. And you text me," he said with a reassuring smile that melted my heart. "You sent your line-up, right?"

Aaron nodded.

Shaw quirked a side of his mouth. "Did you text TJ and tell him he was wrong about starting Mitchell and Reyes in his fantasy line-up?"

Aaron nodded.

The other side of Shaw's mouth drew up. "What did he think about that?"

Aaron shrugged. "He said if I was right, he was going to give me a job."

Shaw's smile was devastating. "Did he now?"

"I'm right, of course. Mitchell won't be able to break through Philadelphia's defense, and Reyes won't be given the ball enough to stack the points. He should've started Gonzalez."

The doorbell rang, and a weight settled over the room.

Focusing only on Aaron, Shaw reached out and cupped his shoulder. "You're amazing. Have I told you that today?"

My son's smile could've lit up the room. It may have been just enough to get me through the next few days of missing him.

Shaw slapped his thighs, standing, and sighed, "God, help us all when you're old enough to start betting. In the meantime, have a great Thanksgiving." He dropped his head to meet him eye to eye. "You text, call, email, whatever, whenever, and I will be here to talk about football or whatever you want. Okay?"

Aaron nodded.

"And when you get back, we will keep working on that spiral."

Aaron nodded again. Shaw straightened.

The doorbell rang again.

"Okay, well, I think that's my cue to leave," Shaw mumbled and nodded to me. Since it was the first time that James had even shown up since Shaw had moved in, we agreed it was better he wasn't here to complicate matters.

"Don't you want to meet my dad?" Aaron said.

"I know your dad, buddy," Shaw said, then added, "I'll catch him another time. It's better for you three to be alone. Happy Thanksgiving, and I'll see you on Sunday."

22

Kelcie

Shaw walked out the back door and over to his side of the duplex just as I was opening the front door.

The dichotomy between my ex-husband and Shaw had never been so apparent as it was in that moment—Shaw's sad smile as he walked away from us and my ex-husband's impatience at me for taking too long to open the door.

"Is he ready?" James said as a way of saying hello, staring at his phone.

"Good morning, James," I said with a forced smile. I'd kill the bastard with kindness.

"We need to get on the road. Traffic is going to be a bitch, and I had to detour to come out this way to get him," he said.

"Yes, well. I offered to meet you—" I said.

He waved me off. "It doesn't matter at this point. Are you going to invite me in?"

I gritted my teeth. He wanted to see the place. That was why he was here. He wanted to report to his parents that he'd checked out where Aaron was staying.

I stepped out of the doorway and invited him in with an arm gesture and a tighter smile.

"Hi, Dad." Aaron's jacket was on, and his bag was in his hand. He was ready to leave.

"Hi there," he said. "How's it going, buddy?" His tone was lighter than the one he used with me, but it was also the same one he'd used when Aaron was five years old. James slipped his phone in his pocket and surveyed our house.

"Are you going to your parents alone?" I asked him.

He walked around the family room. "Yes, Amber and her kids are going to her parents' house." He looked over his shoulder and smiled. "So, it's just us guys this time."

I nodded.

"How about you show me your room—"

"I thought you were in a hurry to leave, Dad?" Aaron said.

"I am, but I wanted to see your room."

"Go ahead, Aaron. Show him your room." I gestured upstairs.

Aaron dropped his bag and trudged upstairs while I stood at the bottom and waited. "This is my room. That's the bathroom. That closed door is Mom's room," Aaron said with the efficiency James would normally appreciate. "Oh! I almost forgot…" Aaron raced down the stairs. "Mom, can I take this with me? Maybe my cousins will help me practice."

In his hand, he held the football Shaw had given him. "Sure. I think that should be fine," I said.

James came back downstairs. "What's that?"

"The football Shaw gave me," Aaron said, running up and showing his father. "Shaw showed me how to throw a spiral. We are working on my distance. He said I've got natural talent, and I'm fast. He said I get it from Pop-pop. I can't wait to show Pop-pop when he gets back from his trip. Wait until he sees what I can do."

Pop-pop was my father, Holden Hammer, who was RVing around the southern states and was expected home in a few days. While only our close friends knew about our change in status, Shaw and I knew my father was going to be less than thrilled with the situation. It would probably be a toss-up between him and James over how bad a reaction they would have.

James's hands went to his hips, and his smile froze. "Shaw? I thought Shaw went back to Charlotte. Shouldn't he be back with the team by now?"

Aaron shook his head, beating me to an explanation. "No, he lives next door. Mom's working on Shaw's body to get him in shape, and he's showing me how to play football."

I stopped any further sharing with, "I think taking your football would be a great idea. It'll be a way to get outside and get some exercise while you're gone. Work off all that pie your grandma will make. I bet she makes the chocolate one just for you." I went and picked up his bag for him. I needed James to go before this conversation went off the rails.

James motioned Aaron out the door, but his focus never left me. "Go ahead and take your things out. I'll be right there."

I helped Aaron shoulder his bag and held the door. "Have fun, honey." I snuck a kiss on his cheek as he walked out.

"Bye, Mom. Tell Shaw I said bye."

I nodded and braced myself for whatever James was going to hit me with as the screen door slammed, and Aaron walked down to the car.

"How long will Shaw be living next door?"

I crossed my arms. "I don't know. Until he's ready to return to play, I guess."

"And when will that be?"

"I'm not at liberty to discuss his medical condition—"

"Cut the crap, Kelcie. Why didn't you mention he was living next door?"

"Because I didn't find it relevant."

"Not relevant. The man who wanted to raise my son moves in next door to you just a few

months after you and I get divorced, and that's not relevant?"

"It's not. It doesn't affect our custody, and therefore, it's not relevant."

"It damn well—"

I held up my hand. "I'm not doing this with you now." I pointed to the driveway. "You are going to get in that car and drive to your parents and spend time with your son." *The son you haven't seen in months.* "What you're not going to do is get bent out of shape all of a sudden about who is living next door to me."

"Amber and I are getting married," he blurted out.

"O-kay…" It was whipped at me without any preamble. I wasn't sure how I was supposed to respond to it. "Congratulations."

"Amber and her two kids will become part of Aaron's life now. I need to make sure he won't be influenced by your outrageous behavior where Shaw is concerned. It's important for him to have stability."

I stepped up to the door, ushering him out. "Go, James." I wasn't even going to touch that asinine statement. He had enough of his own outrageous behavior to answer for. "Enjoy the holiday with our son. He's missed you. Spend some time with him."

He took one step forward. His lips thinned as he tried to hold back any further opinions. "Did you pack his earplugs?"

"Yes, he packed them, but he tries not to use them as much."

His shoulders squared, and he walked past me. "His tablet—did you pack that too?"

"Yes, but he really does like to go outside and throw the ball now."

He banged the porch door open and gritted out, "Yeah. I'm sure he does. But what good is that going to do him, Kelcie? It's not like any team is going to let him play."

The gut punch synchronized with the slam of the screen door, unleashing the toxic wake-up call that had fed my own negative thoughts for a year.

I opened the door and stared daggers at the back of his head. "You don't know that," I muttered. Maybe spending a few days with his son, seeing how much he'd changed, would make him realize that Aaron playing on a team was no longer the impossibility it once was.

23

———

Shaw

With Kelcie's father still off RVing with his wife, and my mother living in Florida, our Thanksgiving plans consisted of my brother and our friends. I was more than a little relieved not to have to sit across the table from Coach Hammer quite yet—although I knew that conversation was necessary. He and I had to have a come-to-Jesus moment about my feelings for Kelcie and his opinion on us being together. We weren't kids any longer, and as much as I respected the man's opinion, I was done living by it.

For now, my belly was "Thanksgiving-full," and the tryptophan was kicking my contentment into high gear. I drew in a deep breath and let it out before taking a swig of the beer Grace had given me. I was lounging on Grace's sofa, Kelcie next to me, my friends surrounding us, and my world was complete—well, almost, since Aaron wasn't with us.

Because there would be a next year. And every year after that. We finally got off our asses, and while we agreed to take things slow—both to savor the new us and to give everyone else time to adjust to the idea—my mind was way ahead of the game.

I surveyed my friends in Grace's cozy family room, the game playing on the television, and was very aware of my arm on the back of the sofa behind her, of the way our bodies weren't exactly touching but how badly I wanted to lean her into my side and kiss the top of her hair. It was where she belonged. Was that allowed? Was that "taking it slow"?

I let my finger caress the back of her shoulder and saw the corner of her lip curve.

The sexual tension wasn't one-sided. Good.

She shifted, straightening her back, and took a sip of her wine. She curled a leg under her and…there—she leaned against my side.

Bingo. I didn't hide my satisfaction as I let my hand lightly rest on her shoulder. I peered up to meet several sets of knowing glances and warm smiles. Our friends were happy.

"Even with Kelcie joining us, our group seems smaller this year," Dylan said.

"Well, the fact that all of us are single certainly slims down the crowd," Grace said.

"I'm not single," Aliya said, coming into the room carrying a newly opened bottle of wine.

While none of us rolled our eyes, none of us acknowledged her statement.

"Where is the love of your life," Dylan said.

Aliya poured a healthy glass. "He's on a guys' trip to the Rockies." She took a sip and did not make eye contact but, faking the casualness of the explanation, added, "It was booked over a year ago."

No one commented on Aliya's boyfriend's constant excuses for not being around us. "What about Wyatt?" Dylan said.

"We are going to do a video call with him in a bit," Grace said, grabbing her laptop. "He got stuck out in Seattle." No one was quite sure what Wyatt did in Seattle. Venture capitalist was our closest guess. Maybe something with investments?

The conversation slipped into the background as I watched the game and enjoyed the warmth of the company. I cued into the conversation when the tone of the women changed to Aliya's latest recommendation.

"So, our friend over here"—Kelcie pointed at Aliya, who flashed an expression of mock innocence—"recommended a new audiobook a bit outside my usual genre. She wouldn't even tell me what it was about. She even went so far as to send it to me as a gift. *'Just download it, listen, and call to thank me later,'* she'd said."

Aliya leaned back on the chair and studied her wine glass. Her hesitancy in discussing her boyfriend switched over into full amusement as she grinned like the Cheshire Cat.

Grace leaned over. "What did you send her?"

"You'll see." Aliya took another sip, hiding her devilish smile.

"I dropped Aaron off at school and had to drive to the next town over for my annual *woman's appointment.*" Kelcie's neck flushed, and the pink traveled up to her cheeks. This was going to be good.

She took a deep, thorough drink. "I can't believe I'm telling you all this story."

"Take another sip." Aliya rested her chin on her hand and giggled. "Keep going…"

Kelcie covered her eyes, ran her hands over her forehead, and leaned into me further. "After I dropped off Aaron, I had my earbuds in and started the audiobook, listening to it all the way over to the doctor's office and…" She let it trail off, not making eye contact with anyone, but her blush deepened.

"What kind of book was this, Kelcie? If it had this kind of reaction, it must have been interesting," Dylan said, leaning forward.

"It was a…ahem… steamy romance." She straightened, waving us off. "That wasn't the part that's embarrassing. I read those all the time."

"Which book was this?" Grace asked.

"The one I told you about with the house contractor," Aliya said to Grace, waving her off and not taking her eyes off Kelcie, to whom she said, "Keep going…"

Dylan held up a hand, sitting up so straight he almost fell off his seat. "House contractor…nice."

Aliya motioned with one hand to get on with it while she drank from her glass in the other one.

"So, when I got to the doctor's office, things in the story were, um…reaching the pivotal scene Aliya had warned me about. So, I paused it and went to check in." Kelcie sipped her drink, and we all sat in silence, waiting.

"Once the nurse took me back, I changed and was sitting on the table, waiting for the doctor. The nurse said he was with another patient and would be in shortly. I pulled out my phone and started checking emails and such." She shifted and, still not making eye contact, continued, "The doctor came in and startled me, and I didn't manage to close all the apps on my phone." She looked up and gestured to the girls. "He darted around the room, getting things together, pulling out the stirrups, and chatting while he worked, and I, um…assumed the position." She gestured with her hands as if she were talking about the weather, not lying buck-ass naked, legs spread in front of a man who wasn't hers.

She continued, "The doctor asked, 'How are things? How's your son?'—the normal chit-chat that he always does—so I didn't think about the fact that I was spreading my naked lady parts open to him, and he was inserting a mini-metal pry-bar inside me."

Dylan and I simultaneously cringed. It was more than either one of us wanted to know about gynecological exams. Our enthusiasm for the story lessened slightly.

"I laid down, holding my phone next to me as he started the breast exam."

Dylan put up a hand and said, "Whoa. I understand that we've all been close friends for a long while, but there are certain images I don't think I need to have in my head, Kelcie."

She rolled her eyes. "Anyway…I went to lift my hand holding my phone, and it slipped, fell, and after a bit of juggling, it landed on a chair nearby. But not before it tripped my audiobook into playing… quite loudly at a very…um…eh…descriptive, intimate moment."

"Which scene?" Grace was on the edge of her seat.

Kelcie took a sip of her drink and said, "The shower scene…"

Aliya's face beamed. "Ohhh—no."

Grace's mouth fell open, and she let out a roar, "No!"

"Yep. Just as the doctor was scooting his stool around and propping my legs in the stirrups, my phone blared out, "Oh, yes, baby! Right there. Please, don't stop—"

Dylan made the rookie mistake of having a mouthful of beer. Kelcie delivered that last description in an overly dramatic falsetto, and beer sprayed from his mouth.

She continued, "There was a good deal of descriptiveness of body parts and moaning before I could work my fingers well enough to shut it off."

Kelcie simply downed the rest of her drink as our friends enjoyed her embarrassment. As her newly minted, self-appointed boyfriend, I took the glass from her, stood, and went to refill it.

Kelcie joined the laugh-fest with a freeness I didn't think I'd seen in…God, in ages. Before Aaron, before James. Her smile was sunshine with a hint of that rascally smirk that told us that she liked the fact that she still had it in her to shock us.

It was my kryptonite.

My eyes burned. "There you are," I whispered without even realizing it.

She turned to me, and our friends faded into the background, discussing the details of the book.

Kelcie leaned into my chest. The alcohol had relaxed her enough, so her estimation of personal space was slightly off, and her lips were centimeters from mine. "What did you say?"

A different kind of light had returned. Uninhibited. Unhindered.

"What are you mumbling about, Shawfield?"

I tucked a piece of hair behind her ear. "There you are," I repeated, taking in every inch of the girl I remembered, the one who'd been hidden behind responsibilities and obligations. Tonight, we'd pulled her out.

"I haven't gone anywhere." Her laugh died, and her smile softened.

I played with the wisps of hair falling out of her ponytail, staring at them, and didn't say another thing.

"Just kiss her already," Aliya yelled at us. "And put us all out of our misery."

I hadn't realized how quiet it had fallen and how all their eyes were on us, like a bride and groom at a wedding. Before I knew it, Kelcie's hand was on my cheek, and she was kissing me, giving them all something to talk about.

"Okay, okay," Dylan said to Aliya. "Do you see what you started?"

A flash went off, and Kelcie drew back, her face flushed, her smile a bit shy and—damn me—flirtatious. I liked it.

"I think it may be time for us to…" I stood, pulling Kelcie off the sofa, ready to make our exit.

"Oh, no you don't," Grace said. "We're doing a video call with Wyatt over pie. Then you can go home to your love nest. You have all night."

"Damn, Grace, with the cock block," I said.

"Anticipation—makes the heart grow fonder," Aliya said.

"I think I've had enough anticipation to last a lifetime," I grumbled, pulling Kelcie's back against my front. I nuzzled her ear.

"Give it a rest, Romeo. Wyatt wants to see everyone," Grace said. "Give him ten minutes."

I sat back down on the sofa, pulling Kelcie down on me and cradling her on my lap. She stiffened at first but then sunk into my chest. We talked with Wyatt as Grace handed out a variety of pies. Kelcie snuggled into me as we caught him up on the latest happenings, but my attention was on holding her, feeling her warmth against me, the scent of her hair, the way her voice reverberated against my chest, and how my hand molded to different parts of her body (of course the PG-13 versions, for now).

She fell asleep on the way home, and I coaxed her into her side of the house, wishing I could hold her in my arms. The indulgence of food, wine, fun, and what I suspected was pure relaxation for the first time in a long time caught up with her. She changed into a strappy nightgown, and I stripped down to a modest t-shirt and boxers, and we both crawled into bed without any discussion of me being there. I held open my arms, and she sleepily crawled up onto my chest.

The moonlight was just bright enough for me to see her beautiful eyes, which were half-open. "Shaw, I—"

"Go to sleep, beautiful. We have all weekend," I said, kissing her chastely on the lips. James wasn't bringing Aaron back until Sunday. That gave us plenty of time, and I wanted her to be well-rested for everything I dreamed of doing with her.

Besides, holding her, knowing this was where she wanted to be… Hell, I wondered if I would be able to sleep in this condition, let alone with this goofy-ass smile on my face.

24

———

Shaw

I awoke to an empty bed. Peering around the room for her, I fell on my back and took in a deep breath of Kelcie-scented sheets mixed with the aroma of coffee and cinnamon wafting from the kitchen. My girl was making me cinnamon rolls.

As if conjured from my dreams, she peeked her head around the door frame. "Oh, shoot, I wanted to wake you."

"Well, good morning to you too." I leaned up on my elbows, the sheet dropping down, exposing my bare chest, and I watched as her eyes followed it.

Then it was her turn. She entered the room wearing a short silk robe, and her hair was piled up in a messy bun. She leaned casually against the doorway, coffee cup in hand. I was a dead man. If I didn't get to touch her, explore her, make her mine…I would die.

"You're not for real…" she said in a breathy, sexy voice. "You just can't be for real."

I cocked a finger at her and bit my bottom lip to stop all the dirty thoughts I had from ruining the moment.

She slowly glided over to the bed, placing the coffee mug on the dresser, then crawled up over my body, her robe opening with each movement and giving me an amazing view of her cleavage. I bit down harder and rolled onto my back, submitting to her every desire.

Her hand brushed my inner thigh as she traveled up my body, settling above me on all fours. Her big brown eyes and twitching lips were playful but hesitant. Was she nervous? I slowly touched her knee, tracing up her leg under her robe, feeling the softness of her thigh. She closed her eyes as I ran it over the flat of her back and back down her round, firm backside. I squeezed slightly, studying her expression. "You are beyond my imagination." With my other hand, I cupped her face and turned her to look at me. "This right here. With you above me…" Even I could hear the tremble in my deep voice. "It's everything I have ever wanted."

Her eyes grew glassy, and I shifted my hand behind her neck, gently guiding her to my lips. With all the reverence I could manage, I breathed, "You are everything."

This was my testament as I dove into exploring her lips. There wasn't anything sweet, soft, or assessing about this kiss. It was want and need and desire. Her body fell against my chest as my other hand squeezed and pulled her down against my hardness.

She squirmed over my body, touching every inch of it. Our mouths shifted as we licked and nipped, tasting and wanting more.

Take a breath, man. There will only be one first time with her. Savor it. Slow the fuck down.

I turned her onto her back, wanting to take control. Her robe had opened, the strap of her nightgown had fallen, and yep…there was one of her breasts. The ones I'd fantasized about since I noticed breasts. I glanced up, and her eyes darkened as I licked my bottom lip. I slowly lowered myself and licked the peak of her nipple. She bowed off the bed. I did it again, this time capturing it for a brief kiss, and she tried to take charge, pulling my head down firmly to her breast, demanding more than a tease.

She sat up briefly enough to take off the nightgown. So much for slowing down.

I lost all words.

I cupped her breast and gave it my full attention as she moaned, and her body writhed beneath me, rubbing up against parts of me that didn't need encouragement.

Beep...Beep...Beep... "Crap. The cinnamon rolls." She gave me a slight shove. The loss of contact was painful, but the sight of her slipping on my shirt had a different, more primal effect.

"I'm not hungry," I said, trying to drag her back down before she playfully batted at me.

"Animal. They are in the oven. I need to get them out." My shirt didn't disguise the sway of her hips as she walked out of the room.

I ran my hands over my face and put them behind my head, propping myself up for her return. Probably good to fuel up—we'd need the sustenance.

25

———————

Kelcie

My new version of heaven was the promise of warm cinnamon rolls and Shaw waiting for me in my bed.

Yum. Shaw covered in cinnamon goodness—yes, please.

I was shaking with giddiness and anticipation. I swayed my hips to imaginary music as I grabbed the potholder and pulled out the cinnamon rolls. Humming to myself, I grabbed the icing and spread it on the rolls, licking my fingers as I dreamed of spreading it on parts of Shaw. My smile could not be contained. With a few rolls on a plate and grabbing the remaining icing, I walked back to the room. This was—

Wait.

Was that James's car? Pulling up out front?

No. No. *No.*

I ran to the room, dropping the cinnamon rolls on the bed, screeching unintelligible words to Shaw—something along the lines of, "Get up! James—Aaron—You—Naked—Icing—" as I flew around the room, picking up the clothes and throwing them at him.

After a moment of confusion, Shaw caught up with my freak-out and jumped out of bed. "Fucking Needle Dick." He slipped on his jeans with amazing efficiency as I grabbed random clothes, shoved them at him, and pushed him down the hallway.

James and Aaron were walking up the driveway.

My hands were all over his beautiful, amazing back. The back I was allowed to touch, kiss, grip, slide down to his—stop!

"Back door." I directed him through the kitchen.

"Kelcie. Calm down. Wait. You can't be serious? Maybe we could—"

"No. Not yet," I said. "Aaron can't find out like this and definitely not with James here." I covered my eyes, trying not to visualize that scenario. "Just go. Get dressed. Come back after James leaves, and we can eat." I gave him a quick kiss and shoved him out the back door onto our shared deck as if we were kids again and it was my father about to walk through the front door.

"Kelcie, wait, my shirt—" Shaw said as I shut the door on him.

There was an attempt to open the front door then pounding. And if it was possible to hear annoyance in a knock, it was there.

I caught a glance of myself in the mirror and smoothed down my hair, straightened my shirt…Shaw's shirt…and no pants.

There was more annoyed knocking followed by the doorbell. "Kelcie, hurry up. It's cold out here."

Screw it. He wasn't my father, and he wasn't my husband. And if it wasn't for my son, I'd have left him out there and dragged Shaw back into my room.

I opened the door and ushered them in.

"Hey, Mom!" Aaron came storming in, dropped his duffel bag, and walked right past me and into the kitchen. "Ohhh…cinnamon rolls!"

James eyed me from my head to my bare toes and caught sight of the shirt. He followed Aaron into the kitchen as if he were more than just a visitor, his head swiveling from side to side, scanning for someone or something incriminating.

Aaron ran back into the room. "Mom, I'm going to go see Shaw. I worked on my spiral with Uncle Mike yesterday. I want to show him."

"Um, okay." He was out the door before I could stop him.

An awkward silence settled over us as James watched Aaron leave.

"I thought you weren't bringing him home until Sunday?"

James nodded at my oversized man's shirt, and then his eyes lifted to the ceiling. "Did we interrupt something?"

"No."

"You made cinnamon rolls just for yourself, then?"

"You know I love them."

He traced the edge of the counter. "Aaron told me you had a date last week. A guy you met at work, he said. I just wasn't sure if you needed to sneak someone out before he came back."

I shifted on my feet. "No. There isn't anyone else here."

He tapped the counter, ending that part of this awkward conversation. "Aaron wanted to watch the games with Shaw." He tilted his head with a forced smile and a change in his tone.

"So, you guys threw the football with Aaron? That sounds fun," I said, walking around the kitchen island to stop feeling so undressed and vulnerable around my ex-husband.

He crossed his arms over his chest, staring down at his shoes. "Mike threw the ball with him." Mike, the older brother he had nothing in common with, the one he was always being compared to…great. "He told Mike all about playing football with Dawson Shawfield and how he was going to be his football coach."

Yikes.

James took in a deep breath through his nose, the way he usually did just before he told me how annoyed he was, and closed his eyes. "This obsession with football…it's a disaster waiting to happen, Kelcie."

The back door opened, signaling Aaron's return. I wasn't about to get into it with him again.

"Why the early return?"

"You mean, besides the fact that Aaron wanted to come back and watch football all weekend with Shaw?" James's tone was laced with scorn that was too light for Aaron to pick up.

"Dad wanted to come home," my son said as he came around the corner, taking off his jacket.

"And Aaron didn't want to do anything but watch football or play football," James said, sounding as juvenile as he often acted.

Ignoring his father, Aaron said, "So, Dad said if I was going to do that, we might as well come home."

It was my turn to cross my arms. I leaned against the island.

Aaron eyed the rolls. "Shaw said he was coming over as soon as he gets dressed."

James lifted a superior eyebrow as he nodded at my t-shirt. "Looks like your mother could use some clothing also."

"Yeah, Mom. What are you doing in a t-shirt? Go get some clothes on before Shaw comes over," Aaron said.

"Yes, why don't you put some more clothes on? Then we can discuss the choices you've been making about our son."

"Fine. But keep your coat on. You won't be staying long."

26

Shaw

I stepped outside and saw Needle Dick talking to Kelcie, his arms crossed over his chest. I told myself I needed to know what he was saying, if only to be there for my girl.

"I don't like this, Kelcie. What the hell are you doing putting Aaron on a talk show?"

"What?"

"Smitty Talk or whatever it's called. Imagine my embarrassment when Mike asked Aaron about meeting TJ Smith and being on his podcast—him and Shaw." His voice deepened, and his face was molten red. "I never gave my permission for anything like that."

"It wasn't a planned thing. He was at Shaw's place to watch the taping and…well…" She shrugged. "You know how he is when he has an opinion."

"Can you imagine how bad it would've been if Aaron had decided he disagreed with Smitty and had a full-scale meltdown while on the air?"

"It's not live. It's a recorded show, James."

"That's not my point. He's a minor, and I should have a say in what he is involved in—and who he's involved with."

He was staking his authority, trying to make it clear he was still in charge. But as far as I was concerned, he had to be present in Aaron's life to have an opinion that mattered.

I had a father who'd walked out, so I knew this type of guy. The only difference between Needle Dick and my father was that Aaron had me.

I wanted to be part of Aaron and Kelcie's life, but James was going to make things difficult. He'd gone weeks without making any effort to see Aaron, but now that he knew I wanted them in my life, he'd obviously decided to be a pain in the ass.

"What exactly don't you like?" I said, stepping up behind Kelcie. "Aaron was fantastic on the podcast. He was smart, sharp, and concise. Have you listened to it?"

Aaron ran out of the house. "Shaw! Did you talk to TJ? Did you tell him about my picks?"

James's eyes burned a hole in my head from the frustration of never being able to completely get rid of me.

"Aaron, why don't you go get your things out of the car," James said. "And don't forget the bag your grandmother gave you."

"Okay." He ran down the stairs, calling out, "I'll be right back, Shaw."

"Sounds good," I said, but James and I were already staring each other down in a silent face-off.

Kelcie broke the standoff. "Hey, if Amber is already home, shouldn't you be going?"

But the asshole wasn't finished yet. He turned to me, inhaling and puffing out his chest—postering. "And why are you here?"

"I live here."

He shot back, "You live in Charlotte."

I shrugged. "I have multiple homes, actually."

"Yeah, and how long is this one going to keep your interest?"

I glared. "We will see what the future holds."

Aaron came running up. "Let me put my things away, and I will come over, Shaw. The pregame should start soon."

I held open the door while Aaron raced in the house.

James continued, "What do you think you're doing?" His posture and expression screamed indignation. "Guarding her or something? Is this another example of that savior complex you play out with her?"

"James, I don't see how that is your—" Kelcie started.

I stepped forward with the smirkiest grin I could muster on my face. "You don't have to worry about why I am around her—why I will always be around her."

James's step faltered at my innuendo. I knew that Kelcie had always maintained there was nothing between us, but I had no intention of giving him that impression—especially now.

"Yeah, well, I think I'll just have a word or two with her before I go—in private, to discuss our son."

Kelcie stepped forward, cutting off the conversation and giving me a pointed look. Then she tilted her head to the house as Aaron came bursting back into the kitchen and grabbed a plate of cinnamon rolls. "Come on! Let's go."

I dropped my head, not happy leaving her with this asshole. I wanted to be there for her, a united front. But right now, she needed me to distract Aaron from this conversation.

"A-man. Those smell incredible. Let's get set up for the game."

"Okay. Hey, what did TJ say? I told you. I told you Dallas' defense wouldn't hold."

I pressed by James, guiding Aaron back to my front door. "You called it, my man."

Once inside, Aaron made his way to my refrigerator and grabbed us both two flavored waters, tossing one to me. "Thanks. So, tell me about your weekend," I asked.

Aaron shouted from behind the fridge door, "Well, I didn't get to throw much, except when Uncle Mike went outside with me. He has an old shoulder injury, so it didn't last long," Aaron said. "But I figured we could do it when I got home."

"Sure. Maybe tomorrow."

Aaron gave me the latest predictions and stats he heard from the commentators this morning as I ushered him out the back to my side of the house. "Go get set up on the couch and turn on the television. I'll be back in a moment. I'm going to grab some more of those cinnamon rolls."

I paused at the door, seeing both James's and Kelcie's body language leaning more to argumentative rather than cordial.

"Shaw…if you want to go check on Mom, just go," Aaron said from behind me. "I may not know much, but I know when my parents are about to fight. Dad was itching for one all the way down here."

"He was? Why do you say that?"

"He was spouting off about all the reasons I shouldn't be so hyper-focused on football. He says I should find other interests that are more in line with my strengths. When I asked him what he thought those were, he said I should explore until I found something else that inter-ested me." He picked at his fingers. "I said football interests me." Aaron's face fell, and he stared at his feet.

That son of a bitch.

"Can you go talk to him? I know he's telling Mom all the reasons why I shouldn't be able to play. He thinks I suck. Can you go tell him that I'm good at it?"

His words broke my heart. How could a man be so blind to his own child?

"Yeah, man. I got this."

He nodded. I swung open the door and went inside, ready to be his proxy.

His parents were too wrapped up in their drama to notice I'd entered the arena.

"There is no way Aaron can play football. You shouldn't be encouraging him—"

"Why not? It's great for his confidence."

"You know why," he said. "Stop making me the bad guy by pointing out the obvious."

"He's not five. He's growing up, and he knows when he needs to back away for a break. He's working with his therapist to identify what triggers him. God, James, he's so happy and independent. You need to come watch—"

"Independent? You can't be serious. Kelcie, come on, stop being so delusional," James said in a tone that I was not going to allow.

I spoke before thinking and stepped into James's space. "The only delusional one is you if you think you even know your son after months of ignoring him," I said, pulling myself up to my full height. I didn't have a short temper, but this conversation was pushing my limit of control.

"Who the hell—" James took a step forward. I stared down my nose at him.

"Shaw. Don't—" Kelcie glared at me and put her hand up to stop my progress.

James wasn't a stupid man. He knew I had fifty pounds and at least five inches on him. He turned on Kelcie and focused his vitriol on her instead. "This is all his influence." James gestured to me. "Is this your lame attempt at getting him to finally notice you?" he sneered. "To climb into his bed and live out the fantasy of being a perfect family?"

"I think you better leave." It was the only warning I was going to give him.

"Is he involved in the parenting of our son now?" He stepped around us, pointing at me. "Tell me, has he lived through some of his monumental meltdowns?"

I spoke before I could even think of the words I formed, everything coming from my heart. "*He* has been here…hanging out with your son." I pointed at myself. "*He* is sharing something Aaron loves and encouraging him. Where have you been? You can't just put him on a shelf and take him down when it's convenient."

Kelcie put up her hand. "Shaw, stop."

Pointing at my own chest, I leaned toward him, causing him to take a step back. "*He* has been fortunate enough to become friends with your son. *He* finds spending time with your son a priority, not a scheduled commitment."

James pointed at Kelcie, forcing out a condescending chuckle. "Are you really so pathetic that you would dangle our son out as a special project for Mr. All-American-Has-Been just to be part of his life?"

He raised his voice. "He's not a normal kid. When are you going to understand that?" Then he turned on me, eyes wide with fury and hands gesturing. "Has he had a game when a play didn't go his way, or an official made a call that didn't go by the book? Have you heard him scream because they were wrong? Have they had to stop a game so Kelcie could escort him off the field kicking and screaming he was right and they were wrong?"

The pain etched on Kelcie's face was all I needed to see. He was resurrecting memories the two of them had shared. Times when they hadn't been able to get through to Aaron when he was young. I reached for her hand, and she flinched.

That cut deep.

James spotted the way she withdrew from me and doubled down. "No matter how much you want a little mini-me running around, it's not going to be Aaron. He has special needs, and not your celebrity or even all your money will change that. He's not a normal boy."

"I'm not a normal boy," Aaron said, once again making a timely entrance. We all froze. He stepped around us and stood in front of his father, his back straight, and purposefully stared him down, which left his pathetic excuse for a parental figure squirming.

Kelcie reached out for him, but I gently coaxed her back to me. "Let him do this."

"I'm not a normal boy. I'm an amazing kid." Aaron looked over his shoulder at me. His voice softened, "That's what Shaw says."

I nodded at him and tentatively reached for Kelcie's hand, and she absently allowed me to hold it.

"TJ Smith thinks I'm brilliant. TJ SMITH! The kids I play flag football with think I'm a fast runner and great at juking." He stared up at his father, who couldn't even make eye contact with his son. The decreasing difference in height between father and son gave this conversation more validity and weight.

Aaron wasn't a little kid anymore. He was growing into a man, and he was well-aware of what people thought of him—including his parents. "Of course my teachers think I'm smart. And then there's my ultrasonic hearing, which is my superpower. You and Mom seem to keep forgetting about it. So, of course, I hear much more than you think I do."

"Aaron, son…" James's pale face was flushed, hopefully with the shame and embarrassment he was experiencing at being caught speaking about his son that way.

Aaron broke eye contact, staring over his father's shoulder instead. "I know you're my dad and that you love me. But I don't understand why you are so angry at me."

Kelcie's breath hitched. "Aaron, I don't think—"

"Honey, let them handle it," I whispered.

She yanked her hand out of mine, letting me know I'd gone too far.

Her focus returned to Aaron and a backpedaling James. "Aaron, your father isn't angry at you. Things are just complicated right now."

James jumped in. "Aaron, it's just that competitive sports in the past were very difficult for you to deal with—"

"I was eight the last time you let me play baseball. It was boring. Of course I had time to argue with the umpire—he was an idiot," Aaron said. "But I don't understand why you're saying these things about me."

Kelcie stepped forward, and this time, I kept my mouth shut. "Okay, I think you gave your father some things to think about. Why don't we sit with this and discuss it later? Maybe you can talk over the phone this week, or he can come up, and you can have lunch together next weekend."

"I'm not sure about next weekend," James said, hedging.

"You can't be serious," I barked and was cut off by another cold stare of death by Kelcie. Obviously, I was to stay out of it.

"Then two weeks," Kelcie said, turning Aaron around. "Good night, James. Drive safe." She nodded at the car.

We all stood silent as he left.

"Aaron, honey. Go on upstairs and give Shaw and me a minute." She opened the door. Aaron stood, throwing me a quizzical look. "But Shaw said we're going to watch the game together."

"Shaw's going back to his place for now."

"Why?"

"Because I think we need some mother-son time."

"But the games—"

Kelcie closed her eyes and took in an unsteady breath. "Aaron, please."

"Go on, my man. I think your mom needs some quiet time with you. Maybe we can catch the later games. It's fine," I said and gave him a wink and a smile. "You know how moms can be." I shrugged and then mocked-whispered, "She missed you."

He gave a dramatic eyeroll and said, "Fine." Then he stomped upstairs as a way of having the last word.

I reached out to turn her around, to hold her and help carry some of the burden. "Honey, it will be—"

She held her hand up to stop me. "I...I just need time to myself right now." With James gone, her shield dropped enough for me to see her anger and frustration transitioning into sadness and even defeat.

She and I used to joke about knowing what each of us needed and when we needed it. I knew when to back off and give her space, and I knew when she needed comfort and support. It was our thing—it was a Kelcie-and-Shaw thing.

"What's wrong?" I asked. "I mean, I know James was being an ass, and Aaron heard some painful things, but he handled him like a champ."

"You shouldn't have interfered," she said, letting out a deep breath and allowing her shoulders to slump. "You just made everything worse."

"Me?" I asked. "Why is this my fault? James swings into town and starts dictating how things are going to be, just to disappear for a few more months until he's required to play Daddy again. How about he tries being a father—"

"He is Aaron's father. That's the point. He *is* his father, and I have to deal with that." She let out an exhausted breath. "I've had to deal with it for years."

"I would've been—" I said softly.

"It wasn't as easy as it appears now." She dug her fingers into her eyes. "Aaron wasn't as compliant and rational as he is now. He couldn't tell me when he was sad, or hungry, or frustrated, or—" Her shoulders dropped before her voice quieted. "He couldn't communicate."

I never took my eyes off her. My girl was in such pain. She'd gone through so much. And where the hell had I been? Licking my wounds. Nursing my pride. Making millions and enjoying the surface, material side of life while she'd raised this amazing child. She had changed. We both had. And we had to get to know who each other had become.

God, I wanted to hold her.

She took in a deep breath and straightened. "Yes, I know James is an ass. But trust me, you wouldn't have wanted to have switched positions with him."

"I would've done it in a heartbeat." I took a step toward her. "If I would've known you were so miserable, I would've been on your doorstep and insisted—"

She shook her head. "It doesn't matter." Pinching the bridge of her nose and closing her eyes, she added, "The fact is I need to deal with him, and you rubbing it in that you have this relationship with Aaron is just making things more difficult."

"I didn't like how he was talking to you," I said, and I meant it. I wasn't going to sit by and let him dictate their lives.

She crossed her arms over her chest and gave me a sad smile. "I'm used to it—and I will deal with him."

"But—" I wanted to tell her she wasn't alone.

She put her hand up to stop me. "I don't want to talk about it anymore. There isn't anything we can do about the situation now, except try to not make it worse."

27

────────

Kelcie

Shaw went back to his place, giving me time with Aaron.

How the hell did all this happen? I slid onto the sofa, and my head fell into my hands.

James probably suspected long ago that I felt more for Shaw than just friendship. And even though we were married, James had had to live with that, though I hadn't realized it myself. Still, his acrimony toward Shaw had been one of the reasons Shaw and I had been estranged for so many years. James just couldn't stand him, and I, in order to keep the peace, had let my best friend drift away.

I remember that time as if it was yesterday. James had called me on the day of the football draft. He'd said he'd spoken to his parents and changed his mind. Through their network of friends, his parents had helped him find a job, and he had a clear vision of his future. He'd said that future wouldn't be complete without our baby and me. It was the first time he'd said, "Our baby." At the same time, I'd been intimidated by the whirlwind surrounding Shaw and all the attention he was receiving. My father had been in my head, telling me I should be with the baby's father, not with a man destined to be a major figure in a top professional football league. Dad convinced me James would be more stable, and I wouldn't ruin Shaw's bright future. I never understood why Shaw was willing to help me, support me, even agreeing to be my baby's father. I couldn't help feeling it was out of obligation. Maybe something he felt he owed to my father and me for our support over the years. I just couldn't do that to him.

I figured if James and I were together, maybe we could make things work. We could be happy. And at first, when Aaron was born, James was the proud dad, showing off photos of him, talking about all the things they would do together as he got older. But that pride didn't last long.

After twelve years of marriage, I knew James. And I knew he hated my friendship with Shaw and was very jealous of his success. So he got back at Shaw by pulling me out of Shaw's life almost completely.

Crap. I saw the resentment and anger stirring in his eyes today with every glare he threw at both of us.

And now he was going to put things together…me in a man's shirt and little else. Shaw was living next door and interfering with Aaron. Shaw's willingness to go toe-to-toe today was the only thing that stopped him from laying into me, but I knew it was coming.

Then there was us—me and Shaw.

God, I barely had the courage to admit to myself that there was an us. Shaw was going to leave and go back to Charlotte, and I couldn't follow. James had had a fit when I moved less than an hour north and settled with Aaron here. If I took him anywhere else…

"Mom," Aaron said from the stairs.

I popped up but kept my back to him as I wiped away the tears I had just realized were forming. "Yeah, buddy."

He was curled up, bent over his knees, and staring at his toes— something he used to do when he was younger. With a voice to match his body language, he mumbled, "I don't want Shaw to leave."

And my heart broke again.

I walked up the stairs and went on my knees in front of him. I sighed. "He will eventually. He has a team waiting for him."

He shrugged. "I know." Then he looked at me. "Was Shaw going to be my dad?"

Dammit.

"No, darling. You already had a father. Dad is your father. He always was and always will be."

He tilted his head toward me, his brow furrowed in contemplation. "Could he be like another father?"

Crap.

"Well, he's a good, dear friend to you—to both of us."

He shrugged. "Okay. That will do…for now." He stretched out his legs. "But if he's my friend, you shouldn't be fighting with him. You should go apologize."

"I didn't—"

Aaron stood and looked down at me. "Mom, you hurt Shaw's feelings. I bet he's upset he's not your husband, and I'm not his son. You shouldn't make him feel worse." He began walking back to his room. "Go see Shaw. I want to watch football this afternoon, and I don't want him sad." He stopped and turned as an afterthought. "Put on some pants first, and give him his shirt back."

It took me a moment to register what he'd said. "What? I mean…"

"Mom, I know it's Shaw's shirt. I also know he ran out the back door earlier."

Stunned, I said, "Um, okay."

"Super hearing, remember? That and I'm super smart," my son added and then continued to his room. "But Mom, go talk to him, because that wasn't any way to treat someone you love."

Love? I wasn't going to respond to that comment. But Aaron was right. I shouldn't have treated Shaw like a dirty secret. If nothing else, I valued Shaw's role in my life—whatever it was—and I didn't want it to be like this between us. I didn't want James to come between us again.

A few moments later, I stood in front of his door—fully dressed now—and knocked. I clasped my hands, raking my bottom lip with my teeth, which was sure to leave a mark.

Nothing.

No response.

I knocked again. A little louder, a little longer, in case he was in the bathroom or bedroom.

Nothing.

I knocked again. My thoughts were racing, and my courage was equally waning.

Before I could talk myself into abandoning the mission, I banged on the door. My fist was descending when the door finally opened, and I was inches away from pounding on a naked chest. Shaw's naked chest.

Oh. My.

I'd seen his chest before. Many, many times. And if James hadn't come home early, I would've had a chance to explore that chest more thoroughly with my lips and tongue. I raked my bottom lip through my teeth and tried to tear my eyes off it and upward to a more appropriate visual field for this conversation.

That beautiful chest was at my eye level, and my eyes drifted down…to the trail of hair that disappeared under a towel around his waist all the way to his large, adorable bare feet, pausing a few breathtaking moments in between.

He shifted, leaning against his door before clearing his throat and studying me with a cocked eyebrow. When I remained unable to form a cohesive sentence, he said, "Is everything okay?"

"Um…I'm sorry." I swallowed, trying to regain my composure. "This divorce, treading these waters…it's hard. I have heard so many horror stories about divorce and how the kids suffer, and I don't want to do that to Aaron. I want to try to keep things amicable."

A cold November wind blew my disheveled ponytail into my face, further loosening its bond and reminding me that, while I'd put on some clothes, I'd neglected a coat or shoes.

My lack of bra—okay, I wasn't *fully* dressed—was screamingly obvious as well.

His eyes darkened as he pulled me inside. "Come in." He stepped aside, and I brushed against him while walking through the entrance. "Does Aaron know you're over here?"

"Yes." I hesitantly walked to his sofa, turning to him for permission before I sat. He gestured to the corner, and I curled into it.

He sat next to me and took my hand. "Kelce, hon, you aren't alone. That's all I meant to do—to back you up. I'm here."

I shook my head. "I need to deal with James alone. Even just you being there ramps up his resentment. Then he starts to throw his weight around."

"I'm sorry, but—" He went to sit on the coffee table in front of me, only to be reminded of the towel that was already being stretched to its limits.

Not that I was about to complain, but it was more than a little distracting.

"Give me a minute," he said, disappearing up the stairs.

Soon, he was back in gray sweatpants. Pulling a t-shirt over his head, he sat on the table in front of me, letting out a deep breath. "Listen. This is becoming more complicated..." Here it was, the gentle letdown. He was cutting off any possibility of us. "More complicated than it needs to be," he finished. He leaned forward, taking my hands and pulling me toward him, so I had no choice but to stare into his eyes. "All I know is that you have always been one of the most important people in my life. All I want is to spend time with you and Aaron." He caressed the backs of my hands with his thumbs, and my mind wandered to other parts of my body where those thumbs could be rubbing. *Get your mind out of the bedroom, Kelcie. Jeez.*

His voice dropped an octave or two as he added, "But now that I know what it is like to touch you, hold you." He ran his tongue over his bottom lip as he stared at mine. "Taste you..."

Realizing I wasn't breathing, I let out a breath.

"I need to kiss you some more." He lifted a hand and kissed the underside of my wrist slowly. "And to hear you say my name in that breathy way you do."

"Shaw." It came out more seductive than I ever thought I was capable of.

He growled, "Yes, like that." He kissed my wrist again.

"We have a lot to figure out, things to discuss, and maybe some boundaries to decide on, but I'm not letting you walk away from me again—and certainly not because of him," he said. "We don't have to figure it all out today. Let's get comfortable with each other—with us being us. Give me a chance to woo you."

"Woo me? Seriously?"

"Seduce you? Romance you? Make you hot and bothered? Show you I'm irresistible so you can't imagine your life without me in it. You get the idea," he said with the cockiest, self-assured smile, as if this was only a matter of time. He leaned forward and gave me a chaste kiss. "Because you already have wooed me, seduced me, romanced me, made me hot and bothered. You are irresistible, and I can't imagine my life without you. And the beautiful, amazing part of all of it is you haven't even tried. It's just because you are my Kelcie.

My Kelcie.

I'd never bought into the possessive type of guy, but…yeah, I wanted to be his Kelcie. Hearing those two words out of Shaw's mouth had me ready to hand over my heart, my soul, and my future to him right now.

Instead, I claimed him. I grabbed him by the head and dragged him to me, kissing him the way I'd always wanted to kiss him. My hand fell on that amazing chest I so wanted to explore.

He let me take the lead for a hot few seconds before his hand dove into my hair and demanded control. He moved to the sofa, pulling him on top of me. It was slow and deep and unimaginably intense because it was so goddamn full of meaning.

This wasn't us just trying on a relationship to see if it fit. This was us finding the courage to admit that being together was essential to both of us.

And with the blaring ring of Shaw's phone on the table, the real world reminded us it was still there, waiting to be dealt with.

We slowly came back down to reality. I immediately thought of Aaron. Crap. He could walk in any minute and see us like this. That was not a good idea. We needed to get a better grip on what was happening before we introduced this idea to him.

I stood. Shaw's phone continued to ring in a special ringtone I hadn't heard often.

"Goddammit," Shaw said, leaning over and reaching for the phone. He stared at it, then said, "Give me a moment. I have to get this."

I began backing to the door. "That's okay. I need to go back and check on Aaron before he decides to drop in on us." I tossed a thumb signal over my shoulder. "Come over when you're done, and we can watch the games with him.

He nodded then stood, answering as he walked into the kitchen, "Yeah, Yaz."

Yaz. His agent.

And there was another hurdle for us. He had to get back to Charlotte. There wasn't much keeping him here in town, and the team was going to want him back, regardless of whether he was starting. They were heading into the playoffs soon, and he needed to get back.

And when he left, we'd be right back where we were before. What would happen to us then?

28

Shaw

Yazmine Silva was the head of YES—the agency that represented me
—and a beautiful ballbuster. As such, she didn't waste time with pleas-
antries. She just jumped into it.

"So, we've got two issues—well, three, really." I heard her power
heels clapping on the floor in the background at a clipped pace. She
was obviously calling me in between meetings. "One, Smitty wants
your boy back on his podcast ASAP. He said his subscribers' rate
jumped by 30% with that week's episode. So, what's the deal with
him? Are you dating his mother or something? I've only caught a few
minutes of it, but I can tell he's adorable and wicked smart. You need
to talk to his parents about representation, and then we can get into
negotiations."

"Wait, what?"

"The boy. Smitty wants the boy back on air. They are thinking of
creating a segment with him for Fantasy Football followers. Many of
his latest predictions have hit, and Fantasy Football blog pages are
actually posting his picks. He's trending as #footballkid and
#Shawsson. Social media accounts are blowing up with discussions of

188

his analysis, and he even has other professional analysts legitimizing his thought processes."

Seriously? A smile tugged at my lips. "That's my boy," I said softly. Wait. What? "The hashtag is #Shawsson?"

The background noise on the other line went silent, and irritation and a tinge of panic laced her tone. "Holy crap. Shaw, is he your child? I thought it was—"

"No. No. Nothing like that."

"Okay." The sound of her footsteps started back up as she stressed, "If there is anyone out there who can call you Daddy, I need to be your first call, got it?"

"Excuse me?"

"That came out wrong. You know what I mean," she said, annoyed at my innuendo.

"Of course," I agreed, mollifying her. I didn't need Yaz poking at me any more than what she was about to do.

"The next item on my list: your former girlfriend is making waves. I guess her fifteen minutes of fame wasn't as profitable as she had hoped it would be, and she wants a settlement out of you for your break-up."

"You can't be serious. She left me—cheated on me, technically."

"I know, but a girl needs to pay her bills, and it's either you pay, or a tabloid will. We think leaning into helping the boy with the podcast will help boost your image before she tries to take it down for profit."

"Riley wouldn't do that," I said with more conviction than I felt.

"Trust me. Let's get some photos of you and the boy—TJ mentioned he was autistic or something. Maybe we can get you working with a non-profit autism program."

Red filled my world.

"Yaz, we've worked together for years." My voice was as thick as concrete. "So take what I'm saying as a line drawn in the sand. Nothing about Aaron or his mother is up for discussion. I will be severing all ties with the YES agency and all your agents the next time it's considered. Do you feel me?"

She quieted herself and said softly, "Shaw, I didn't mean it that way—"

"They are family to me. Not a prop."

"I understand. I am sorry. I didn't mean to offend or imply you meant to capitalize on them." Her tone was placating. "How about we just get photos of the three of you working on the podcast? We don't have to mention the autism or anything, but this is a great opportunity for Aaron if he's interested in it."

"I doubt his parents will even let him go back on."

"Most teenage boys would kill for this opportunity. Hell, most men too."

He would love to do it regularly, but James would shit a brick. Then again, that might be the perfect reason. "I will talk with Kelcie."

"Ah, Kelcie. I talked with Davy the other day, and he mentioned you were ga-ga for an old girlfriend."

"She wasn't my girlfriend—just my best friend."

"Tomatoes, tomatoes… When is she coming to Charlotte?"

"Don't know. Next topic."

She spoke to someone in the background and then refocused on me, as if I hadn't just threatened to drop her. A door opened and closed, and I imagined her settling into her desk for what was bound to be her piéce de résistance. "Okay, now for the important stuff."

Oh, jeez, she thought Riley going after me for money wasn't important?

"I know you're happy in your cozy small-town alternate reality, but you need to get back here and defend your job."

"Hold up. What?"

"Shaw, hon. You've been out half the season. The doctors are telling the staff you should be ready to return—"

"I am, but—"

"They need you. It's clutch time." She referred to our team's prospects of being in the playoffs and the team's current lackluster performances. "The pendulum could swing either way, and they need their best players back in the pack."

"Okay, fine. I was going to get the sign-off at my doctor's appointment in Baltimore tomorrow, anyway. But what is all this drama about defending my job?"

"Come on, Shaw. You're not naïve. You know there are younger guys behind you who are gunning for your position for less money. And your contract takes a chunk of change out of the salary cap. You need to justify it. So, stop playing house with—"

"That's none of your business, Yaz."

"Darling, everything about you is our business. It's our job at YES to know about everything before anyone else. Of course, I've already done a background check on her. I have an NDA ready for you to give her to sign—"

"You are getting precariously close to that line again, Yaz."

"Don't be an idiot. If it weren't for that NDA breathing over her, Riley would be spilling all about the two of you to any gossip podcast she could find, just to extend her five minutes of publicity."

"She's still threatening to sue me, so what good is the NDA?"

"The lawyers are dealing with it."

"Kelcie has known me since we were pimply faced kids. If she wanted to smear me or cash in on old photos or secrets, she would've done it already. No NDA."

Yaz let out an exasperated sound. "This won't make legal very happy."

"Tough shit. If an NDA was effective, they wouldn't be dealing with Riley."

She refocused. "Regardless, it's time to get your ass back down here—and not just for a visit. Time to get back to work." The sound of a door opening and voices entered her background again. "Gotta go. Let me know about the kid and what plane you're arriving on."

And as fast as she'd disrupted my life, she exited it, leaving behind a wake of problems for me to figure out.

Later, between games, we ate dinner. As we were cleaning up, I approached the subject with the hesitancy of a teenage boy asking a girl out for the first time. "How would you feel about going to Charlotte this weekend?"

Kelcie was bending over to put away a pot. She froze, and I caught her before she fell on her ass and helped her stand. "Wh—what? Why?"

I took a small step back, ran my hand over my jaw, and said, "Well, it turns out I have a job, and some people are anxious for me to get back to it."

"But you haven't been cleared to play."

I lifted my good shoulder. "Yeah, but I'm still expected on the sidelines. And truthfully, I have no reason not to be there. I'm still on the team—at least for now." I leaned my back on the counter and crossed my arms over my chest—the epitome of cool casualness. "So, what do you think? I'd love to take you to Charlotte for a few days… You could see the game and meet some of my friends…" I lowered my voice. "I could have some time alone with you."

"What about Aaron and school? He'd be so jealous that I saw a game and he didn't get to go."

"Aaron could stay with Grace. You know she'd love to have him," I said, wrapping my arms around her waist, afraid she was going to run, figuratively and literally.

"But—"

I leaned over and kissed her. "We will never have time alone with him here, and James isn't coming for another two weeks. Besides, we need to figure this out." I kissed her again, deeper this time, and cupped her face in my hands. I wanted her to say yes.

"Let's have some fun. Tell Aaron you need to meet with my doctors. I will promise to take him to another game—maybe even playoffs, if our team makes it. I could even get him a pre-game field pass."

Her eyes widened. "I may be able to buy a lot of good behavior with that reward."

"So? You, me, my place…alone?"

"Let me talk with Grace about it and check with work."

No doubt Grace would push her out the door.

"I have to leave tomorrow after my doctor's appointment and get down there for a team meeting and talk with the trainers. Why don't you fly down Thursday? That will give us the weekend together," I said, giddy as a schoolgirl. I could get the place ready for her. "Just let me know when you want to leave, and I'll get my assistant, Matt, to book your flight." The first thing I was doing was making sure nothing of Riley's had been left in the house, including that gaudy bed she'd bought for us. In fact, I was going to call my housekeeper, Cora, about getting it out now. I don't know why I hadn't thought about it before.

"Matt?" Kelcie said. "You have an assistant? I thought Yaz was your assistant?"

The bark of laughter that escaped me shocked both of us before I reeled it back. "Oh no. And please, for the love of God, don't call Yaz my assistant. Even though I hired her agency, Yaz thinks I work for her instead of the other way around."

Kelcie's brows furrowed.

"Yaz is my agent. Different from Matt. Matt schedules my calendar, books flights, and oversees the houses and cars—you know, the day-to-day stuff," I said. "Yazmine Silva and her staff at YES Sports Management are my go-between with the team, business contacts, media, marketing, trainers, etc. Basically, she handles everything business or football related."

"How many employees do you have, Shaw?"

"I don't have employees, really—well, maybe just Matt. Then there's my housekeeper. The others are kind of, I don't know… Matt and Yaz have different people working on my behalf.

She threw up a hand. "Hold up. Houses? As in, you have more than one house in Charlotte?"

I leaned back against the counter and pulled her between my legs. "I can't believe I haven't told you about this." I held her hand. "Yes, I have a condo close to the stadium and a lake house on Lake Norman. I have a few friends who also have homes on the lake, so it's a place I go to relax. I have a boat too. Maybe we could go there with Aaron once the season is over."

She stared at me for a moment, her mouth slightly open. "I know I shouldn't be surprised you have more than one house. I guess we have a lot to learn about each other." I gave her a quick kiss. "I'm just so excited to show you everything and have a chance to introduce you to my friends. I want to show you what life is like in Charlotte."

And I want you to see what our life could be…if you would just give it a chance.

I couldn't wait.

29

Kelcie

Breathe.

He wanted me to come home with him to Charlotte. See his place
—no, *places*. Go to his game. Meet his friends. He had friends besides
us. Of course he did. He probably had a ton of friends. I'd have alone
time with him for a weekend. It sounded like bliss.

All I had to do is call his assistant to book a flight…and decide
which house we wanted to stay at so he can tell his housekeeper to
prepare the place, and then his chef can stock the kitchen with some
meals—unless we want to go out to eat. Then he could get Matt to
make some reservations.

*Breathe in and let it out. It's not like you thought he lived in a two-
bedroom townhome in Charlotte. The guy is worth millions. Millions—
with an 's.'*

"What kind of car do you drive?"

"Huh?" He was typing on his phone—no doubt sending a text to
his assistant. "Oh, um, at the condo, I have a Mercedes AMG 63, and
at the lake house, I usually keep my Audi R8 Spider. I guess I'll leave
the truck here so I can use it when I visit."

Visit. I turned my back on him so I could process this idea properly.

Because he wouldn't be living here anymore. He'd be living there. Two states and several hours away from me—from us.

Why was I doing this?

His arms wrapped around me from behind, and Shaw's breath was warm against my neck. "I can feel your apprehension. What are you thinking?"

He turned me around to face him. His eyes were so green and still the most beautiful thing known to me. This boy—this man—had held my heart for as long as I'd known him. He wanted to show me his life, and I was holding back.

"I'm just thinking about logistics," I said, then flattened my hand over his warm chest, longing to lay my head over his beating heart every night.

"Shaw! Come on, the Dallas game is starting!" Aaron yelled from the other room.

Shaw kissed my forehead and whispered, "Just the two of us together, okay? No outside influences, opinions, or expectations. Just us."

I smiled a genuine smile and nodded. Because it did sound like the closest thing to heaven I'd heard in a long time.

30

Shaw

Later that evening, as Kelcie and I fixed dinner, we discussed what needed to be done to manage our weekend away.

"When are we telling Aaron? I don't think we can go away together without telling him what is happening between us," I whispered. Even with the television blaring in the other room, we were both paranoid about being overheard.

"Tell me what?"

Speak of the devil…

Startled, Kelcie dropped a bag of chips, and I bent down to pick them up.

"Holy cow, Aaron, you are sneaky," I said.

He shrugged. "Don't mean to be. I want a Coke. Can I get one, please?"

Kelcie nodded. "Sure, why not." She went to grab one out of the refrigerator.

I nudged her a little with my elbow, and she shook her head vehemently. I gave her the big eyes—universal for "say something."

She shook her head faster. "I'm not ready," she gritted out.

"Not ready for what?" he asked.

"For dinner. It's not ready to be served yet." She wiped her hands on a towel and turned, bracing herself against the counter. "Hey, what do you think about staying with Grace this weekend?"

"Why?"

She shifted. "Well, I need to make a trip down to Charlotte for work, and—"

He lifted an arm, pointing at me. "Well, I can stay with Shaw."

I quirked a smile, "Actually, I will be out of town as well."

He opened his soda and took a sip. "Where are you going?"

She clasped and unclasped her fingers, and a nervous smile graced her face. "We both are going to Charlotte…actually."

He took another sip. "So, you're going together?"

"Yes," I said as she simultaneously said, "No."

The more he studied us, the more uneasy Kelcie became, so I took pity on her and said, "The team needs me back." His face fell slightly, and he straightened.

"So, you're leaving us?"

Man, I hadn't even thought of it that way. "No, not really. I need to go down and see what the trainers have to say, as well as what their doctors and coaches have to say. So I thought I'd take your mom with me."

"But what about me? Why can't I go too?"

Kelcie softly reminded him, "You have school."

"It's going to be all work. Boring stuff." I waved a hand then added, "But I will be traveling back and forth from now on. As soon as your winter break starts, I could bring both of you down to Charlotte— if we can arrange it with your father's schedule, of course. We can even go to one of the games. Okay?"

The disappointment, the upturned bottom lip, gave me a glimpse of what he must have been like as a little boy. "I promise I will save all the good tours for your visit. This will be business stuff that won't interest you."

He grumbled, "You know I like the business stuff too."

"Yeah, but I don't think the team is ready for your genius just yet."

I winked. "Let me get back in the groove and whip them into shape before we pull you in."

"Okay."

"So, I'm going to ask Grace to stay with you, if that is okay—"

"No, I want Pop-pop to stay with me."

"Pop-pop is out of town."

He shook his head, taking another sip of his soda, and as he stepped out of the room, he threw over his shoulder, "Nope. He called me. When I told him Shaw moved in with us, he said he was on his way over."

I closed my eyes and pinched the bridge of my nose. Why did I feel like I'd been caught in her bedroom with my pants down? I stared down at myself—yep, I was fully clothed.

But entirely vulnerable.

Oh, crap. Kelcie stared at me and said, "Guess we *are* doing this, after all."

"Yeah, well, let's hope I come out of this conversation intact, or the trip to Charlotte may not be what we were both hoping."

31

Shaw

I remember walking onto the football field the summer before my freshman year—well, actually, Tyler dragged me there—and that had been the first time I'd met Coach Hammer. I'd been a knobby-knee, reed-thin, awkward teen with big feet and, without a father in my life, virtually no idea how to play the game.

I'd also met his fire-plug-sized daughter that first day and admired the way the other boys—some twice her size—followed her through drills, listened as she yelled at them from the tackling sleds, and watched teenage boys fall to their knees while she passed them running suicides uphill.

I knew then that I had to be friends with her.

"No one touches Coach's daughter, so don't get any ideas," Tyler had said.

I didn't even know what to do with a girl back then. But I knew she was special.

And so was her dad. Coach Hammer had filled a void in my life, giving me direction and discipline. He'd believed in me and pushed me to my limit. He'd taught me the very basics of throwing a spiral and, later, called recruiters, begging them to come see me play. I owed him the career I have now.

One thing that had always been a touchy subject, though, was my friendship with his daughter. He'd been fine with our group of friends, but he hadn't liked Kelcie and me being as close as we were. More than once, he'd sat me down, reminding me there were plenty of girls out there that weren't his daughter.

I'd tried not to be hurt by his uneasiness with our relationship. Hell, I'd even teased him about my unworthiness. But he'd never wavered, even though we'd reassured him repeatedly—by dating other people, even double-dating sometimes—that we were just friends.

He hadn't had trouble with her dating—just with the idea of dating me.

Yeah. That wasn't insulting or anything.

Not more than twenty minutes after Aaron gave us the heads up, Holden Hammer was on our porch. I opened Kelcie's front door to meet him eye to eye. He hadn't changed much over the years. His walrus mustache was perfectly trimmed but downturned, and his hair was unruly under his Carolina baseball cap. Coach Hammer was probably two inches shorter than me, and even though I was stronger and more fit, just his glare could still halt me in my step.

"Coach." I forced a pleasant smile. "Come on in. Aaron told us you were back in town." I would normally go in for a hug, but I could tell that he wouldn't appreciate it. His body was rigid as he rocked back on his feet.

"Why don't you join me outside for a moment first?"

It was cold enough to see your breath outside. But his tone brooked no room for dispute. "Okay."

I closed the door behind me and walked a few steps away from the door, knowing this wasn't something Aaron needed to overhear.

"How was your trip? You've been gone since the summer, right?"

He leaned against the porch railing and crossed his arms over his chest. "Last I heard, you were going to rehab that shoulder and get back to Charlotte. Why are you still here?"

Straight and to the point. "I am going this week. The clavicle takes longer to heal than other bones. I still can't play. But yes, I'm heading down tomorrow—"

"Dad?" Kelcie walked out, closing the door behind her and wrapping her arms around herself against the cold. I just caught myself from reaching out to her. Given our audience, that would throw me in the deep end of the pool before I could swim. "Why don't you come in? It's freezing out here. I just made some dinner. Where is Maria?" Maria was Coach's wife of twenty-some years.

Kelcie's mom hadn't been part of her life since she was a baby. I learned from Kelcie that she'd expected Coach to be a big football star. However, that dream disappeared when he blew out his knee shortly before the draft and after Kelcie was born. Inevitably, her mom decided she could do better than being the wife of a high school football coach.

"Home. Unpacking." His eyes shifted, measuring the distance between the two of us as if daring me to touch her. He pointed back and forth at us. "What's going on here? Aaron said you're living together?"

"No, Dad. Shaw is living next door." She nodded toward my house.

He eyed her, remaining silent, as if waiting for our real explanation. Finally, he asked, "Then why is he answering your door at night?"

"He's having dinner. Jeez," she said, motioning to the door. "Which is probably burning. Can we please go inside?"

I shook my head. I was fine with her wanting to take some time telling Aaron, but I didn't want to lie to her dad. I stared up from my shoes and said, "Kelce…"

She caught my gaze, and one of those heavy moments passed between us—the kind that occurred between people who knew each other's thoughts and didn't need to put words to them. This meant something to me—to tell her dad. It was a step to making this real.

She drew in a breath then walked back over and stood between the two of us. Staring up at her father, she said, "Fine. Dad, Shaw and I are dating. We're…together."

And with those words, my smile couldn't be contained.

"Aaron doesn't know yet because we are still figuring things out, and I don't want to tell him yet. So, please don't make this a thing."

Coach opened his mouth to say something, and she stopped him. "I know you don't approve, but know this: Shaw has always been the closest person to me. You know that. It's always been us. We're older now, and we've held back our feelings for each other for too long."

The entire time she talked, he shook his head and began to pace. "Just because you are both lonely and living next to each other, that isn't a reason to do…this." He waved his hand between us. "He's heading back to Charlotte, for God's sake, and you have a son who just got acclimated to town."

"Dad, I know. That is why we are taking things slow, allowing some time to figure it out. We have things to work through. But you have to know that we've had feelings for each other for a long time.

It was like he didn't even hear us. He just turned around and stared into the yard. "You live in different worlds. He's a goddamn celebrity, and you—" He pointed at her. "You aren't meant to be anyone's arm candy. You're a professional woman with a special needs kid. That is where your priorities should be."

"I would appreciate it if you didn't lecture me about my priorities, Dad. I'm in my thirties, and I think I've figured them out pretty well on my own."

He gestured at me wildly. "He doesn't have a 9-5 job. He won't be home for dinner. He will be on the road. Trust will be an issue. That wears on a marriage—a relationship."

"Kelcie and I aren't you and her mom," I added. "In fact, her relationship with James wasn't like that, either…even if it was a disaster," I couldn't help saying.

"You think the reason I don't approve of you two together is because of her mom?"

"Isn't it?" I asked. "I mean, her mom married you and then took off when you discovered you couldn't go pro. She went in pursuit of greener pastures. But you are still here coaching football, never having the chance to reach for your own dreams."

"Shaw!" Kelcie's surprise at my bluntness gave me a moment of pause.

"Sorry. But we are grown-ass adults, and whatever issues he has with me being good enough for you—"

"I raised her to be her own person and not depend on riding anyone's coattails or, worse yet, being left behind. I wanted my daughter to carve her own path, her own future. I didn't want her chasing a man who was chasing his own dreams."

Kelcie whispered, "You thought I was so shallow that…" The pain on her face was striking. She stared at her father as if it was the first time she'd ever really seen him.

Her father laid out his reasoning, "James was from a good family. He was consistent and dependable, and he had a successful career ahead of him."

"Yet he made me miserable and ended up dumping me anyway."

Her father ran his hand over his face and turned away. "You didn't exactly come with a manual when you were born, Kelcie. I did what I thought was best."

He stepped toward Kelcie but then froze in place. "If nothing else, he was your son's father. It was his responsibility," he said, tilting his chin up.

Then he turned to me. "Shaw, I wanted you to chase your dream without hesitation or commitment."

He held out his arms to us both. "I just didn't want to see you hinder each other or resent each other." He looked at Kelcie. "I'm sorry if I pushed you into a loveless marriage. I'm sorry if I projected my own experiences onto you. I did what I thought—as your father—was the right thing for both of you."

Kelcie and I exchanged a look, and she slowly gripped my hand. I cleared my throat and sat forward. "I can appreciate your intentions, Coach—er—Holden. Um. Mr. Hammer."

"Coach is fine."

"Coach." I stared at the man who had been more than a teacher, but a coach, a mentor, a friend. He'd been the only adult who'd truly believed in me, but he'd also been the reason Kelcie and I could never see a future together.

"I've been in love with your daughter for most of my life. I've waited years to show her—and prove to you—that I am worthy of her." I brought her hand to my lips, kissed her fingers, and opened my heart…my soul…to her. Right there in front of her father.

I should've done it when we were alone. I should've saved those words for her ears when we were by ourselves. But I had to show her how serious I was about us. Unleashing years of unrequited feelings for her in front of her father… It was the only way I could think of to show her—to show *both* of them—how much she had always meant to me.

Because while I respected the hell out of the man and could never repay the confidence he had in me, I was never again going to let him interfere with my relationship with my Kelce.

But it was her reaction I needed. Not his. So, I repeated my words —those oh-so-important words—directly to her. "I'm in love with you, Kelcie. I think I have been since the day you outran me in suicide sprints at my first football practice." Tears filled her eyes as she bit her bottom lip. "I loved you when you helped me pass my high school literature class so I could graduate. And then there was chemistry…and well, trig too, come to think about it." She let out a tearful laugh, and that was fuel for me to continue. "I loved you all the times I knew I shouldn't. But how could I stop loving someone who is my best friend, my home, the person who inspires me most? You're the most beautiful human being I know."

She put her finger gently over my mouth as a tear escaped.

Still staring at me, she said, "Dad, I know your heart was in the right place…" She turned to me as I put my arm around her. "But I think we can take it from here."

Her father stroked his mustache and studied his feet. "I'm not a man who believes in fate, and Lord knows I'm not a romantic sort." He looked down at Kelcie and then up at me. "Fine. I'll admit you're different people than you were fourteen years ago…" He stepped back. "And I'm not saying I wouldn't do things differently, if I could. But I probably would've told you the same things back then."

Both Kelcie and I opened our mouths to protest. But her father stopped us with his upturned hands.

"However, if you love each other and think you can make this work, then who am I to criticize?" he asked. Kelcie leaned forward, breaking her hold with me to hug her father. "But be smart about this. You aren't the same people you were, and life has become a lot more complicated. It's okay to make sacrifices for each other, but don't lose your own way." He looked up at me. "That's all I ask."

I nodded once. Kelcie was re-establishing herself, her goals, and her priorities. The last thing she needed was my lifestyle, my career interfering with hers. "Message received, sir."

That wouldn't be a problem. I hoped...

32

Kelcie

After another round with James about his planned visit with Aaron this weekend, I was ready to scream. He spilled that he and Amber were eloping and then taking her kids on a mini-vacation, planning a better honeymoon in the summer. I asked why Aaron wasn't part of their plans—didn't he want Aaron at his wedding? His answer? "We are flying out Friday morning, and I don't think he could handle the plane. Besides, I'd have to get him his own room, and that wouldn't work."

I didn't ask why Aaron couldn't share with Amber's kids. James didn't want him there. There was no purpose in trying to understand why. Nevertheless, didn't he realize that Aaron's feelings would be hurt?

"I had plans this weekend, James."

"I'm getting married. I think that trumps any plans you could've had."

I closed my eyes and prayed for divine intervention to stop me from tearing into him. Nope. Not giving in to that. "Okay, well, I'll let you explain your reasoning to him." He wouldn't. I would tell Aaron in order to spare his feelings as much as I could. "I'll see you in another two weeks, then?"

"Yeah, sure," he said, noncommittal.

Luckily, Grace was so excited about me going away with Shaw for a "romantic weekend," she'd jumped at having Aaron.

I'd sat in first class, on my way to Charlotte for the most romantic weekend of my life…and all I could do was worry about Aaron. I wasn't the least bit surprised at James's selfish behavior—it had always fallen on me to "handle Aaron." It was James's favorite phrase whenever we went into a new public setting.

But I decided I had to let it go. Dealing with James would be another problem for another day.

I was going to enjoy the here and now. Flying first class to Charlotte was just a taste of what awaited me. Not wanting to draw any attention by picking me up at the airport, Shaw had sent a car to drive me to his "place in town."

Charlotte wasn't New York City, but I wasn't exactly a city girl either. Now here I was, staring up at the top of Shaw's building, and I had to take in a deep breath. This trip was about showing me who he was and what his life was like. This journey was about getting to know who we had both become.

I didn't know what to expect as I entered the elevator to access the penthouse floor and entered the code he gave me. My apprehension settled when the elevator doors opened to Shaw's stupid-adorable grin. Even as he stood there, with his boyish, shaggy hair, barefoot in navy sweatpants and a plain white t-shirt, I couldn't believe my luck. You couldn't take this man for anything but striking. "You made it," he whispered. Then he grabbed my hand and pulled me into his arms.

"It's not like you live in Timbuktu, and I had to scale a mountain to get here," I answered dryly, breathing in his cedar scent and dropping my bag to return the hug.

He cupped my face with enthusiasm and kissed me soundly, his grin dialing down just slightly. "Yeah…" He studied me as if I'd been gone for years instead of a few days. "I know."

I held onto his forearms. "You were afraid I was going to back out."

The smile dimmed a bit more, and he shrugged one shoulder.

"Shaw…"

"Let's get you inside," he said, wrapping his arm around me. "No need to give Davy a show."

"Davy?"

"Yeah, my teammate, Davy Johnson, lives in the other unit." He nodded behind us.

"You mean this entire floor is only two apartments?" I said, my gaze flicking back and forth down the marble-covered corridor that was tastefully decorated in neutral colors and soft lighting.

"Yeah." He picked up my luggage with his other hand. "Our friend Harper lived there"—he motioned to Davy's place—"before getting engaged. He told me about this unit going up for sale, and it worked out this way."

He opened the door and ushered me in. I didn't know what to expect—maybe dark wood bordering on man-cave—but Shaw's home was open and airy without feeling overwhelming. The two-story great room was framed by windows that overlooked the heart of the city. That was all the decoration any room would need. A large white, plush sectional, white area rug, and glass coffee table had my mom-heart wincing at the thought of trying to keep an area like this so pristine— but of course, he had a housekeeper for that.

The rest of the space was also beautifully decorated with glass, cool wood, and neutral tones, but the design still felt welcoming without being cold and stiff. A custom mural caught my attention amid all the white and neutrals. It was a landscape that ran down the main hall. And I recognized it immediately. There was a creek and—

I briskly walked over to it and whispered, "Wait…" The trees, grass, and the water bending around that large tree where a rope swing would usually be found. My words took a moment to form as my fingers drifted toward the wall, reaching out to it. "Is that Maeve's creek?"

His hands were in his pockets as he rocked back on his feet, but the pink in his cheeks was all the confirmation I needed. We'd spent most of our summers at that spot. The trees that surrounded the area had sheltered us from the sun most days and kept us dry enough in the wetter months. The rope swing hanging from an old oak along the bank gave it away.

Maeve had always been pretty cool about all of us kids hanging out at her property, figuring it was better to keep an eye on all of us that way. It was our clubhouse, without the house. It was our space where we'd made so many memories, dreamed about our futures, cried over heartbreaks, strengthened our bonds, and laughed so damn much.

I stared at the mural and then back at him, waiting for an explanation.

He nodded. "It centers me. I walk by it every morning as I'm leaving, and it reminds me where I'm from and who I am."

I walked down the hall, trailing my fingers and continuing to study the mural. "We used to sit down there by that creek—just the two of us —and not say a word."

"I know," he said. "I used to have photos of all of us I would put up, but as the years went by and we all grew further apart… Well, I just thought this would make me happier."

I reached over and squeezed his forearm. "It's beautiful."

"Would it be cheesy to say, 'So are you'?" He latched onto my hand and pulled me gently toward him. "I'm so happy you are here."

Overcome by his sentimental confession and unable to speak to it, I wrapped my arms around his neck, pulling on him while I raised onto my toes to meet his lips.

The kiss was long and languid, unlike the stolen ones we'd had on the back porch, because we didn't have to worry about interruptions.

His hands wrapped around my waist and trailed down my back, settling on my backside. He groaned. Then he stopped kissing me, rested his forehead on mine, and said, "I have my hand on your ass." His breathing was heavier, his voice deeper, and I loved it.

"You have both of them on my ass," I whispered in a tone that was more seductive than I'd ever dreamed of being.

His hands roamed up and down my ass, and his groan turned into a sexy moan of delight. "Do you know how long I've waited to put my hand here? Right here." He slapped my butt with a playful smack that made me giggle and jump. "You couldn't even begin to imagine."

His sweats weren't hiding anything, and I resisted the urge to check him out. Instead, I reached behind him, spread my fingers as wide as they would go, and squeezed as much of his deliciously solid gluteus maximus as I could grab. His eyes darkened and narrowed, but his mouth grew deliciously devilish as his teeth scraped across his bottom lip.

I wanted his teeth on me.

Whoa—we're into biting now?

With him. Yep.

With his hands fixed on my ass, he dragged me even closer. His sexy voice growled, "Kiss me."

He didn't have to tell me twice.

I released my grip and wrapped my arms around his neck again, reveling in the fact that I was here, and he was mine.

"Hold on," he warned before he moved his arms farther under my legs to—

I pushed at his shoulders in complete panic. "Don't!" I yelled. "Have you lost your mind?" I slapped his chest. "Don't you dare lift me with that shoulder the way it is. You shouldn't be lifting heavy objects."

But up I went. Most of my weight was distributed to the uninjured shoulder, but both hands cupped my thighs, and I straddled him high to distribute my weight and avoid strain on his shoulder. "First, you aren't a heavy object. You are the only thing in the world that matters to me right now." He turned to a door and opened it. "And I want to find out if you are as bossy in bed as you are out of it." He sat me down gently on the bed, pulling off my shoes, staring at me under lowered lashes.

I pretended to smack him again, but he dodged it.

"I need to hear you moan. I need to feel you writhe with pleasure. I want to speak dirty words and tell you all the things I want to do to you. I want to hear you tell me all the things you want me to do. I want to touch you with my hands, with my lips and tongue…with my cock. I want to hear you pant my name, and most of all, I want to see you straddling me when you come."

Images flashed through my mind of satisfying all of those desires. "Someone is quite specific."

"I just want..."

He pulled up my sweater, his eyes going to the new, expensive, lace pink bra I'd spent a fortune on to give "the girls" the illusion of firmness that had been lost with time and pregnancy.

He traced his hand over the top of each plump breast with such tenderness it sent a shiver down my spine. "I want it all."

It had been worth every penny.

I closed my eyes and begged for patience not to jump him.

His voice deepened. "I've had dreams—dirty, teasingly orgasmic dreams. Imagining how you'd look under me, over me...but not knowing your scent or the way you taste. Never knowing how you sounded."

I was done with descriptions. I yanked him closer to me and slipped my hand into his sweats.

"You know girls have dirty dreams too," I said. "Now shut up and make them real."

His eyes grew wide as he guided my hand to the bulge in his pants, showing me what he wanted, moving my hand up and then down. Because he was still standing over me, I was granted a gorgeous view as he let my wandering fingers explore him. Obviously wanting to prove himself useful, he drew his shirt up and off, giving me an eye-level view of his abs and the cock that was now peeking out from his pants.

"Yes..." I drawled. Damn, was this empowering. There was over two hundred pounds of muscular, elite athlete standing in front of me. A man whose job involved aggression and physical dominance. And I had him literally in my hand.

I licked my lips, staring up at him. "You okay?"

He shook his head, his lips thinned.

I tilted my head, continually stroking him slowly, up and down. "Shaw." I deepened my voice. "Get. On. This. Bed."

He yanked my hand out of his pants then gently pushed me down. I crawled back over the bed as he followed, crawling on all fours over my body—like a predator.

The slightest wince flashed over his face—his shoulder wasn't as healed as he wanted everyone to believe. As he hovered over me, he said, "Bossy…even now."

I ran my hands over his chest, marveling at the definition and hair he'd never had before. I reached up to kiss a nipple and felt my jeans loosen. While I'd been busy admiring his body, he'd undone my pants and was tugging them off. Only, the movement didn't happen without some wincing as it caused him to support his weight on his bad shoulder.

That wouldn't do. I knifed up, pushing him onto his back. "I don't think you will complain," I said. "At least I hope not."

I shimmied out of my jeans, my panties still in place, and slung a leg over his hip before I realized his pants were still on. Still, straddling him connected his hardness to my center, and before long, we were both making obscene noises that would definitely qualify as dirty if we had been capable of forming words.

His pelvis and mine moved in a rhythm that was a prequel of what was to come. He moved his mouth away from mine, pushing me up so he could trail kisses down my chest. He whispered, "Are we doing this?"

I took off my expensive bra and tossed it aside—it had done its job. "Yeah, we are doing this. I dare you try to pull me off you now," I said, grinning.

"Not a chance." His eyes were fixed on my breasts as he reached out, gently cupping one of them and stroking his thumb over it…before he took me in his mouth.

The sensation of his lips on my nipple was so intense I almost lost my mind. I threw back my head as I wrapped my arms around him, essentially burying his face in my breasts.

Both of his hands played with my breasts as he suckled, and I continued to gyrate over him until he slipped one hand down my belly, and a thumb went into my panties.

"Oh, Shaw…" I clamped my hand over the hand in my panties, and he pulled his face out from between my breasts to stare up at me. My breathing was so heavy, the sensations rushing through me so intense…I needed a moment to breathe. I wanted to be naked with him, I wanted him inside me, but fuck I never wanted his hand to move from that one spot.

My eyes struggled to stay open, and his pressure and rhythm increased. "Not yet…" I weakly protested.

"We got all night. I want to watch you."

He sucked the other nipple in his mouth, applying the smallest pressure with his glorious thumb, and that put me over. My hand clamped over his, and I cried out his name as he drew out the best orgasm I'd ever had. And technically, we still had our pants on.

33

____

Shaw

"Ride it out, honey," I said with the minimal breath left in my lungs. I had to remind my heart to beat because I was sure it had stopped. That moment would be tattooed on my brain forever. Shudders continued to run through her body, and my dick was out of patience and about to rebel.

She slumped over me as I pulled my hand from her panties, and our breathing synced. I caressed her back, memorizing every detail of that moment so it would always be with me.

"I think you've destroyed me."

I chuckled. "Not quite." The heat between me and her wetness was causing my dick to demand we pick things up. Kelcie slowly pushed up on me again, and holy shit...I needed her to stop riding me before I embarrassed myself.

She trailed a hand down my chest to my boxers. "My turn." The confident grin she shot me as she gripped my dick, the way she trailed herself down my abdomen, was mesmerizing.

I wouldn't survive getting past her lips. "Kelcie, I don't think I can..."

She trailed kisses all over my abdomen as her hands pulled down my pants, cutting off my ability to protest.

I gritted my teeth and failed to notice that she had also removed her panties.

We were both naked.

"Wait, Kelce. Let me get a condom."

"I went to the doctor. We're covered," she breathed. "Are you—?"

"Yes, I was tested last week as part of the physical," I said, and we simultaneously grinned. This was going to happen.

Leaning over me, she said, "Is this okay?"

I cupped her face but was unable to form coherent words, so I kissed her. Her hair was disheveled and barely retained any shape of a ponytail. I pulled the tie out of her hair, throwing it aside and letting her thick waves fall between us.

My God, she was the beauty that was meant for me. I tucked a few strands behind her ear.

"I just figured…with your shoulder…it would be better if I was on top," she said softly as she licked her bottom lip.

"Bossy, even in bed."

"That's not true—"

I put the thumb that had previously been in her panties to her lips, and she sucked it into her mouth.

She nipped my thumb, positioned herself over me, and all I could do was watch as she guided me inside her. And then she began to move —*we* began to move—captured in a hypnotic dance.

My breath hitched as I marveled at this unimaginable connection we'd never had before. A new level of us we'd never breached. It was the missing link.

She was mine.

She braced her hands on my chest for leverage, and her nails bit into my skin. My hands gripped her hips, afraid she'd disappear.

Did choirs of angels sing? Did the heavens part?

Hell, yeah, they could have—but we wouldn't have known.

In sync, we moaned each other's names, tethering us to the world as we found our release.

I rolled her over to her side, and she nuzzled into me, her head dipping under my chin and warming my chest. We held each other with as much skin touching as possible.

She turned to face me. "So, I guess you're happy to see me?"

"Woman, you laid me out. I'm barely conscious." I leaned up, catching her lips.

"Well, then, I guess it's safe to say we are definitely doing that again."

"Now that you're here, I may never let you go," I said, only half-kidding.

A shadow fell over her face, and her smile seemed a bit forced. She snuggled down into me as if she were burrowing to safety.

And why did I sense that was the wrong thing to say?

34

Kelcie

"Tell us everything," Aliya said, her face beaming over the screen she and Grace shared on my computer. It was Friday afternoon, and Shaw and I finally emerged from the bedroom. "Where's the stud muffin now? Do you have him tied to his bed or something?"

"He's at practice," I said. "They cleared him this week and are starting him this weekend. They want him back in time for the play-offs." While the team had managed to squeeze in a shot at the playoffs, they'd been plagued with injured players. For there to be any chance of the team advancing, they needed him back.

He explained it to me while we were curled up in bed this morning, and I expressed my misgivings about him returning. While he sat out for the suggested recovery time for a normal man, his demands on his body weren't normal. He was a well-paid athlete in a contact sport. Football players were expected to heal faster. But as a PT, I couldn't help but compare it to reassembling a stock car with duct tape and a prayer, sending it out on a racetrack and expecting it to not only hold together but perform at a high level as it was tossed around the track, long enough to capture the checkered flag.

In the early morning hours, he kissed the top of my head, whispering softly, "This is my job, hon."

I didn't have the heart to break our bubble of happy contentment by suggesting that maybe his thirty-something body was ready for a career change or ask how many more years of this he thought his body could take.

Grace voiced my concerns. "Isn't it too soon for him to be back?"

I shrugged. "He said it's just a few more games, and then he will have the off-season to fully heal." I stood and took the laptop with me into the kitchen. "From what I've heard, his contract is up at the end of this season, and his agent has concerns."

"Well, at least you're down there with him," Grace said.

"Yeah, you can kiss his boo-boos and rub him down afterward," Aliya said.

I rolled my eyes at her. "He has an entire training and medical staff here to do that. I'm here strictly as his…um—"

"Girlfriend," they said in unison.

I began to shake my head when Aliya added, "Uh-uh…you're Dawson Shawfield's girlfriend. You need to get that through your head. Because you're going to be around a bunch of people questioning who you are to him."

"I know."

"No, I don't think you do," Aliya said, sitting closer to her screen. "You need to own this. You're his. He is yours. This isn't our small town where he's just Shaw. In Charlotte, he's Dawson Shawfield—a football star. You need to be ready to pull out your bad bitch self."

"She gets it. Don't freak her out," Grace said quietly.

Aliya wasn't pulling any punches. "I'm serious. You need to find that confident, take-no-prisoners self you haven't used in a while and dust her off. There are a lot of women who would want to be in your place—women who dream of being the center of his focus, his desires." She wasn't letting up. "Many who think they should be on his arm, in his bed—"

I held out my hand, not wanting to think of the gorgeous women he'd probably had in his bed before. "I know, I know. I dealt with that all throughout college and even high school."

"Yeah, but these women make a profession out of it."

Grace stepped in. "Don't worry. It will be fine. Just be yourself, and don't let anyone get in your head or push you around. What are your plans tonight?"

"We're meeting his friend Davy and his girlfriend. She lives in Chicago but is in town for the weekend."

"See. Another long-distance relationship." Grace's face lit up with positivity, "Good. You can see how they handle it."

"Sounds like Shaw has the right idea," Aliya said. "So, now the good stuff. How's the sex?"

Grace shook her head. "I don't want the graphic details. This is Shaw."

"I don't need to know what his dick looks like. I'm just wondering if all the years of banked chemistry and anticipation were worth it," Aliya said.

I put my hand over my mouth in a ridiculous attempt to stop my smile.

Both my best friends' smiles widened. "Oh, yeah…" Grace said. "It was worth it."

Aliya erupted into a laugh as she fist-pumped the air. "Yes! I want at least some details!"

The door to the penthouse opened and closed. "Kelce?"

"Saved by the man of the hour." Grace winked.

"This conversation isn't over," Aliya said. "But I'm so happy you both finally jumped each other."

Shaw came into the kitchen and peered over my shoulder to our friends, "Hello, ladies. Am I interrupting girl talk?" He kissed my cheek as if it was a part of our daily activity, before grabbing a bottle of flavored water from the fridge.

Grace sighed, the goofiest grin on her face.

Aliya said, "Yeah, Kelcie was describing how big your dick was and how many times she orgasmed last night."

He stopped in his tracks, unfazed by Aliya's attempt to shock him.

He hit her right back. "She didn't tell you about this morning, too?" Not missing a beat, his brow furrowed. "I thought I did some of my best work in the shower. Remember that shower scene you were telling me about in Addison's book?" Then he walked out of the kitchen to the gasp of all of us.

Addison was another member of the group who was a best-selling romance novelist. She always sent Grace, Aliya, and I advanced copies of her latest release. My cheeks burned as both my friends' mouths dropped open. Aliya whispered, "The shower scene?"

Grace's voice hitched before she cleared her throat. "I think this is too much information for me." She pinched the bridge of her nose. "Great, Shaw, you ruined that book for me now."

His laugh from the other room was infectious, and I was floating on a cloud of pure bliss. Having never done drugs before, I had nothing to compare it to, but this time with him seemed perfect. The intimacy, the mind-blowing sex, the friendship, the laughter, being with our friends, and Aaron having another man to guide him in his life—I didn't think life could get much better.

Later that evening, Shaw held my hand, stroking it with his thumb, as we rode down the elevator to the restaurant on the floor below his penthouse. We were meeting a few of his friends for a quiet, private dinner. "It's easier than going out, plus the owner will give us a room to ourselves," Shaw explained, holding the door for me as I exited the elevator.

"Well, that's convenient," I said, taking in the skin that showed beneath the open neck of his shirt and the broadness of his sports jacket. He wasn't just gorgeous; he was breathtaking…and more than a little addictive. Even though I'd memorized his features over the years, our physical relationship just made everything that much…*more.* "Must be nice to just pop down here for dinner in a private room."

He shrugged, held the door for the restaurant, and ushered me in with a hand to the small of my back. "It's difficult sometimes for me to go out for dinner downtown without being recognized." He nodded at the maître d'. "And it's damn near impossible for a group of us to sneak into any establishment together, because someone is always identified. Then word gets out, and we are inundated with well-meaning fans."

We walked through the dimly lit restaurant, passing the open kitchen to one side and the scattering of tables to the other. An entire wall of ceiling-to-floor windows overlooked what appeared to be a large rooftop patio that spanned the entire restaurant and undoubtedly had an amazing view.

"Who exactly do you hang out with around here?"

He smirked as we walked to the doorway toward the back of the room. "What do you know about stock car racing?"

"Not much, I'm afraid."

He lowered his head to whisper in my ear, his breath warm against my neck, "Good. They'll love you." He winked and pushed the door open. Two couples sat at the rectangular table inside a room that was meant for a much larger group. Davy Johnson's build would always be the first to catch someone's eye. Shaw's teammate was kicked back, his leg crossed over his knee with his arm resting on the chair of a stylish, curvy woman with thick, jet-black hair cascading down her back, dressed in a form-fitting brick-red dress and heels I could only dream of remaining upright in if I'd been wearing them.

She sat forward, talking animatedly to a woman with a brilliant smile and gorgeous, tawny-colored, thick corkscrew curls. The man beside her absently played with her hair while listening to their conversation. His attention shifted when he spotted us walking in the room, and he nodded in our direction. "There he is. The wayward son found his way home."

His woman added, "We weren't sure if you were ever going to come back."

Both couples rose and walked over to greet us.

Shaw's hand reassuringly moved from the small of my back to my shoulder, where he possessively drew me into his front. "Well, I won't lie. The thought had crossed my mind." He squeezed my shoulders.

"Yeah, but all those zeros on your paycheck, not to mention the endorsement deals, are worth it, right?" Davy said with a smirk.

Millions. Shaw was worth millions. I worked on a body that was worth millions of dollars. He was worth more money than I'd probably see in my lifetime.

"She's worth it," he said, wrapping his arms around me and settling his chin on top of my head.

"Well, then, introduce us," the beauty with the black hair said, gesturing to me. "I want—no, I need—to hear this monumental love story."

I laughed. Finally finding my voice around these strangers, I said, "I'm Kelcie Byron." Then I held out my hand.

Davy took it first. I knew of Davy already—both from Shaw's stories and from following the team. I was surprised to find his hand was as large as Shaw's, but his grip was firm but gentle. "I'm Davy Johnson. I live across the building from this guy."

I nodded. "Yes, he told me yesterday. It's a pleasure to meet you. My son is a big fan of yours."

"Cool," he said, rubbing his hands together and lowering his voice. "More mine than Shaw's?"

I shook my head. "No one is cooler than Shaw."

Davy's grin widened. "Good answer."

The black-haired beauty jumped in. "Since Davy and Shaw are caught up in their bromance, I figure I should introduce myself. I'm Shyla Stern."

As if he'd been poked with a taser, Davy jumped in, "Oh, sorry. Yes, this is Shyla, my girlfriend."

She crossed her arms over her chest. "Yes. And somehow, you forgot about that? Hmm?" She shifted on her feet and pushed her hip out.

He put his arm around her waist, pulling her into his body. "Of course not. You're unforgettable." He kissed her cheek enthusiastically.

"Shaw said you're here for the weekend also?" I asked.

"Yes, I actually live in Chicago. I'm a resident at a hospital there."

"My girl is a miracle worker," Davy added. "She works in the emergency room, saving lives." His pride in her was almost as big as he was.

"I'm Mia St. James," the one with the pretty smile said, shaking my hand with both of hers. A flush spread across her face as she shifted her gaze between me and Shaw.

"Soon to be Quinlan," a man who could be on the cover of a magazine added over her shoulder.

She rolled her eyes. "Gus, Shaw already knows we're engaged."

"Yes, but I never miss an opportunity to tell people." He beamed. "And we just met Kelcie."

"Well, we aren't competing for the cutest couple contest. Besides, these two may win," Mia said, waving her hand toward us.

"Let's get them a drink as an award," Shyla said.

"You know the drill," Davy said as we all took seats around the table. "No alcohol for us—not this close to game day."

"Shaw can indulge," Gus said. "Can't you? Are you suiting up this week?"

"Well, that's still being tossed around the locker room," he said. "So, to be safe, I'm going to stick with water. But Kelcie would probably like a drink."

After the waiter left with our order, Shaw turned to Gus and Mia. "So, how is the rest of your gang doing? Congrats on having such a successful season." Then he turned to me, explaining, "Gus and Mia work for rival stock car teams."

"Right. Shaw was telling me about that. I think what you, CJ, and Harper have accomplished is amazing. I wasn't a racing fan, but I love watching the three of you take the industry by storm. I'm sure there is a lot more interest in the sport because of it." As an afterthought, I said to Gus, "Of course, I'm sure your team did well too."

He rolled his eyes. "No respect. I'm just another pretty face."

Mia ran her hand over his stubbled cheek. "Yes, but you are nice to look at from the backside as well."

I smiled at their banter.

"But enough about us. I've been waiting months to hear this story," Gus said.

"As if you're a romantic," Shaw said.

Gus gestured toward me. "This is Rock Woman. If it wasn't for her

—if Shaw hadn't still been hung up on her—he might never have taken pity on me, and we may have had a different outcome."

"Rock Woman?"

Shaw's hand went over his face.

Mia pivoted her body and glared at her fiancé. "You had to go there."

"What?" Gus said, possibly as clueless as I felt.

"What does he mean, Rock Woman?" I asked.

Shaw sighed and glared at Gus. "I never should've told you about that." Then he leaned to me and said, "Can I get a reprieve until later on explaining this?"

Shyla leaned forward and put a hand over mine. "Tell us about you, Kelcie. I love your name, by the way."

Shaw picked his head up. "She's an amazing physical therapist. I credit her for being able to suit up."

Mia turned to Shaw and said, "That's wonderful. But I'd like to hear more about Kelcie from Kelcie." She gave me an encouraging nod. "I understand you have a son?"

"Yes, his name is Aaron. He's in seventh grade, and no joke, he's probably Shaw's biggest fan," I said and nudged Shaw, who stared at me with that side smile I loved so much.

"And you two knew each other in high school?" Shyla said.

I nodded. "We met when we were Aaron's age, actually." I enjoyed telling our story—where we started and what we'd become. Shaw joined in with his funny tidbits, and we entertained them through appetizers and ordering dinner.

"So, how long are you going to be in town for, Kelcie?" Davy asked.

"Just until Sunday. I need to get back for work and to Aaron."

Gus shifted to Shaw. "What are you doing then?"

He studied the tablecloth. "We are still working out the logistics. I'm probably going to have to spend more time here until after the playoffs, but I'm hoping Aaron and Kelcie can come out. I know Aaron wants to get to some more games." He winked at me.

"The team definitely needs you back. With Payton out with that knee injury and the hit Jones took last week, making him questionable, the post-season is not going well for the offense. They need to be able to pull you up."

Shaw smoothed the imaginary creases from the cloth. "Yeah, that's what I'm being told." The table went quiet for a moment. "Like I said, we are still working out the logistics."

"But you're staying until after the game?" Shyla asked me.

"Yes, of course," I said. "I wouldn't miss watching him in action. I mean, after all that work I put in to get him there." I swallowed hard, trying to put on a brave face.

"Good." She tapped the table. "You can sit with me, then. Do you have a seat for her, Shaw?"

Shaw shifted in his seat. "Yeah." He cleared his throat. "The same one."

The same one Riley had with the other girlfriends and wives.

Shyla's eyes narrowed at him. "Good. I'll let the other women know."

She smiled and told me, "Some of the players rent a suite for their wives and girlfriends to use for the season." She pulled out her phone and handed it to me. "Give me your info, and we can coordinate."

As I entered my information in her phone, panic gripped me. I would be taking Riley's seat. I was going to be sitting in a seat formerly held by a model. A B-list actress, sure, but she was gorgeous and stylish and, even at games, perfectly put together. I was just…me.

I handed the phone back to Shyla, insecurities overwhelming me. Being married to James hadn't exactly been a boost to my ego. He hadn't been one to shower me with compliments, and over the years, I guess I'd had less reason to worry about how I appeared to others. But now…

Now, it wasn't just about Shaw and me. I was going to be sitting in his seat, walking beside him, being seen with him—a place held before by supermodels and accomplished beautiful women. I wasn't saying I was ugly, but I was the poster child for normal and forgettable.

And OMG, what would I wear? Did these women dress up for games? I was always decked out in Shaw's jersey and jeans. Was that okay? Shaw was talking to the rest of the table about Aaron and his time on the podcast with TJ. Shyla leaned over and whispered, "Hey, are you okay? You've gone pale."

I fidgeted with my napkin in my lap. "I feel like I'm out of my depth." It popped out of my mouth before I could even stop it.

"How so?" Shyla said, a hand on the table close to me. "Why would you say that?"

I shook my head. "I'm not Riley, and I couldn't even begin to imagine how to dress like that. I mean, this…" I ran my hand up and down, indicating my plain blue sheath dress and low heels. "This is the extent of me dressing up. I rarely take my hair out of a ponytail simply because I hate having it in my face."

"My girl over here"—she motioned to Mia—"is a reformed tomboy. If I can get her in make-up, I'm sure we can find you some confidence with clothes. Don't worry, girl. We got you. It's just a game. I'll be dressing for warmth anyway. I'll call you tomorrow, and we can discuss it." She patted my hand. "Listen…I've only known Shaw for maybe two years, but we all know he's been holding out for someone—or something. Sweetheart, it was you. You could wear a burlap sack while all the other girls wear lingerie, and that man would still fall at your feet."

"You just met me. How could you know that?"

"Because I know men. Anyone can see how he feels about you every time he looks at you. It's in his eyes. And he hasn't stopped touching you since you walked into the room. Honey, sometimes he forgot Riley was even with him."

I cocked my head at her and gave a weak laugh. I knew she was exaggerating, but I loved that she was trying to reassure me. Shaw's friends were good people—I loved that for him.

His hand slid over my knee—not sexually, just proprietary—and I rested my hand over his. It was the most natural movement. The gas firepit came to life outside on the patio, and I thought how different this life was from the one we had at home. First-class flight, pent-houses, a private dining room on top of one of the tallest buildings in Charlotte, eating an expensive dinner with two professional football players, two of the best-known names in stock car racing, a glamorous emergency room doctor…and me.

How small my life must have seemed to him. I squeezed his hand to reassure myself that this part of our story was real as he continued talking about the draft class coming up. He was practically a household name. I was a divorced physical therapist raising a son alone, driving a sensible car, and living in a duplex—one my friend had given me a discounted rate for.

I didn't voice my concerns to Shaw when we rode back upstairs to his apartment. Instead, I attacked him in a frenzy, trying to drown out the negative voice in my head that listed why this relationship didn't make sense.

We laughed and loved and licked and languished, and I fell asleep in his arms. But my fears and concerns only spread like a virus the rest of the weekend. No matter what I did, no matter how perfect everything was, the shadow of inevitable destruction was never far behind.

35

Kelcie

It was the day before game day, and Shaw got the call earlier that they were going to start him. As if they flipped a switch, his demeanor changed. Yes, he'd been back on the practice squad for a little over a week, but still, it seemed fast. His back straightened, and his face became locked in concentration. He was still affectionate and sweet, but he was focused, and his mind was on the game ahead.

Shaw geared up to head to the hotel for the night, a ritual the players all had to adhere to before a game. A pit formed in my stomach. I had never been the nervous type. Hell, I was an athlete myself and had been raised by a man who'd instilled toughness and perseverance in me. There hadn't been any whining in my house. 'Shake it off' had been the household mantra long before Taylor Swift became a household name. And now, as an adult, my job was to help people regain strength, recover, and bounce back after injury.

So why did the idea of seeing him on that field cause such a knot in the pit of my stomach? I'd watched him get hit millions of times and rarely even winced. I'd seen him break his arm, twist an ankle—hell, I was there when he decimated his collarbone and saw what he went through to recover. I'd never been squeamish before. But that was the problem. I knew too much. I knew the impact the game would have on his spine. I was familiar with his medical record—the concussions, the injuries—and I knew the toll it was taking on his body.

I didn't want to see him get hurt, and my fear was outweighing my excitement over seeing him play. Was it because of what was between us?

"Hey, hon, I need to get moving. I have to meet with the trainer and a few others before our team meeting," he said. He came into the room wearing only a towel while water dripped down his muscular back. I sat on his bed cross-legged and watched the muscles in his rear flex as he walked into the closet, coming out with a few hangers and throwing them on his bed. "Don't give me that look." He went back into his closet and grabbed a duffel bag.

"What look?" I said, straightening and biting my bottom lip. I knew 'what look.'

"The one that will make me very late to the stadium and in need of another shower," he said, bending over and kissing me. I tried to grab onto him, but he pulled away, and I was only able to trace my hand down between his pecs. "You'll be the death of me, I swear."

He went to his dresser, discarded his towel, and grabbed a pair of boxer briefs, covering the evidence that I was very close to getting my way.

"Now, you're not being fair," I said, giving him my best pout and lying across his bed, my head propped up in my hand.

He side-eyed me and did a double-take, rolling his eyes heavenward. "You're more tempting than the devil himself." He drew on his briefs but not without needing a bit of tucking and maneuvering to get everything inside them. He pointed to his groin. "How am I supposed to get dressed like this?"

I shrugged. "You're the one in the hurry." I bit my lip again, looking up at him. "I could help you out with that." I pushed up to my hands and knees.

He took a step back. "No. No. Get back, temptress. I need all my energy. That's why they make the team stay in hotel rooms the night before a game."

"It's stupid. You're here. You live literally a few blocks from the stadium. Hell, we can see it from your patio."

"I know, but it's their rules, and given the paycheck they give me, they're allowed to make them," he said, putting on his pants—as if to put another barrier between us. "I promise to make it up to you."

I leaned back against the headboard, arms and legs crossed. "That's fine." I sighed. "I could use a little relaxation. In fact, I have a few hours before I have to meet Shyla. You have that fantastic, powerful handheld showerhead. I'm sure I could..." I stared up at him from under my lashes and lowered my voice, "Entertain myself."

Dead stop. He was halfway into putting on his shirt and stood still, halfway turned away from me. "You wouldn't."

A dare? Did he not know me at all?

"Darling, I have years of entertaining myself to draw from. I'm well-versed. Don't you worry about me."

"It's my job to...entertain...you. If that showerhead is going to be used to bring you pleasure, it will be in my hand. Use it without me and see what happens."

I shrugged. "Okay. There are other ways I can relax, other places..."

"This unit has security cameras throughout so I can check on the place when I'm out of town. You'd be surprised what fans will try to do."

"Well, now you just made it more interesting."

He pulled me up into his arms so quickly I gasped and let out a squeal when I felt his hardness between us, evidence that the idea was more than a little interesting to him.

He kissed me sweetly. "Wait for me?" he asked with the hint of a plea in his tone.

I traced his jaw. "Always."

Those important three words were screaming out from inside me, but I refused to let them out. Even though he'd declared he loved me—

in front of my father—neither of us had uttered those words to each other—at least not directly.

He kissed my forehead then went into his closet and grabbed his toiletry bag before disappearing into his bathroom. He poked out around the corner. "I'm sorry. I wish I could stay with you—believe me."

"I know," I said.

"Maybe you and Shyla could do something."

"I don't want to burden her. Besides, I think I'll just take it easy. I don't get many nights to myself," I said.

"Okay. I just hate leaving—"

"I'm a big girl, Shaw," I said.

He moseyed over to me, his eyes soft. "I know. I just wanted to take advantage of every minute here with you, and I feel like I'm abandoning you."

"Shyla told me she was going to give me the lowdown on what it was like to be a WAG. I'll be fine."

"Did you have fun meeting everyone at dinner?" Shaw was folding some clothes into his bag and making room for his toiletry kit.

"I did. You have some great friends here." Then, I remembered something Gus had said. "Hey, why does Gus call me Rock Woman?"

Shaw paused his packing and glanced up at me. A blush spread up his neck and to his cheeks.

"Shaw?"

With a hand on his hip and the other one wiping at his brow, he let out an uncomfortable laugh.

"What?" I said, knowing I stumbled on something. "He was saying you were responsible for him being with Mia and something about a rock."

Shaw slowly moved and sat down beside me. His hand on my knee was a warm assurance.

He let out a big sigh, "Mia and I moved into town around the same time. Gus and his friends are a tight group who all grew up together—like we did—so while we were thankful they befriended us, we were still outsiders. He rubbed my thigh distractingly. "We decided to start hanging out."

"You dated Mia?" My eyes were frozen open in shock. "*You* dated Mia? For how long? Did you sleep with her?" Green and red alternated as colors that blinded me. Why did I have to ask that question? I didn't want to know that answer. Mia was gorgeous, a natural beauty and nothing like Riley—or me, for that matter.

He let out a breath through his nose. "Yes, we dated. No, we didn't sleep together. I think we were both lonely, and honestly, she was hung up on Gus, and he had his head up his ass."

I just stared at him. Was I always going to compare myself to the women he'd been with? God, I hated feeling so damn insecure.

His hand squeezed my knee. "Anyway, watching those two dance around each other reminded me of you and me in a way. Well, him with his head up his ass reminded me of me—being an idiot and not having the balls to lay it all out for you. So…" He let out a pathetic, self-deprecating chuckle as he stood and went to his highboy dresser, opening the top drawer and reaching inside. "I told Gus to stop being a coward and to go after her. To tell her how he feels before he was left with regrets—like me." He reached for something inside and came back to the bed. "I told him my 'Mia' was married to another man because I hadn't had the balls to tell her she was meant to be with me." He sat next to me, our thighs touching. "Hold out your hand," he said softly.

I did.

"I said, 'Instead of holding her heart in my hands, I was left with this rock,'" he said, handing me a plain, smooth, gray granite rock.

I was immediately transported back in time. I stood quickly with the rock in my hand, studying it as if it were an artifact, long believed lost and forgotten.

"It's the pet rock I made for you," I said. I looked up at him as he sat on the edge of the bed, elbows to his knees, hands clasped together. It was from the creek on Maeve's property, where we all used to hang out. I knew he'd been nervous about leaving for college—about all the expectations set on him—and I'd wanted something he could hold onto, something from home, but not sappy.

I think I drew googly eyes on it at one point and maybe wrote a few inspirational words on the other side. I turned it over. All the writing was long gone. I'd given it to him before we left for college. A little token from home—from me.

"You gave me that rock as a joke, but I held onto it as a talisman, a reminder." He sat up straight. "It was granite, hard and tough, just like you. It was enduring, just like our friendship. And I held it when I needed a way to center myself, just like you used to do for me."

He gestured at it. "I carried it with me in my pocket. I got a few strange looks from people in the TSA line at airports, but I just explained it was my lucky charm. No one ever knew the story behind it. That's why Gus called you my Rock Woman. He knew you were the one I thought about—the one that got away.

I gripped the rock in my hand, tested its weight, and thought of this man. The rock represented the proof that I'd been in his heart for years. Years he'd wished I'd been there to hold his hand.

A tear ran down my cheek as I stared into a face that had handsomely aged with time. Through the sun-worn skin, small laugh lines, and thicker scruff of beard, I still saw the softened lines of youth that had been there the day I'd given him that rock. I loved him then, and I loved him now.

Holding the rock, I bent over and kissed him, the three words banging incessantly in my head and my heart. I deepened the kiss, throwing my arms around his neck to keep my mouth from uttering them.

His hands roamed up and down my back, then he turned as if to throw me on the bed.

Then his phone rang.

"Goddamn it," he said. "That's probably Davy. We are going over together."

He pushed himself up off me, and the entire time, his eyes blazed with lust. We both lowered our gaze to his groin and made unsatisfied noises.

I stood and helped him zip up his bag while he grabbed his jacket and shoes. "Damn, you look good," I said.

The smile he shot me while walking out the door was arrogant and sinful. "Hey, I left some gear for tomorrow, in case you forgot to pack anything." He snuck in one last kiss. "I'll call you tonight. And Kelce—"

"Yes?"

"I won't be very happy if I find out about any 'self-entertaining.'"

I rolled my eyes. "Fine."

36

Kelcie

It was game time and my first time attending as a girlfriend. I won't lie; I felt a little like the high school girl dating the football superstar. Except, the stadium sat 70,000 people, and it was a major network.

"I gotcha, girl," Shyla had said when I called her after Shaw left that night. I needed to talk to someone. I was beyond nervous about meeting the other wives and girlfriends. "They aren't that bad. Just stick with me. Besides, it's a freaking suite."

And that felt like being forced to sit at the cool girl's table. No pressure.

"Um, what do I even wear?" I asked her.

"Carolina gear, but cute," she said.

"I have no idea what that means."

"That means wear a Carolina sweatshirt or jersey but not one your grandfather would wear. What do you have with you?"

"A jersey Shaw gave me a few months ago," I said.

"Is it a woman's cut, or does it go over shoulder pads?" she asked.

"Um, I have no idea. It's big enough to wear over my jacket," I said.

There was a pause. "You know what…are you at Shaw's?"

"Yeah."

"I'll be right over. I'm at Davy's, and I keep most of my Carolina gear there. I have some things we can use to put an outfit together for you."

"But I just wanted to know if I needed to do my hair and wear make-up."

Another pause. "Oh, boy," she sighed. "Yes, hon. You need to be "sport-glam"—cute, sporty, with a touch of glamorous that sets you apart. You are the girlfriend of one of the best-looking tight ends in the country. If you're going to be on his arm, sitting in his seat, you need to look the part. I'll grab a few things and be over." And then, as if to herself, she said, "Now, where did I put that Bedazzler…" before she hung up.

Bedazzler? What the hell had I gotten myself into?

True to her word, Shyla decked me out in a cute Carolina outfit, insisted I wear my hair down, curling it in effortless waves, and applied makeup in a way that I could only dream of reproducing. She deconstructed the blue jersey Shaw had given me and reformed it to be more slim fitting, cutting a low neckline into it. I wore it over a long-sleeved, slimming body suit. She paired it with jet-black skinny jeans because she said my ass looked amazing in them, making sure Shaw's jersey was cut off short enough to showcase it. She kindly suppressed an amused smile when I put away my gym shoes and grabbed the heeled boots Aliya insisted I bring. She had me go to his closet and find a Carolina jacket because the whole team had merch like that. I pulled out one that was twice my size but had his number on the sleeve and his name across the back. With a few more touches on the hair, it was fluffed and sprayed. I stared at myself in the mirror.

I looked good. Damn good. But would Shaw even recognize me under this? Hell, he rarely saw me with my hair down, let alone all wavy and cascading down my back. Was this who he wanted me to be? The glam girlfriend?

With lipstick and other necessities tucked in a cute purse she gave me to use, Shyla surveyed me, smiled, and said, "Perfect."

"I feel like I'm being branded."

Her smile grew as she grabbed both my hands and twirled me around, then with a playful wink said, "Darling, that's because you are."

Later, on the way over in her car, Shyla explained, "It's a bit of a club, and there is a hierarchy that will become apparent as you watch. Most of the women are nice and inviting, if not a little shallow. But there is a huge difference between being a wife and being a girlfriend. The wives have commitments and are more involved with the organization than the girlfriends."

"Why is that?"

"Because the girlfriend isn't committed to sticking around."

"What about you?"

Shyla sighed, and her shoulders dropped. "Well, this is where Davy and I are at a crossroads," she said. "I'm on vacation right now, which is why I'm down here staying with him. We try to alternate and find time to see each other when we can. But in-season is very hard for both of us. I'm an emergency room doctor at a metropolitan hospital in Chicago. It's not like I have a lot of free time to jet around to his games, nor is it easy for me to get the time off just to come down here."

She glanced over at me as we turned into the parking lot. I nodded in understanding. "To be honest, we are at the point in our relationship where the distance is becoming a problem," she continued. She followed the attendants, motioning for us on where to go to park. "He wants me to move down here. But honestly, I like living in Chicago. And besides, he doesn't know how much longer he has in the league. What if I uproot myself from Chicago and move down here to start over in a local ER, and then he gets traded or decides to retire?" She shook her head. "Anyway, it's an impasse."

It brought up the nagging reminder of my situation with Shaw and the way it lingered like an unanswered question. What would happen after this weekend?

Even when we were in heaven, snuggled in his suite, I missed my boy and was looking forward to going home to more familiar ground.

Charlotte was the road I could've traveled if things had worked out differently. But my reality was Aaron and the life I was rebuilding back home. However, part of that rebuilding had become Shaw living next door. He'd become an integral part of our lives—a cornerstone.

But the status quo wasn't possible any longer. He was needed here. I was needed there.

When we pulled into a parking spot, she said, "Enough talk. Let's go have a good time, drink some beers, and cheer on our boys!"

I walked into the WAGS suite and was suddenly surrounded by a wide range of beautiful women who were hugging and gossiping like old school friends. I tried hard not to cling to Shyla.

Although there was a wide range of beautiful women, they all had one thing in common. Whether it was their eyes, their hair, their shape, their smile, their intelligence, or their confidence, something about each of these women called to a man whose job required a lot of grit, perseverance, and talent.

Shyla introduced me around to a few women, even though I had little hope of remembering everyone. Darius Stoker's wife, Tasha, was the unofficial welcome committee. Darius was the quarterback of the team. He and Shaw had a good connection, both on and off the field.

"So, Darius hasn't told me much about you, except that you are an old girlfriend from high school Shaw reconnected with while he was recovering," she said. I couldn't glean her sincerity and glanced at Shyla. "Let's get a drink, and you can tell me the full story. Come on, Shyla, I'm sure you have some dirt on this already. I love a second-chance romance."

She walked over to the bar, which was stocked with a variety of drinks, including beer and vodka seltzers. I grabbed a soda while the other women went for the vodka seltzers. "Come on, have a drink,"

Tasha said. "We can get you a ride back to Shaw's, I'm sure." She quirked an eyebrow. "You are staying at Shaw's, right?"

"Yes, but I have to be up early for a flight tomorrow, so I'm going to take it slow. Maybe later in the game, I'll have one." Besides, I needed to keep my wits about me.

"No worries," she said, ushering us to seats by the full wall of windows that looked down over the field. The team had just come out to do warm-ups. "Some of the women have gone down to wish their boys luck, so it will get more crowded in here in a bit," she said, popping open the can. "Darius doesn't like the distraction." She rolled her eyes. "I'm surprised Shaw didn't have you come down for a good luck kiss."

"He said something about it, but I told him I was afraid I'd get lost," I joked. "Besides, I want his head in the game. It's his first time back since getting hurt."

"Yes, I heard you were his physical therapist. Is that how things happened with you two?"

"Oh, no," I said, not wanting her to think I was unprofessional. "It didn't happen like that at all. I—"

Tasha giggled and took a deep draw of her drink. Shyla rolled her eyes. "She's pushing your buttons. Stop it, Tash."

"What?" Tasha's eyes got wide with mock innocence. "One day, Riley is here. Shaw is injured, and she disappears in the wind. Then he comes back here with a physical therapist as a girlfriend. Rolling rocks gather no moss, I guess."

Wow. That was about as bitchy as any woman had ever been toward me.

"Tash, what is wrong with you?" Shyla stood and pulled me with her. "Let's get some food, Kelce."

"I was a news reporter. Did you know that, Shy?" Tash said over her shoulder. "When I met Darius, I was working for the local channel around Miami." She turned in her seat to follow me as I walked away. I stopped to listen to her. She took a healthy sip from her can. "I had a chance to be an anchor, possibly in New York or DC."

She took another sip of her drink. "But then I fell in love with

Darius and came down here. I thought I'd get a job locally. I mean, it's Charlotte, not LA or something." She ran her hand through her beautiful, thick black hair. "But here's the thing. When you marry the player, you marry the organization. The team comes first, especially in season. There are charity events, and social events, and networking..." She counted off on her fingers. "Pop out the babies, sit on charity boards, plan events, and smile on his arm. That's what I've become."

Shyla and I side-eyed each other. Clearly, this wasn't Tasha's first drink.

Shyla sat down next to Tasha. "Tash, hon. This isn't like you. Are you doing okay?"

The door to the suite opened, and the other women rolled in with smiles and good energy, which was just want the room needed. Tasha pasted on her best cheerleader face, and I tried to forget everything she and Shyla had shared with me.

Everyone was entitled to a bad day. Relationships were tough. There would be bumps Shaw and I would have to figure out. Except, from where I was sitting, those bumps seemed more like mountains.

I turned away from the chatter behind me, sat at one of the outside seats, and stared down at my man—my Shaw—the man I'd been in love with since the moment he stumbled onto my father's football field.

The players ran off the field and back into the locker room to prepare for the game.

Tasha and Shyla had inadvertently stirred up those nagging questions that I'd been trying not to think about in the euphoric swirl of our new relationship.

How would we ever see each other? How could I balance my career and Aaron's custody schedule with James? I'd just gotten out of a marriage where I'd lost my direction and myself. Was I ready to commit so much energy to Shaw's career? How would such a schedule affect Aaron? Would we have to move? When was Shaw going to retire? If he was thinking of getting out next year, that would be one thing...but he didn't seem inclined to stop playing anytime soon.

"Hey..." Shyla came over with a fresh drink and sat by me.

"What's going on? You're not letting what Tash said get to you, are you?"

I thanked her for the drink and took a sip, slapping on my game face. "No. Just taking it all in."

"Good. Don't let them chase you off," she said.

A few more women sat down, introduced themselves, and drew me into the group, asking about my history with Shaw and then oohing and ahhing about our friends-to-lovers romance. They were welcoming and helped me forget my interaction with Tasha, at least for the rest of the game.

We cheered on the team as they were introduced onto the field. The crowd grew louder when Shaw's name was introduced—a wonderful welcome back that surprised me at the intensity. I knew he was popular, but not living in Charlotte—and not having walked in the spotlight with him—I guess I'd never realized the level of it.

They had one of their better games since Shaw had left—winning 24-10, with Shaw having some amazing plays, including one touchdown near our suite.

He did his patented Shaw Shuffle—a basic two-step shuffle and butt shimmy—that didn't seem to fit his hulking figure. But then, that was what made it comical and endearing. The crowd, already on their feet, roared with elation. He pivoted, grinned, and winked. Then, with the football gripped in his hand, he pointed up to our suite. The roar of the crowd increased as his gesture was caught on the Jumbotron along with the direction he was aiming.

"Oh my God!" Shyla said. "Look!"

Sure enough. There, up on a Jumbotron, in front of seventy-thousand people—and millions televised—was me, my mouth agape, gasping like a fish out of water as I stared at myself on a screen as big as a building.

Oh. My. God.

So, what did I do?

Did I wave and make a cute, coquettish grin at my superstar boyfriend in front of millions of at-home television viewers?

No, I screamed as if shot, with a level of drama Riley could've only dreamed of, and dropped to the floor on my hands and knees.

That was me. All class.

And that was my first strike as a professional football player's girlfriend.

Never let it be said that I did anything half-assed.

37

Kelcie

"It wasn't that bad." Shyla patted my back as we walked down the corridor to the locker room.

My head down, a hat pulled down low over my face, I had to watch her steps to know where we were going. I bit off another piece of pretzel to avoid answering Shyla's reassurance with four-letter words.

We waited outside the team's locker room for the guys to come out. Davy came out first, kissed Shyla, and accepted congratulations from those around him for having a good game. "Shaw's on his way," he said. "He got held up by some reporters. He'll be out soon. Do you want us to wait with you?"

"No. I'll be fine." I shrunk further into the wall. "I'll just wait here for him."

Shyla turned to me and said with a slight grimace, "I hope you had fun tonight."

"I did, and I can't thank you enough for holding my hand through it." I ran my hand over my face and forced a self-deprecating smile. "And literally picking me up off the floor." I shook my head.

She laughed. "Girl, no problem. Give me a call when you get back home. We can compare schedules and see when we will both be back. We can try this again, with regular seats and without the spotlight. Or maybe we could just get together again, with or without these monsters." She patted Davy affectionately on the chest.

I leaned over and hugged her. "Sounds great." I waved them off, tossed the remainder of my pretzel away, and checked my texts.

And my hopes of no one seeing my exit were dashed.

I give that dive a 9 out of 10. I couldn't see the landing. That was from Wyatt.

Is that what they call 'falling for a man'? From Aliya.

Are you okay? From Grace.

Mom, why did you do that? From Aaron.

What the hell, Kelcie? Did you have to make such a spectacle of yourself?" From James. And as an afterthought…*Is Aaron in Charlotte with you? I didn't agree to that. What the hell is going on?*

Great.

I only texted Aaron back. *I'm fine. No need to worry. I was surprised, that's all.*

I gripped my phone as a lifeline, stood against the wall, stared down at myself, and surveyed the area. The friends and families of players were waiting for them to come out, and I begged the fates not to let anyone recognize me.

I didn't think I'd ever felt like such an imposter.

Why was I there?

The sandy-blond threads in his hair caught my attention, a beacon of light as he came closer to me. The smile on his face was just as bright. He dropped his bag and picked me up in the air, catching the attention of everyone around us.

"Kelcie," he growled into my hair before gently putting me down on my feet, immediately cupping my face and kissing me as if I was going to disappear. Flashes went off around us, and I vaguely sensed people watching. But when Shaw kissed me, especially with the voracity and passion he was showing now, everything else faded. My concerns, my fears, my limitations. He was happy. I wanted to let go and be that happy too.

Why did that seem so terrifying?

38

Shaw

I had everything I'd ever wanted in front of me…and it terrified me.

I had to get out of that locker room as quickly as possible. I had to know—to reassure myself that she was there. That she was waiting for me. That she hadn't left.

I smiled for the cameras, gave brief, vague statements about my recovery—yes, I was happy to back, to see what the future holds, one game at a time—and then politely skirted past people as if they were linemen.

We could do this. I knew we could. Her, me, and Aaron.

It wasn't until I had her in my arms that the niggling of doubt disappeared, and I breathed in her scent, felt her warmth, and was able to believe in this happiness that was descending on us. I kissed her because I couldn't not kiss her. It was as necessary as breathing at that moment. I needed the connection to dispel all my doubts.

I didn't care how many sites this kiss ended up on. I didn't care how many rumors or PR issues it would bring up. I needed to kiss my girl.

So, I did. It was a great kiss. Possibly in the top five of all our kisses. Possibly slightly indecent. I stopped my hands from roaming over her ass, but just barely. My hand loved resting there—sue me.

Coming out of our lust-induced fog, I said, "Let's go home."

We barely made it in the house before I was tearing her clothes off her. Call it the potent mix of an adrenaline rush from the game, or the blissful high of her being there...I don't know. But I never needed anything more than to be a part of her.

Jacket gone. Shirt gone. I gently pushed her on the ottoman in my living room, and she giggled at my domineering move as I undressed her down to her lace bra and panties that were sheer enough to leave nothing to the imagination.

"Fuck," I mumbled as I surveyed her, my hands stroking the inside of her thighs as I knelt in front of her. My hands traveled up higher until my thumbs met at her apex, tracing it lightly. I roamed up her body until our eyes met, and the lust in her eyes was a jolt of an aphrodisiac I didn't need.

"Shaw," she moaned as she sat up on her elbows.

I moved my thumbs lightly, teasing her through the silk panties as I kissed up her thighs, never breaking eye contact until my mouth replaced my thumbs and softly kissed her panties, changing the timbre of her moans. Encouraged, I grinned and replaced my thumbs with my mouth.

"Take them off," she pleaded.

But I continued my ministrations, my hand claiming her breast and teasing her nipple through the bra, as her hand dove into my hair, gripping it tightly, sending a jolt straight to my already on-edge dick.

She arched her back and breathed out, "More." Her free hand went to her panties, yanking on them, attempting to pull them down.

I rubbed her center with my hand and said, "Allow me."

I pulled off her panties, spread her legs, and didn't hesitate, going straight to her center as a personal challenge to find out how high I could take her.

Her screams were so satisfying that I came embarrassingly close to joining her. She laid back on the ottoman, her legs still spread in front of me, panting nearly as hard as I was for a few moments before sitting up, grabbing my face, and kissing me deeply, tasting herself on my lips and tongue.

Pulling back, she looked at me, vulnerability and something else I'd never seen before etched on her face. Those three words I'd already given her…were they hiding behind that expression?

I wasn't going to ask. But damn, I wanted to hear them.

I caressed her face, her mussed hair, tucking a strand behind her ear. I liked it down. Sure, the ponytail was usually her moniker, but her hair was beautiful down, cascading over her chest.

"You're so damn gorgeous…" My voice hitched, and I cleared it as I skimmed my hands over her body. I threaded my hands through her hair and confessed my truth, "God, I love you."

Her bottom lip trembled slightly before she grabbed my shoulders and pulled me close to kiss her again. "Take off your clothes."

No argument here. Clothes gone. I couldn't wait to get to a room. She slowly turned over, bent over the ottoman, her hair cascading down her back, and bit her lip as she stared at me over one shoulder. She couldn't wait either.

I ran my hand over her ass and up her back, between her shoulder blades, moving her hair to the side so I could kiss up her neck. I breathed into her ear and felt her shudder. "You want me like this, baby?"

"Yes, so much."

I reached my hand around to cup her breast, pinching the nipple and causing her back to arch. She reached her arm back, pulling me into her neck more.

"Don't tease me. Do it."

We both pushed into each other, not wanting any hesitation. As I gave her a moment to adjust to me, I ran my hand up and down her abdomen from her breasts to her mound teasingly.

Her breathing was ragged and heavy. "Move," she demanded. I loved it.

I pushed her down on the ottoman, spread her feet…and I moved. The rest was a lust-filled blur. Thank God for the soundproof walls they installed because of the nightclub downstairs. We were both vocally describing our pleasure—boldly.

I ran my finger down between her legs, and she tightened around me. Her soundless moment of ecstasy had her insides gripping me, and her arm snaked back around the back of my neck, both things tipping me over the edge.

Through the fog of bliss, I wrestled my way back to reality.

I scooped her up and carried her languid body into my room—our room.

She was mine. She'd always been mine. And she would always be mine. And God help the person who ever got in the way of that.

The next morning, we enjoyed another memorable shower experience. I didn't know how I would ever be able to use that shower without her. I laid on the bed, drifting off and pulling her back in my arms, when her phone rang.

Her head popped up. "That's Grace. I can tell by the ringtone. I need to get that." She sat up and grabbed her phone, smiling down at me. "Hey, Grace."

Her smile disappeared, and she jumped out of bed. "What do you mean he's there?"

Silence. I covered my eyes with my hand. Needle Dick. It had to be.

"No. No. I didn't agree to that." Kelcie's voice rose, and she began to pace. "He said he was getting married and didn't want—I mean, couldn't take Aaron." Kelcie halted. "What? He said what to you?"

I begrudgingly pulled on some pants. Our bubble had burst, and that toxic weasel was ruining it.

"He said that?" Kelcie's face was red. "Are they still there? I want to talk to him. NOW!"

I reached out my hand to give her strength and reassure her she wasn't alone. She pushed it away and walked out the bedroom door.

"James. No. No. You can't—"

Even from six feet away, his voice came through the phone, chastising her.

"Yes, I was—I am visiting Shaw in Charlotte."

I hated just sitting here listening to her fight. I wanted to put my hand through the phone and strangle the bastard.

Her voice rose. "That's not any of your business!" She let out a deep breath. "James, don't put Grace in the middle of this. I am coming home now. We can discuss it tonight. What? James, you can't just take him. He's fine with Grace." Her face was pale, and her voice hitched when she said, "I thought you were going away for the weekend." She covered her eyes with her hand, as if that could stop what was to come.

"James, you're being ridiculous. Of course I want custody of my son. I don't see how my being out of town for a few days negates anything."

Kelcie began to pace again. "You can't even bother to keep your scheduled visitation dates, and now you want to take me back to court for full custody?"

I needed to do something. I couldn't just stand here.

"I'm not behaving erratically. I merely came to watch a game."

Now, her face began to redden again. His intentions scared her, but they also angered her.

"Who I date—or choose to sleep with—is *none* of your business."

James's voice was louder, but I could only imagine the insults he was throwing around. I leaned over to grab the phone from Kelcie. She didn't have to listen to this asshole.

She dodged my grab and turned her back on me. "Wait." She closed her eyes and put her hand to her forehead. "We can re-visit the visitation agreement if you want. But James, you're being irrational." Tears formed in her eyes. "You can't just take Aaron because you're mad at me. You can't pull him out of his routine. He's happy at school —" There was a hitch in her voice. "James, don't do this. You're going to freak him out."

He was making her cry. I was done. I reached over her head and grabbed the phone out of her hands.

"Kelcie will be talking to you through her lawyer. And don't you dare leave town with that boy, or it'll be the last thing you do." I didn't give him a chance to say anything else but hung up the phone and tossed it on the bed.

"Fucking asshole." Then I glanced up at Kelcie's stricken face.

"What have you done?"

"Cut off that nonsense. He can't just show up and take him."

"He's his father," she said, as if that was enough of an explanation, tears rolling down her face.

I reached for the phone and handed it back to her. "Call your lawyer."

"It's Sunday. I don't think he will—"

"Fuck what day it is. Call him," I said, grabbing my own phone. I was going to find her a better lawyer. I'd find her ten lawyers. Fuck this. He wasn't going to get away with this bullshit.

"I've got to go." She made a beeline for the bedroom. "I have to get home and sort this out."

I followed her. "Why did he show up?"

"He saw me on television last night." She began shoving clothes in her suitcase. "He heard about me on the news. And then, to get him even more ramped up, he said he got a contract agreement from Smitty's people for Aaron to appear as a regular guest."

"So?"

"He said I was capitalizing on my son's disability and behaving like a ..." Tears coursed down her face quicker than she could wipe them away. "He said he and Amber think—" She cut herself off.

"What did he say?" I gritted.

She took in a breath. "He's going to try for full custody. They came home from their trip so he could take Aaron and demand emergency temporary custody."

I was going to kill him.

"That's not going to happen," I growled and began punching the buttons on my phone. "Yeah, Matt, it's Shaw. I need a plane. Now. As soon as possible. There's an emergency." I went into my closet and grabbed my duffel, shoving miscellaneous clothing items in it.

"Yeah. Sure. Let me see what I can do," he said. "Hey, man, is everything okay?"

"No. Call Lieberman and ask him to find me the best family law practice in the area. I need that name immediately."

"Yeah…okay. Let me make a few calls, and I'll get back to you," Matt said. "Anything else?"

"No, but call me back with the plane information first," I said. "We're going home."

39

Kelcie

"This is ridiculous. You can't go back. You have practice and play-offs to prepare for," I said as Shaw packed his car for the airport.

He slammed the trunk and motioned me to the passenger door. "Of course I'm going. I'm not letting you deal with this alone."

I really didn't need to be fighting with him. I had enough on my mind dealing with James, especially now that I'd likely have to go to his place to pick up Aaron.

"His visitation ends this evening at 9:00 pm. He is supposed to have Aaron back at my house by then," I said, downplaying the situation as I climbed in the car.

He grunted like a bull. "That's fine. I will be there with you when they return. I need him to know you aren't alone, that you won't be bullied any longer. If he wants a relationship with Aaron, he'll need to co-parent with you." Once I was seatbelted in, he slammed my door.

"Having you there will be like pouring gasoline on a fire," I said as he settled into the driver's seat and started the car.

"Yeah, well, I'll bring the matches, and we can get this shit over with," Shaw said as he pulled out into traffic.

His phone rang, and he answered it with his earbuds, "Yeah." He listened for a moment while I pulled out my phone and tried to text Aaron. "I want someone at Kelcie's house when we get there for back-up. Can you manage that? Also, can you check into the financials for James Byron?"

"What are you doing?" I asked.

"Checking on a hunch," he said before returning to the caller. "I'll get you a copy of Smitty's contract as soon as I can get my hands on it. Because Aaron is a minor, the office was required to send it to both parents. We haven't been home to see it yet."

He listened to the other line for a moment. "Okay, hold on."

Then he turned to me. "Tell me what Grace told you."

"According to Grace, James showed up with Amber and her kids in the car, packed up Aaron's suitcase, told Grace that Aaron wasn't any of her damn business and if she tried to stop him, he was calling the police."

"Did you catch that? Yeah, Grace is fine. She was just pissed she couldn't stop him. Please stay by the phone, and I will get back to you," Shaw said. "Thanks, Wyatt, I appreciate it."

"Why is Wyatt involved?" I asked.

"Because Grace called him, and I asked for his help. Trust me, Kelce, please."

"I do, but the more people in my life who get involved, the messier James is going to make this."

"I don't give a rat's ass. He isn't going to touch you, Kelcie, and he isn't going to take Aaron. We need a copy of your custody agreement so our lawyer can familiarize himself with it."

I stared at him, open-mouthed. "What the hell. I have a lawyer," I said.

"Has he called you back?" he said. "This can't wait until business hours tomorrow. We need to be ready to handle James and get Aaron back immediately."

I stared out the window, Shaw unable to see my face as we drove in silence to the airport.

40

Kelcie

I tried texting Aaron again to check on him. Before he finally responded, I'd been about to call James again to find out if he had taken away Aaron's phone.

AARON

Mom, Dad made me leave with him. Are you going to come get me?

ME

Yes, honey, don't worry. Your father and I had a miscommunication.

AARON

I don't like it here, Mom. This wasn't the plan. I was supposed to watch the games with Grace tonight. She was making chili. I want to come home.

ME

I know, honey. I'll be there this evening.

AARON

> Is Shaw coming? Dad is saying bad things to
> Ms. Amber about you and Shaw. I can hear
> him from the other room.

I'm sure he was. James's anger was in full tilt.

AARON

> Dad and Ms. Amber are arguing about where
> I'm going to live. Mom, I don't like this.

Son of a bitch. I decided to call Aaron and let him hear my voice. I didn't care what James thought.

"Hello?"

"Hey, honey. I know you don't like to talk on the phone, but—"

"Mom. I don't like them talking about you, and I don't want to live here."

My boy's tone was edgy and panicked. I needed to be there to talk him down, to hold him tight and help him calm down.

"Honey, it's okay. Your father is…" I said and then realized I was going to make excuses for this man—again. Well, not this time. "Your father is being a jerk."

"He's being an asshole," he said, and I heard the tears in his voice.

"Okay, yes, you're right," I said, and we both got quiet for a beat.

James's voice broke the silence. "Aaron, get off the phone. You're supposed to be doing your homework."

"I'm talking to Mom," Aaron said. "And I don't have any homework."

"Give me that phone," he said to Aaron, and then to me, he said, "Where are you?"

"I'm at the airport. I'll be home in a few hours."

"It will be too late to bring Aaron back. He will stay here this evening," James declared. "You shouldn't be giving in to his demands all the time."

Aaron began to yell in the background, "No. I won't. I won't stay here with you. I need to get home. I belong at home. This was not the plan."

"Do you see what you did now?" James sneered at me. "You had to call and ramp him up. Now, I'll have to deal with the fallout—again. You spoil him by letting him win all the time."

"This wasn't the plan. I'm supposed to watch football. I'm not staying here!" My son was screaming at his father.

"James, let me talk to him," I said.

"I think you've done enough."

Click. He hung up on me.

I called back immediately, and it went to voicemail. "James, I will be there at 9:00 to pick up my son as per our custody agreement."

I disconnected and stared at my phone as tears ran down my face. What had I done? My poor boy was having a meltdown. His father couldn't handle him, and I wasn't there.

"Kelcie?" The car had stopped in front of a small plane. We were on the tarmac, and Shaw was trying to take my hand. "Babe, we're here."

I jumped out of the car. "Open the trunk."

Shaw was in front of me, saying words I didn't hear.

"Open it. I have to leave. I have to get home," I said, refusing to look at him. I didn't know why—probably because he was the person in front of me and the only one I could take out my fear and anger on.

Shaw grabbed the suitcases and motioned for me to the plane.

We were at the stairs, and Shaw greeted the man who had taken our baggage.

I made it up a few steps before rounding on him. "You're not going," I said. "You need to stay here, and I don't need you—"

"You don't want to need me to be there for you," he shot back. "This isn't about you. It's about Aaron. And from what I heard, he needs both of us. So stop wasting your energy arguing with me about this. I'm going to see you home. We will decide what happens after that."

I stood a few steps above him and glared down at him.

"You're wasting time. You can glare at me on the plane. Move it," he said, glaring right back.

After we were belted in our seats, the stewardess took our drink order.

I stared out the window and didn't say another word as Shaw continued to make calls. A stray tear would occasionally run down my cheek, and I would try to casually catch it before Shaw could see it.

It wasn't rational, my hostility toward him. But right now, I couldn't worry about him…I couldn't worry about us. My only thoughts were about Aaron and what he was going through.

"God, he must be so confused," I said to myself.

He reached over, took my hand, and broke our stand-off by saying, "Grace said James was ranting about several photos of us out together this weekend on the internet. I guess, with Riley trying to milk more publicity out of our break-up, the media has found us…interesting."

"What kind of photos?" Horror filled me. Oh my God, did someone get a photo of us in his condo?

"Nothing like that." He put his hand over mine. "They were innocent, just catching us kissing and laughing. Nothing inappropriate."

"Then why is James doing this?" My voice broke.

"Because he's a jealous bastard."

"My son is losing his shit right now, and his own father doesn't seem to care. I told him what would happen. Hell, he knew what this would lead to—Aaron losing his shit. What is wrong with that man?" Thank God we were on a private flight because I was losing my shit now too. "What does he hope to accomplish from this?"

Shaw held my hand, squeezed it lightly, and said, "I don't know, babe. But I'm sure we will find out."

41

———

Shaw

It was dark out when I finally pulled the rental car up outside a two-story colonial brick house in a neighborhood with perfectly manicured lawns and trees lining the road. It was the quintessential DC Suburb with mid-range luxury cars in the driveways.

The drive had been almost as quiet as the flight.

I'd never been to Kelcie's home when she was married to Needle Dick. It was a surprising glimpse into the life she used to lead.

I didn't bother with the driveway in case we needed to make a fast exit, and saw a dark-blue Explorer parked across the street, just as Wyatt had indicated.

"Let me go get him and see how quickly we can leave. Stay. Here. No matter what," she said, glowering at me. "I don't even want him to know you're in the car."

I stared back. "Remember what the lawyer said? Do not engage. If you want me to stay in the car, then there won't be any witnesses to what was said. So just don't say anything."

She didn't answer me, just got out of the car and slammed the door. She faltered for a moment, staring up at what used to be her house. I walked around the car to join her, wanting to reach for her hand. "We got this," I whispered.

We were a few feet from the door when Aaron came bursting out of the house, his arms outstretched and his face a blotchy mess. "Mom! You came. Let's go home. I want to go home."

The boy was in the house he grew up in, but it wasn't home to him any longer.

"Aaron, come get your bag," James said, walking out on the porch, hands in his pockets. He didn't give two shits what emotional upheaval he had caused. He'd managed to get her to leave me and run home. That was all he'd wanted—to see if he still could sway her.

Aaron ignored his father and held onto Kelcie like a child clutching his favorite teddy bear that someone threatened to take away. He was almost the same height as her, making her wrap her arm around his waist and whisper soothing words to him.

Amber came out onto the porch, carrying a backpack. James took it from her and walked it down to Aaron.

"Aaron, I will talk to you tomorrow. Remember what we talked about," he said, pushing the backpack at Aaron, who was refusing to let go of Kelcie.

"I'm not talking to you," he said loud enough for all of us to hear.

James glared at Kelcie and then over to the car, where I'd gone back to wait. He was no longer able to maintain his passive expression. His anger was cold and calculating.

Kelcie took the backpack and turned Aaron to the car.

"Don't forget what the custody agreement says, Kelcie." He smirked then raised his voice and added, "He can't move without my permission."

Kelcie opened the door to the car and helped Aaron get in it. "Hold your bag, honey. We are heading home."

"You'll be hearing from my lawyer." James walked toward the car with the confidence of a man who thought he had us by the balls. "I would suggest you hold off on any trips out of state."

Aaron rolled down his window. "When Shaw goes the Super Bowl, I'm going too. And you can't stop me."

Oh jeez.

Kelcie cringed and hurried up to situate herself then turned to me. "Let's go. Now."

Aaron fell asleep before we were on the beltway.

Kelcie was silent, leaning her head against the window. Lights from overhead and the oncoming cars caught random glimpses of her fear and anger.

I didn't know what to say or what to do to help her.

She rubbed her hand over her forehead, her voice weary. "When do you have to be back?"

Tomorrow morning. I had workouts and meetings. "Don't worry about it."

"Why don't we drive to the airport, and I'll drop you off so you can get back—"

"Don't be ridiculous. I'm driving you two home and making sure you are good."

She let out a sigh. "There isn't anything you can do, Shaw. Especially not now. Just go back to Charlotte."

It sounded like a dismissal. "I can—"

She put her hand up to stop me. "I have to deal with this, and you being here is just going to make it worse. He's going to do anything he can to gain leverage over me. You are the catalyst to all of this—just me being with you."

What the hell?

"I didn't do anything."

"You exist. I almost replaced him with you."

"He threw you away as soon as you became pregnant—like you were a burden."

"And you are more successful than he could ever hope to be. His son worships you. He probably knows you would've been a better father than he is—though he would never admit it."

"That's his issue."

"No, it's mine. Because until Aaron is eighteen and no longer a minor, James gets a say in Aaron's life and, by extension, mine."

"He's remarried. He has his ready-made family." She gave the smallest flinch, accentuating the point that I wasn't helping, even now.

She stared back out the window, her hand over her mouth as if stifling what else she wanted to say—needed to say.

"What?"

"We need to take a few steps back. I can't be involved with you—with anyone—until I can figure out a way to get James to back off."

I gripped the wheel again, and this time, I felt the fancy leather wrapped around the steering wheel start to give. I bit out, "You are giving him exactly what he wants, you know that."

She remained silent.

"Fine, I will stay away for a little while—"

"It's not going to work. You heard him. Even if I was able to maintain custody—or even joint custody—he's never going to let Aaron move to Charlotte."

"So, I'll commute during the season—many players do it."

She shook her head. "It won't work."

I glanced at the backseat to see if Aaron was awake. He didn't need to hear me getting dumped on top of the drama his father and mother were fighting. I pulled into a well-lit parking lot and got out of the car. I walked around and opened her door, giving her my hand to help her out of the car, and closed the door, trying not to slam it.

She still wouldn't look at me.

I paced and ran my hand through my hair. "It's like the universe is determined to keep us apart."

Her arms crossed over her chest, and she stood with her back to the car.

I stepped up to her, fencing her in with my hands on the door behind her. "I love you. Do you get that? I love you, and all I want to do is make a home with you and Aaron."

The gasp of air she let out was the only indication I was getting through to her. I tipped her head up. "Babe, look at me."

"Do you—" She put her hand over my mouth before I could ask, *Do you love me?*

"Don't. Don't do this to me. I need to focus on Aaron and the nightmare his father is about to make his life. I don't have the mental capacity to analyze our relationship. Not now."

"Let me help you."

"You can't." She pushed past me. "I don't need you to come in and rescue me."

"I know you don't need me." And damn, if that didn't hurt to say. "But for Christ's sake, Kelcie, sometimes it's good to have support from the sidelines, someone who's there for you, waiting to be called in as back-up when you need him."

She turned and wiped her hands over her eyes. Then she drew in a deep breath, straightened her back, and said, "We—I mean, I need to get Aaron home, and you need to get back on that plane to get ready for this weekend's game. You are probably on thin ice with the team as it is."

That was true. If Yaz found out I took a night flight out of town, she would have my balls.

I was particularly attached to my balls and my career. Screw it.

She stepped close but didn't touch me. Her arms wrapped and folded over her chest, her eyes determined and decided. That made the distance between us real.

"Fine. Get in the car," I said, my heart growing cold while my knees weakened. I couldn't believe she was doing this. "I tell you I love you, and you tell me to leave. I don't think it gets any clearer than that. I guess I should just be thankful you didn't just drop me another Dear Shaw note."

I didn't wait for her response. We both rode to the airport in silence. I had the plane on standby, not knowing what the evening would hold. Maybe deep down, I knew this would be the outcome.

When we reached the tarmac, I got out of the car and popped the trunk.

"Shaw? Where are you going?" Aaron's sleepy voice said from the darkened backseat. He straightened up and leaned into the light from the overhead light in the car.

"I got to get back to Charlotte, buddy. Your mom is going to take you home and get you settled. You have school tomorrow, don't you?"

"When will you be back?"

I didn't have the strength to answer that, and I refused to admit I didn't know. "Not sure, but hey, you call me or text me. Okay? About anything."

"I wish I could go with you," he said, his tone hiding his real age and sounding like a small child.

I put my hand in the car, mussed his hair, and said, "I know. Me too."

Kelcie was behind me, ready to get into the driver's seat. The wind had picked up, and she tucked the hair straying from her ponytail behind her ears. With her back to the light, it was hard to see her face. "Good luck this week." She shifted on her feet, probably anxious for me to leave.

I put my unused duffel bag over my shoulder and stared at the plane. There wasn't anything left for me to do except fulfill the one thing asked of me. I left. "Drive safely."

Then I walked up the stairs to the plane, my eyes burning, and lied to myself that it was the wind.

42

———————

Kelcie

"It just doesn't make any sense. Why now?" Grace said.

I dropped Aaron off at school and called in to work. I was sick to my stomach.

"I don't know. He's a jealous asshole," I said, rubbing my hand over my forehead in a vain attempt to stop my mind from reeling. "He just got married, and he has a happy little family. Why all of a sudden does he care?"

"I don't know, but girl, we need to get in front of this. Did you call your lawyer?"

"I did. He's supposed to call me back."

She let out a deep sigh. "I'm sorry you are going through this. What is Shaw doing?"

"He's back at practice today. There isn't anything he can do. Truthfully, having him involved just pissed James off more."

My phone beeped with an incoming call. It was from a law firm I didn't recognize. Great. James probably hired new attorneys. He wasn't wasting any time.

"Grace, let me get this," I said. "Just hold on a moment."

"Yep. Sure," she said.

I answered the other call. "Hello?"

"Hello, Ms. Hammer. This is Susan from the offices of Brown and Epstein. I wanted to set up a tele-appointment with Mr. Epstein for today. We were wondering if you were available around 1:00 this afternoon?"

Um, what?

"I'm sorry, I think there must be some misunderstanding. Who is this?"

"Susan from Mr. Epstein's office. Dawson Shawfield contacted us on your behalf about your custody issue."

I gritted my teeth. "Oh, I'm sorry, I was unaware of—"

"Mr. Shawfield said it was a time-sensitive matter, so we made room in Mr. Epstein's schedule for today. I was hoping to get the name of your previous representative so we could obtain the necessary documents to bring Mr. Epstein up to speed."

I took in a deep breath. "Could you hold for one moment?"

"Yes, ma'am."

I flipped back to Grace. "Grace. Shaw hired a new law firm."

"Good. Because it's probably the best."

"I told him not to get involved."

"Hiring the best lawyer you could have is probably the best thing he could do for you. I mean, your other lawyer hasn't called you back yet, and this one is ready to meet with you today," Grace said. "Don't cut off your nose to spite your face, Kelcie. If this helps you out of the situation, who cares who is helping you? It's not about your pride, honey. It's about Aaron."

Well, crap. I gritted my teeth. I didn't know why I was being so obstinate. "Give me a moment." I flipped back to the lady.

"Yes, 1:00 should be fine." I gave her the information for my previous lawyer and said I would call and ask them to forward all files to the new firm.

I texted Shaw to thank him.

> **ME**
>
> Thank you for the referral.

SHAW

They are the best in the area. Please, just talk to them.

I stared at the screen for a moment.

> **ME**
>
> I can't afford a big firm, Shaw.

SHAW

I can. And don't fight with me about it. It's not negotiable. Did you get the contract from Smitty?

> **ME**
>
> Yes, but I haven't looked at it yet.

SHAW

Forward it to me. I'll have some people look at it.

> **ME**
>
> Okay.

I didn't want to deal with a contract that wouldn't ever get approved by James. There was no point in getting everyone's hopes up.

SHAW

Tell Aaron I said hi. He can call me this afternoon if he wants.

If that is okay with you.

> **ME**
>
> Okay.

The dots danced as Shaw continued to type, and my eyes burned in anticipation of what else he'd say.

Then they disappeared, and my heart sank. Dammit, I had to focus on other things. I couldn't get wrapped up in what was happening with Shaw. I had to put all my focus on Aaron.

———

"So, your new boyfriend is buying you a new lawyer, huh?" James said as a greeting when he called the next day.

"I don't see how that matters to you," I said quietly and closed the door to my bedroom.

"It doesn't. I want to see Aaron this weekend."

"It's not your weekend," I said.

"Nonetheless, if you want to make this more amicable, you will start to be flexible. I want him here this weekend."

"Why, what is the big deal? I couldn't get you to adhere to the other scheduled dates."

"My schedule is always changing. Between work, Amber, and her kids' activities, I have to rearrange things sometimes," he said with irritation.

"That isn't my problem. We have an agreement. I'd like to stick with it," I said.

His tone darkened with exasperation. "My parents are coming this weekend, and I would like my family together."

His family.

"I see." His parents had always liked me, and they adored Aaron. I'm sure he'd had a lot of explaining to do with the divorce and his marrying Amber so quickly. "I will talk with Aaron and see if he'd like to come visit your parents. I think he wanted some quiet time after last weekend."

"You mean after you left him for your fling in Charlotte."

"Again, none of your business. I told you I had plans."

"If I'd known you were going to abandon him to—"

"I didn't abandon him. You know what? It doesn't matter. I will talk to Aaron," I said. "I will text you later."

"Kelcie—"

I hung up on him. There wasn't any point in arguing.

Later that evening, after dinner, I approached Aaron with the idea of going to his father's that weekend to see his grandparents.

He dropped his spoon in his ice cream bowl and, without looking up, said, "Do I have to?"

"Technically, no. It's not his weekend."

He straightened. "Then I don't want to go. I want to stay home."

The wave of unhappiness that hit him had me prying more. "Honey, is everything okay when you go there?"

"It's so loud, Mom," he said, the floodgates opening. "Amber's kids have televisions and video games in their bedrooms, and they're always so loud."

I put my hand over his as he continued, "And Dad gave Brent my room. He moved me out of my room and put me in the den."

Excuse me. Was he kidding? One of the reasons I'd agreed to sell the house to James was so that Aaron could have some continuity when he went there.

"He said it was selfish of me to want to keep my room since I was only there every other weekend, and Brent needed it," he said. "Now my room is the den, and it's never quiet down there. They always are yelling and loud, and when I get upset, Dad gets angry at me."

I held it in. I bit my tongue, and I watched my son shovel ice cream in his mouth, his eyes glassy.

What was James's deal? If he made so little room for Aaron in his life, why was he insisting on custody?

43

Shaw

Practice sucked.

Coming home to an empty home sucked.

Not knowing what was going on with Kelcie and Aaron sucked.

I'd driven myself into the ground with practice and PT and anything else that could distract me from jumping on a plane.

I made a beeline for my shower when I got home, and that made it worse. All I could think of were the moments we'd had there. It was a very cold shower. When I came out, I found a text from Wyatt.

WYATT

Any word from Kelcie?

ME

No. Did you find out anything?

WYATT

Still working on it. I have a guy who is looking into things.

Wyatt always had "a guy." He always had a way of getting information—and information was a weapon if used correctly.

WYATT

So far, there may be some issues with the asshole's finances.

ME

How is that?

WYATT

It seems the new Mrs. Byron came into the marriage with some debt, and they just finished refurbishing the house. My people said there were a lot of contractors in and out of there in the last six months.

ME

Do you think it's his child support?

WYATT

Could be. But my money is on TJ's offer to Aaron. It was a pretty sweet deal.

That two-faced son of a bitch…

WYATT

I'm still looking into it.

ME

Alright, man. I appreciate it. Anything you can do.

After pacing around, I dialed her.

"Hey," I said. Great opening.

"Oh, hey," she said. "I…um. Did you want to talk with Aaron?"

"No, honey—I mean, of course I want to talk with him. But I want to talk to you first. Is everything okay?"

"As well as it could be," she said.

"Did you talk with the lawyer?" I asked.

"Yes, and there is a meeting set with him, James, and his lawyer for next week.

But James wants him this weekend again."

She went on to explain the situation with his parents coming and that they'd moved Aaron out of his room and into the den. Images of Harry Potter living under the stairs flashed through my mind, and my anger grew. So did my determination.

"I hate that I can't be there to help you," I said. And it was true. I loved her, and I loved Aaron. Nothing would change that.

"You focus on what you need to do, and I will focus on what I need to do," she said.

"And then what?" The words spilled out of my mouth before I realized I wasn't ready for the answer she might give.

"I don't know, Shaw. I just don't know."

———

I was walking to my car after an early morning workout when my phone rang.

Aaron.

"Hey, man, how's it going?"

"Shaw. Can you come get me?" The hitch in his voice made him sound so incredibly young.

I froze. "What's wrong? Where are you? Did you call your mom?"

"No. If she comes, they will just fight more, and my mom will cry. Can you come?"

I raked my hand through my hair. This had to stop. I couldn't just stay here in Charlotte. But if I went, Kelcie would kill me. "I tell you what. You call your mom, and I will see what I can do. But buddy, you need to tell your mom. I can't just come get you."

"But—"

"Buddy, these are your parents," I said. "Have you tried to talk to your dad about how unhappy you are?"

He sniffled on the other end of the line. "I tried. He said you and Mom have put things in my head. I don't know what that means."

"Call your mom. I'm going to see what I can do, okay?"

"Okay. But, Shaw, I think they want to send me to a different school. I heard Amber and Dad talking about it. They said I had to go visit it on Monday. But I have school on Monday. I'm supposed to go back home Sunday."

"Call your mom, and I will see what I can do about coming home for a bit. Okay?"

"Okay."

"We have a plan, then. Listen to your father, but call your mom. And Buddy, what school were they talking to you about?"

"It's called the Tucker School, but I've never heard of it."

"That's fine. We'll figure it out. Are you going to be okay?"

"Yeah. I guess."

"Call your mom as soon as we hang up, and I will call her afterward."

"Okay, thanks, Shaw."

"Hey, my man. We will figure it out. I've got you," I said.

My hands were shaking as I hung up the phone and was barely able to dial Wyatt's number.

"Yo," he said as a way of greeting.

"Yeah, I need your person to find out what they can about a place called The Tucker School," I said.

"Is this about Aaron?" he said.

"Yeah, and I don't think it's a good thing."

———

After showering and packing, I drove straight to the airport and was on a flight that afternoon, barely managing to keep my anger banked under my need to see them. To protect them.

I didn't think this was going to go over well, but I needed to tell her what I'd found out in person. I needed to have her back.

Come hell or high water, she wasn't in this alone.

I pulled up to the house and knocked on the door.

"Shaw?"

There she was, with bags under her eyes, a messy ponytail, and still wearing her robe. But damn, she was so beautiful. My stomach dropped with the weight of how much I missed her.

"What in the world are you doing here?"

"We need to talk. You need to get dressed." I kissed her forehead in a friendly greeting as I pushed past her.

Within an hour, we were on James's front porch.

Amber opened the door, the fake smile disappearing from her face when she asked, in a tone laced with hostility, "What the hell are you doing here?"

I stood behind Kelcie, hands folded in front of me, trying to look as inconspicuous as a 240 pound, 6'5" man could be as she stepped forward with a backpack in her hand. "Hello, Amber. I was in the neighborhood and thought I'd check in on Aaron. I brought his homework. He seemed to have forgotten it."

She yanked the bag out of Kelcie's hand. "Fine, I'll give it to him."

"Amber, who is at the door?" another feminine voice sounded, and a pretty, older woman appeared.

"Hello, Vivian," Kelcie said with a soft, hesitant smile.

"Oh! Kelcie, dear, how wonderful to see you." She wrapped Kelcie in a hug and escorted her out onto the porch. "What are you doing here, dear?"

"Just dropping off—" she started to say before Amber walked out, closing the door behind her.

"She forgot to give Aaron his backpack and was just dropping it off."

"And who is this big guy?" the petite, older woman asked, surveying me.

"This is Shaw…I mean Dawson Shawfield. An old friend of mine," she said. "Shaw, this is James's mother, Vivian Byron."

I held out my hand, and she promptly shook it with a dazzling smile that was more than just polite. "Oh, so this is Shaw. We've heard endless stories about you from Aaron."

"What is going on—" James walked out and gauged the situation. "You aren't supposed to be here."

"Yeah, well, like Kelcie said, we thought we'd just bring Aaron his—"

"Shaw!" Aaron ran out and threw himself into my arms. "You came! I'll just be a moment and get my things."

"Your mom brought your bookbag, Aaron," Amber said as she shot James a look.

He straightened with a poorly practiced smile. "Aaron, this wasn't part of the plan."

Aaron turned on his father. "Well, you're always saying plans change, and I have to learn to deal with it." Aaron ran back in the house, running and dodging everyone like a running back.

I stifled back a laugh with a cough.

Ignoring his mother's presence, James turned on Kelcie. "I told you my mom was visiting. This was not what we agreed on." With his teeth gritted, he added, "I thought you wanted to make this go smoother."

"I'm not doing anything wrong, James."

"Oh, yeah? Then why is he here?" He glared up at me.

I spread my legs and crossed my arms over my chest, knowing damn well the position made my biceps bulge.

"Oh, my…" James's mother cooed. She flushed, and I swear she clutched her pearls—real pearls.

"Don't worry about Shaw. But since you want to discuss an agreement—"

"I'm not worried about him." His eyes bounced between Amber and his mother. "But it just goes to show how far up his ass you are."

"James Monroe Byron," his mother scolded him. "Language."

He raised his voice and ignored her. "It doesn't matter, because he's going to drop you like yesterday's news."

"I didn't come here to swap insults, James."

"Then leave." Amber's expression, even under her Stepford-Wife persona, was smug and not at all attractive.

"Amber," Mrs. Byron scolded, "that isn't how you greet a guest. Why don't we go inside so we don't give the neighbors anything to gossip about?" She motioned to us toward the door.

I put my hand on Kelcie's back, encouraging her to say what she needed to say before Aaron came back.

"I wanted to know why you suddenly have a problem with our custody arrangement?"

"That isn't your concern. The lawyers will handle it. I think you need to go," Amber said.

But Kelcie didn't take her eyes off her ex-husband.

"Is it the child support? Is that it? You don't want to have to pay for child support?" she shot at him.

"Of course not." James shifted on his feet, glancing at Amber and his mom.

His mom stepped forward. "What is this about the custody agreement? I thought—"

"It's nothing, Mom."

Kelcie turned her attention to James's mom. "He is taking me to court for primary custody."

"He's what?"

Amber stepped in, saccharine-sweet sugar lacing her words. "We believe we can give Aaron a better, morally sound home life. I'm a stay-at-home mom, and he would have the two boys as brothers."

James jumped in and added, "It would be better for him to have stability."

I stepped up next to Kelcie, and she grabbed my arm to hold me back. "That's rich. You cheat on me—"

Mama Byron clutched her pearls again. "What? James?"

"He didn't cheat," Amber said

"I never slept with her!" James yelled.

There was a pause. We all stared at Mama Byron, who was obviously gobsmacked. She probably hadn't known about that piece of information. Then she straightened. "Oh, my word. The one day your father decides to play sick so he doesn't have to come down here, and I have this dropped in my lap."

She reached for Kelcie's hand and walked her to the swing on the other side of the porch. "Tell me."

"Mom!" James whined.

Mama Byron held up her hand. "You had your chance to tell me and didn't. Now I want to hear from my daughter-in-law."

"But I'm your daughter-in-law!" Amber squealed, pouting.

Kelcie sat down beside her. "I went to Charlotte to see Shaw's first game back since being injured. You know Shaw and I—"

"Oh, yes. James's father was watching the game."

Kelcie gave her former mother-in-law her side of the story and then added, "I didn't know where it came from. It was out of nowhere. James was supposed to have Aaron that weekend but backed out—like he always does," I couldn't help but drop in.

"You stay out of this!" James sneered. "If it wasn't for you, my son wouldn't be so difficult to deal with."

I'd had enough of sitting on the sidelines.

"What is The Tucker School, James?" I said.

He froze.

Amber went pale.

"I don't know," he said and turned to his mom. "I have no idea what he's talking about."

"It's a boarding school in Connecticut. They were planning to send Aaron there," Kelcie said quietly and then pierced Amber and James with her gaze. "If you knew your son, James, you'd remember that Aaron hears everything. He heard you two discussing your plans. Tell me, where were you going to find the tuition for that?"

And then Kelcie spilled all the tea. "It's going to be difficult since you just spent so much on the house renovations and all the trips you and Amber have been taking, isn't it?"

"My finances aren't any of your business, but you know what is? Aaron. He's mine, not yours."

"Cutting my child support wasn't going to put a dent in that amount," Kelcie said, standing next to me.

"I know where it was going to come from," I said, scanning the group. "The offer for Smitty's podcast. A few appearances on his show would've paid for the tuition with a fair amount of money left over. Plus, if you didn't have to pay child support, you'd be sitting pretty…

at least until you found yourselves in debt again. But then, Aaron could just do a few more podcasts, and you'd be set."

"You shouldn't even be here! Get off my property!" James yelled loud enough that the man in the Explorer across the street definitely caught it.

Amber held him back. "He needs to be in a structured environment. Tucker is a great school for autistic kids," Amber piped in, justifying their actions.

"Aaron doesn't need to be sent to a boarding school. He's fine with me," Kelcie said.

"Bullshit," James said.

James's mom peered down her nose at Amber and James. "I know he's unhappy here. He tells me, and he hears more than he should. I don't blame him." She waved at the house. "It's bedlam in this house." She folded her hands. "Amber, dear, I think you should stay in your lane and take your own guidance about structure and discipline."

She stepped up to James, causing him to take a step back. "I don't want to ever hear you talk about sending my grandson away again. And taking him from his mother? What has gotten into you?"

James's mouth was so tightly drawn that his lips disappeared. "He isn't a normal boy. He needs—"

"I am a normal boy."

We all turned to see Aaron standing on the porch with his belongings. "You need to stop bullying me and my mom." Aaron narrowed his eyes at his father and Amber.

"Aaron—"

"I want to go home with Mom. I want to watch football with Shaw, and go to the playoffs, and play with my friends in the park."

"You aren't going anywhere with him," James said. "Your mother can chase Shaw like a pathetic football groupie, but I won't have her dragging you all over with her."

Aaron lunged for his father, but I grabbed him. "Don't you talk that way about my mom!"

"We are done here," I said, gently moving Aaron into Kelcie's arms.

"If you choose to continue with this asinine behavior, James… If you keep harassing Kelcie and Aaron, you won't just be taking on my lawyers, but I will have Wyatt Fortner so far up your ass, your breath will smell like a dirty sneaker."

James's eyes widened.

"Yes, Wyatt has a remarkable way of finding out everyone's secrets," I said.

Amber grabbed James's arm. "Forget it, sweetheart. We don't need this aggravation."

Aaron piped in, "And you aren't going to be able to squeeze Shaw for money either. Because I'll tell any judge about everything I've heard while in this house." He gave Amber a knowing smile. "Everything."

That had Amber backing up. "Fine, take your brat and leave. We don't need his spoiled fits here. Our life was perfect without—"

Mama Byron stepped up into Amber's space. "Complete that sentence, girl, and you will regret it. I don't care who you are married to. Get me?" Mama Byron's Dirty Harry tone could have scared a defense lineman into submission.

I wrapped my arms around my girl and her boy and led them away from that house.

Kelcie turned to Mama Byron and said, "Vivian, you are welcome to visit any time. We'd love to see you."

"Thank you, sweetie. She smiled her grandma smile at us, walked down the stairs, and gave Aaron an exaggerated hug. "I'm so sorry you've had to deal with this. You are our grandson, darling. You are loved beyond measure."

Then she gave a weary smile and rolled her eyes before saying to Kelcie and me, "I'm sorry for whatever this has cost you…both of you."

"No problem, Mrs. Byron. Tell Mr. Byron you are both welcome to come see any of my games as a personal guest," I said.

We all ignored James's outburst. "My father hates Charlotte."

Mama Byron kissed Kelcie and Aaron. "We'll be in touch." As we walked to the car, she added, "Shaw, take care of my family."

"Of course," I said. "They're my family too."

44

———————

Kelcie

We were going to drive Shaw back to the airport before heading home. But a few blocks from James's house, we pulled over. A dark-blue Explorer pulled up, and Shaw introduced me to my new bodyguard.

It was Nick, the bartender from the bar in town. My surprise had me asking, "You moonlight as a bodyguard?"

He shrugged, his scruff, dark eyes, shaggy hair, and adorable dimples giving him the look of the boy next door who had a wild side…and a past. "It's one of my many talents," he said, glancing up at Shaw. "We good?"

"Yeah, man. Thanks. I think we made our point." Shaw reached out and shook his hand. "Thanks for the information."

"No worries. It was nice to get out from behind the bar for a bit. It was actually very easy—the neighbors around here love to gossip. It didn't take much to find the info you needed about his finances. Amber had been blabbing her mouth to anyone who would listen about that school and her plans for wrecking Kelcie's life." He turned to me. "She's a vindictive bitch. The neighbors told me about the school drop-off story."

I rolled my eyes.

Nick chuckled. "Hilarious."

Shaw grinned, and it took my anxiety down a few notches for the first time in days.

"Well, see you back in town. Bring those friends of yours around, and I'll buy the first round of drinks," Nick said.

"You mean bring Aliya around?" I teased.

He hit me with a dazzling smile. Then he walked to the door of his truck. "Good luck in the playoffs, Shaw."

"Thanks, man."

Shaw and I watched him drive off.

"Wait…how did you know to talk to Nick?" I asked.

Shaw shot me a knowing look as he walked to the driver's side door of the car. "How do you think?"

"Wyatt," I said. "Of course, what Grace knows, Wyatt knows."

"I was the one to call Wyatt this time. I mean, of course he spoke to Grace and got the story, but I called Wyatt for some help. We will all move heaven and earth to protect you and Aaron. You know that now, right?" he said.

I clicked on my seatbelt. "Yeah, I guess there's no avoiding you all."

Aaron popped up between our seats. "Mom, are we going home with Shaw?"

"No, honey. Shaw is heading back to Charlotte, and we have to stay here. You have to go to school and—"

"But when will we see him again?" He turned to Shaw. "When are you coming home for good?"

Shaw side-eyed me, staying tight-lipped and waiting to see how I was going to answer.

"Shaw has a few games left before he can leave Charlotte. He's probably going to get in trouble with the team just for flying up here again."

I had no idea where we stood, and I didn't want to ask. He needed to get on a plane and try to get back before his team noticed he was gone.

"Why don't we see how things go? Take it week by week," he said, glancing in his rearview mirror to Aaron.

Aaron pursed his lips, contemplating that for a moment. "Yeah. You need to focus on the game. Are we going to come see you?"

I couldn't leave that up to Shaw. So I said, "We'll see. We have to wait until we iron out an agreement with your father. Besides, you have school, and I work here in Maryland."

Shaw changed the subject, distracting him from what had happened that evening. He talked football with Aaron, and I stayed quiet, just listening to them both and contemplating what to say to Shaw now. I was frustrated with his heavy-handedness in interfering when I'd told him to stay out of it. But I had to admit, he'd come through for me. I didn't doubt his devotion to Aaron.

But every time I tried to think about us together, my insecurities got the better of me. How could someone like me ever hold onto a man who was larger than life and literally worshipped by people all over the country?

We pulled up to the drop-off at the departure terminal, and Shaw put the car in park. Aaron had fallen asleep about a half hour earlier, so we both stepped out of the car. Shaw grabbed his backpack, the only thing he brought, knowing he couldn't stay.

I stepped onto the curb, waiting for him to walk around but still not sure what came next. Did I hug him, hold onto him, never let him go? My heart filled with dread at the thought of him leaving. I wanted to jump in his arms, wrap my legs around him, and never let him go.

But my mind was still reeling with the events of the day and the uncertainty of what would happen next. One thing I knew for sure: he didn't need to be distracted by my neurotic, messy life. Not when his head needed to be in the game if he was going to save his career.

He stepped close to me, his backpack slung over one massive shoulder.

I decided to go with honesty. "I don't know what to say… Thank you. For everything you keep doing for me—for us."

"What are friends for?" he mumbled, unable to look at me as he said it.

Our relationship wasn't going to be solved in the drop-off area at the airport.

He locked eyes with me. A soft sadness permeated the air between us. He took my hand, leaned forward, and slowly kissed my cheek. "Nothing has changed for me," he whispered.

"I—" *I love you.* The words were caught in my throat. "I'll miss you," I said instead, and a tear I didn't see coming snuck out from under my lashes.

He squeezed my hand and brushed his thumb over my cheek, taking the tear with him as he walked away.

45

Shaw

Super Bowl.

We made it to the Super Bowl.

Over the last few weeks, I'd put all my focus into achieving my lifelong dream. We'd made it to playoffs before, only to fall short of the actual championship.

But it was bittersweet.

While I'd been in communication with Aaron and Kelcie, they'd maintained that I needed to focus on my moment and not be bogged down with their daily lives.

Aaron was back at school, playing pick-up games with the guys in the park—even in the cold.

Things with the podcast had been sidelined until the custody agreement negotiations were over.

While James was being less aggressive, he wouldn't allow Kelcie to take Aaron to any of the playoff games because they fell on the weekends he had him. Kelcie refused to discuss anything else pertaining to James. "I don't want you jumping on a plane again," she'd said when I pushed it. "If you lose focus, you'll never forgive yourself—or me. Your very expensive lawyers and I have it handled."

The unaddressed issue was us. What was going to happen to us?

When I brought up the idea of getting them a suite for the Super Bowl, Kelcie lost her mind when she found out what it would cost. "We'll have a Super Bowl party in your honor," she said.

My heart sank, knowing they weren't going to be there. Aaron was just as upset, but I told him my first touchdown would be for him. If he saw me fist bump the air, it was for him. That was our signal.

With my nose to the ground, I reminded myself that it was just a few weeks. And if I won the Super Bowl, my career would be complete, and all my time would be devoted to figuring out how to make Kelcie mine permanently.

The noise inside the Superdome was immense—like jet fighters taking off. For players used to it, it was white noise. For a boy with ultra-sensitive hearing, it would've been horribly difficult. Still, I'll admit to being disappointed that my two favorite people weren't here to share it.

Stepping out during player introductions just made it worse. I put on my game face and focused on the task ahead. The team we were playing had better odds than us. We were the underdogs.

Our team was announced with all the flash and fanfare of a Super Bowl, and the wave of cheering hit me as I ran out of the tunnel and onto the field. I made a beeline to the sidelines, where some players were staring up at the Jumbotron. Davy's face was lit up as if we'd already won. "Looks like someone brought your fan club." He pointed up at the screen.

And there she was, with my jersey on, jumping up and down with a smile that could light up this entire stadium, and waving around a cardboard sign. "I LOVE YOU!"

My eyes were burning, and my cheeks hurt. I was grinning so hard —like a fool. A fool in love.

Guys patted my back as they walked by, but I was frozen, staring at that screen until they panned out and showed the rest of the suite— Kelcie, Aaron, Dylan, Grace, Aliya, Maeve. I even caught a glimpse of the back of Wyatt on the screen. Kelcie flipped her poster around, and it said, "Go kick some A$$!" The camera panned away—probably concerned about the censors.

"Come on, head in the game, Romeo," Darius, the quarterback, said, slapping my helmet as he ran onto the field for the coin toss.

I couldn't stop smiling long enough to form a comeback.

"Channel it, man," Davy said. "Let's get this done so you can go kiss that woman and make her yours."

It was probably the longest game of my life. Knowing she was here —they were *all* there to watch me—drove me harder and made me more determined than ever.

On my first touchdown, I sent a fist bump to Aaron, as promised. Each time I rolled over a defense, I jumped up and down like a rookie —adrenaline coursing through me like a drug.

The second half of the fourth quarter, I broke through two linemen, outran the linebacker to catch an over-the-shoulder pass, and then juked the defensive back that was between me and the goal line. I was getting another touchdown—for her.

I did my shuffle, and the dome went wild. A kind of radar turned on inside my head, and I pivoted to a suite near the 45-yard line. I pointed at it and then tapped my heart. With my other hand, I closed my fist, opening up my thumb, pointer, and pinky—I love you.

The noise in the Superdome amplified. And there she was again on the Jumbotron. Her hands over her mouth, her shoulders shaking, her face beaming. It was a surreal moment. Just her and me making googly eyes through the seventy-foot Jumbotron with seventy-thousand fans watching.

The extra kick was good, and we were up 27-24. Our defense did its job, and as the clock counted down to the end, my mind reeled.

We'd done it. It had been the longest, most intense season of my career, and my team had won.

Pandemonium broke out with streamers and so much confetti filling the air it was almost hard to see more than ten yards in front of you.

I cheered with my teammates, walked around thanking the coaches, and hugged random people who'd searched me out to congratulate me.

Out of the streamers, like a vision, was a brunette barreling into me so fast her infamous ponytail couldn't seem to keep up. I held out my arms, and she launched herself at me, causing me to take a step back as I buried my face in her neck to hide the tears I couldn't control.

"Baby, I'm so proud of you," she said into my ear. "I'm so damn proud of you." She pulled back to look at me, her hands cupping my face, and I held her, wrapping her legs around my waist. "You were amazing." Tears filled her eyes as she kissed me—the kind of kiss the cameraman should've had to cut away from.

Our foreheads together, I closed my eyes and said, "Say it."

Because she was her, and I was me, she knew exactly what I wanted to hear. "I love you."

I threw my head back and roared. Her tears fell, and her laughter was infectious. Aaron came up and threw his arms around both of us as I lowered her to the ground. A circle of friends, teammates, cameras and reporters, and well-wishers formed around us. This moment was ours—me and my best friend, my love...my girl.

EPILOGUE

Shaw

"And...we're back with our resident prognosticator, Aaron the Analyst, and his sidekick, Dawson Shawfield. Aaron, thanks for getting Shaw to come on the podcast today. He's always so busy to spare a few minutes for us," TJ said, and I gave him a side-eye smirk.

Within a month after the game, James and Amber had backed down, withdrawing from demanding custody. Kelcie said she caught Aaron talking to Wyatt at the game about things he heard around the house and around the neighborhood. The next thing we knew, Amber was yanking James away from having anything to do with us.

Plausible deniability was probably the best for me. I'd keep my nose clean—at least until I was out of the league. Knowing Wyatt's modus operandi, I wouldn't have been surprised if Nick had been moonlighting again, digging up more of Amber's skeletons.

Aaron had pointed out that he was old enough to speak with any judge they dragged him in front of and that he would tell that judge his preferences. James knew it was a lost cause.

I didn't doubt James loved his son. I just didn't think James knew his son. He wanted to fit Aaron in a slot that wasn't big enough to hold him.

I bought both sides of the duplex from Dylan, and we decided to keep Kelcie's side for when we visited off-season. Dylan was going to work on finding someone to rent the other side.

We looked at houses in Charlotte and enjoyed the summer at my lake house.

Life was good.

One point of contention we finally settled with James was Aaron's appearance on TJ's podcast. An agreement was reached that Aaron would appear once a month, recorded from our home and on his schedule, with a nice compensation package set up in an air-tight trust for when he came of age.

In those podcasts, he interviewed players and utilized his statistician brilliance to impress TJ's fan base. Being the off-season, I went with Aaron to TJ's studio that first time so Aaron could interview me as a guest.

The minute I walked in the door, I smelled a rat, especially when I saw the size of TJ's grin.

"Sidekick?" I said to both TJ and Aaron. "Really?"

"When we're at the stadium, that's what you call me. It seemed fitting," Aaron said.

Kelcie was off to the side, her hand over her mouth, pretending to bite a nail in order to cover her smile.

"Your beautiful bride is here today, too?" TJ added, waving to Kelcie.

"Yes, that's my mom," Aaron said. "Shaw's going to marry my mom, and I will be his stepson."

Sitting back in his chair, TJ plastered on an over-the-top curious expression. "What is it like, having Shaw as a stepdad?"

Aaron shrugged. "Pretty much the same as before, except he sleeps in my mom's room."

This was going into dangerous territory, and TJ's grin turned wicked.

"I heard you all went on vacation after the Super Bowl," he said as he eyed me with the threat hanging of asking about me sleeping in his mom's bedroom.

"Yeah, we did. That's when my mom and Shaw got engaged.

"Congrats, my man," TJ said to me.

"Thanks," I said, still uncertain and rightfully nervous of where he was going with this.

"While we were gone, my Uncle Dylan worked on the house. He put in soundproof walls for me."

"Really, why?"

"Because I have very sensitive hearing, and I guess Shaw makes a lot of noise."

TJ's eyes shone, and he bit down on his lip, and his jaw ticked in an effort to control himself. "Shaw makes a lot of noise? What kind of noise?"

I was sweating like a whore in church. "Didn't you want to ask about the draft and the upcoming season, and…stuff," I asked. Jeez, this was such a bad idea.

"Okay. Let's break down the stats, then. Aaron, what do you have?" TJ handed it off to Aaron for one of the bits he always did— giving his analysis of the draft picks and who each team picked up in the off-season.

I sat back in my chair, watching my boy go. He was my boy. He was James's son, but he was my boy. I loved and thought of him as my own.

And Kelcie? I didn't think I'd ever seen her so happy. Knowing I was part of that made me want to beat my chest.

Aaron listed off his stats for the Super Bowl from memory like any ESPN announcer.

"So what do you think? Do you think he's going to retire?" I whipped my head around to see TJ leaning forward on the table that separated us, as if in private conversation with Aaron and shooting me a side-eye.

Aaron tipped his head thoughtfully. "I'm not sure. He doesn't talk about it. When are you going to retire, Shaw?"

Nothing like being thrust into the hot seat. I knew this was coming.

It was TJ's purpose of getting me in the chair. I'd been bombarded by calls and questions about my imminent retirement.

"Only time will tell, but you will be the first to know," I said, which was my standard answer.

Aaron leaned over to TJ and whispered directly into the microphone. "He needs to ask my mom. He passes everything through her now because they are together, and she's in charge."

TJ let out an audible guffaw, practically choking, before clearing his throat, "She is?"

"Yeah, after I went to bed, I heard him tell her that he would do whatever she wanted," Aaron said. "When I told them I heard him say she was in charge, we got new walls."

I yanked back on Aaron's chair, rolling him away from the microphone, and glared death rays at TJ, who practically fell out of his chair with suppressed laughter. Kelcie was suddenly nowhere to be seen, probably burying her head.

"Shaw, I can't reach the microphone. Stop being so unprofessional," Aaron scolded me.

"Are you happy with the idea of having a football player as a stepfather?" TJ asked.

"Yes. I'm happy, but I'd been meaning to talk to him about retiring."

"Oh, really. Do you think it's time?" TJ asked.

"Well, yes. If he wants to be with my mom…" He turned his attention to me. "I thought it was important."

"I know. Your mom and I discussed it," I admitted. Because she *was* in charge, and I loved it.

"Because I want a sibling—a brother or sister. I'm not going to be picky about it."

I choked on my reply before it made it out of my mouth.

He nodded and, dead serious, said to my face, "As long as you get working on it. Because I'm not getting any younger, and before you know it, I'll be off to college and won't be able to bond with the baby."

"Baby?" Still playing catch up, I wasn't prepared for his next wave of thinking.

"Yes, and in order for you and my mom to have a baby, a few things need to happen." He straightened. "First…" He held up his index finger. "You need to be in the same place, preferably married, but we have that covered."

I searched for my bride, hoping for backup.

He smiled and continued, "Second, you need to be mindful of taking hits to your groin area. You don't want to hurt your testes."

Did he just say testes? I was too stunned to facepalm or even cringe. I was being lectured about the well-being of my cojones by a teenager. TJ's head dropped, and his shoulders shook with suppressed laughter.

"And third, I know you like your boxer briefs, but you really should think about regular boxers. Just let yourself hang out and help increase your motility."

TJ gave up the fight, hitting the table and screaming, "Motility!"

Yep. That did it. I was mortified. Amused and strangely charmed—but horribly embarrassed. I didn't know whether to laugh or put tape over his mouth, but a chuckle or two snuck through my indignation.

I prayed for Kelcie's reappearance. "Back up a minute, Buster. First, don't you worry about my testes. You don't talk about another man's junk, okay?"

"Why not?"

"It's…it's rude."

"Mom and her friends talk about their women parts all the time."

"Well…well…we are on a public podcast, and I'd rather not discuss my boys." I gestured at my crotch.

He tilted his head, staring at me, and then said, "Okay."

"Also, where did you learn about motility."

"Health class."

"And boxers versus briefs?"

"Google." He folded his hands in front of himself. "I also learned what can happen if you don't wear a jockstrap and a cup. Do you wear one?"

The laughter of thousands of listeners took up real estate inside my head.

Undaunted, he said, "Did you know some athletes can suffer from testicular torsion—that sounds worse than just getting kicked in the balls."

I straightened and cleared my throat before saying, "Yes, well. Let's get back on topic, shall we?"

It took some time for TJ to regain his composure. I said to Aaron, "Why don't you check and see if your mother is still standing, or if she's left us both and run for the hills?"

My head was on the desk. I couldn't breathe. I wiped my eyes. This kid was killing me. Somehow, we went from my retirement, to him wanting me to procreate, to testicular torsion. I squeezed my legs together in an involuntary response.

Just then, Kelce sheepishly walked back into the room, being pulled by Aaron. Her face was several shades of red. "I am so sorry," she mouthed. "Testicular torsion? Really, Aaron?"

He shrugged. "It's a legitimate concern."

TJ choked out, "Shaw, are you going to retire?

I pulled her to me and settled her on my lap, squeezing her gently to let her know it was okay. Aaron returned to his seat. I looked at TJ and said, "We'll see. Like I said, when I know, Aaron will have the exclusive."

Aaron stood next to me while I kissed Kelcie's cheek. "It sounds like they have concerns about a few parts of my body," I said. "I guess we're going to have to have further discussion."

Kelcie and I shared a secret smile.

We weren't ready to admit that Aaron's wish was already granted and that the soundness of my testes would be proven by the beginning of the season.

Maybe this was a good enough reason for this to be my last season. Kelcie had pulled me off the sidelines and into a future with her, handing me something more precious than a Super Bowl ring. I won the only thing I ever wanted—her love.

The End

ALSO BY LARALYN DORAN

The Driven Women Series

A Fast Woman

Boss Lady

Clever Girl

For other formats—Linktree

AFTERWORD

Aaron was heavily influenced by my experiences raising my own neurodiverse children and the range of challenges they faced. The perseverance and courage they've shown, and the perspective they've given us, have been awe-inspiring.

I would like to thank the multitude of therapists, doctors and teachers who have helped us navigate the many different roads we traveled.

The road for each family is as different as each child, but there is beauty in the journey.

And, yes, car rider lines are the worst.

ABOUT THE AUTHOR

Laralyn Doran is one dog away from being the "crazy dog woman".

Even as a self-professed non-athlete, being a boy mom has led her down the path of becoming a NASCAR and football fan. Having a sassy daughter with physical challenges, she's always loved strong-willed female characters who blaze their own path. Between Diet Coke, Starbucks Chai lattes, and disconnecting with fun audiobooks, she maintains her sanity.

She loves posting audiobook recommendations, talking dog videos, and other nonsense when she should be writing or engaging in the outside world.

Sign up for her newsletter to stay on top of her latest releases and sales: LaralynDoran.com.